"You...haven't even asked why someone would want to kill me."

Jared's gaze moved over her face, lit briefly on her bandaged arm and met her eyes with renewed grimness. "Doesn't matter why, just that someone's trying."

She didn't know whether to be flattered or insulted.

"I know that arm is hurting like hell. I'll do what I can to help you, but we've got to keep going. The best way to conserve your energy is to use the 'rest step.'"

Hope rolled her eyes. "I can't move fast, walking like Frankenstein's monster."

"Yeah? Well, pretend the villagers are right on your butt and the sniper's carrying the lead torch."

She suppressed a shudder. "I'd rather just focus on *your* butt, if you don't mind. I've always thought you had a tush worth following." She tried for a cocky grin and failed miserably.

"Aw, hell." He scowled and a steely arm circled her waist. "I'd die before I let him hurt you," Jared said gruffly. Then he kissed her.

ABOUT THE AUTHOR

Jan Freed is proud to write in a genre that presents a "hopeful view of life without diminishing its hardships." She loves the great outdoors and describes herself as an urban camper. "I enjoy hiking and don't mind a little dirt and sweat—as long as there's a hot shower waiting for me at the end of the day." Her attitude led to the creation of a tough executive heroine wrenched out of her preferred environment and forced to focus on elemental issues. "Spending time in the wilderness tends to make us step back and get our priorities straight. I had fun opening my workaholic heroine's eyes and placing the Boy Scout/bad-boy hero smack-dab in her line of vision."

Jan lives in Texas with her husband and two children. She loves to hear from readers and invites you to write her at: P.O. Box 5009-572, Sugar Land, Texas, 77487.

Books by Jan Freed

HARLEQUIN SUPERROMANCE
645—TOO MANY BOSSES
676—THE TEXAS WAY
713—MY FAIR GENTLEMAN

NOBODY DOES IT BETTER
Jan Freed

Harlequin Books

TORONTO • NEW YORK • LONDON
AMSTERDAM • PARIS • SYDNEY • HAMBURG
STOCKHOLM • ATHENS • TOKYO • MILAN
MADRID • WARSAW • BUDAPEST • AUCKLAND

ISBN 0-373-70741-X

NOBODY DOES IT BETTER

Copyright © 1997 by Jan Freed.

This edition published by arrangement with Harlequin Books S.A.

® and TM are trademarks of the publisher. Trademarks indicated with ® are registered in the United States Patent and Trademark Office, the Canadian Trade Marks Office and in other countries.

Printed in U.S.A.

To Philip and Phyllis Freed,
who opened their hearts and let me in.
Every daughter-in-law should be so lucky!

CHAPTER ONE

HOPE MANNING slouched in her back row seat and undressed Jared Austin with her eyes.

Not completely, of course. That was a man's sophomoric trick. She'd fine-tuned the technique to suit her own purpose. Lechery was not involved.

The key to her satisfaction hinged on picturing a man's clothes replaced with...inventive substitutes. Black kneesocks and a red Speedo swimsuit, for example. Or high-heeled gold mules and a pink feather boa. Many an investment shark had lost the teeth to intimidate her after such a poignant Kodak moment.

Smirking for the first time in hours, she visualized the speaker up front wearing black cotton and red spandex. Her spine slowly straightened.

She'd forgotten about Texan men. Forgotten that daily outdoor labor beat the Armani pants off hailing cabs as a muscle-toning exercise. And this particular man had spent years working out in his Big Bend wilderness gym. Hoo-boy.

She should've gone with the high-heeled mules and pink feather boa.

"Some of you have traveled thousands of miles to take our Wilderness Leadeship course," Jared was saying. "I can guarantee that you're in for the challenge of a lifetime..."

Yeah-yeah-yeah, Hope thought, ignoring his welcoming speech to look him over with his clothes intact.

The founder of MindBend Adventures stood in a relaxed pose, one hand thrust deep into his khaki shorts pocket, the other pressing a clipboard against his matching camp shirt. Sandy brown hair worn shaggy over the collar, gold wire-rimmed glasses and dun-colored hiking boots completed the unassuming portrait. Nice-looking, in a nerdy sort of way. Nothing to blow her skirt up. About an olive's worth of description over martinis with Debbie Stone—*if* Hope ever spoke to her vice president again.

Debbie's blackmailing threat to resign would be hard to forgive.

Hope's narrowed gaze refocused on Jared. The man's body *was* good, she conceded. Not an ounce of fat on him that she could see. Sniffing, she tugged her linen vest over the five extra pounds super-glued to her hips. Clothes could hide a lot of body flaws. Any thirty-five-year-old woman worth her weight knew that.

Inner flaws could be hidden, too. She stared at Jared's glasses, trying to penetrate the reflection of overhead fluorescent light. No clues there.

But he smiled too often to be trusted. And those teeth, startling white against his deeply tanned skin, had to be capped. Mr. Natural Man was a hypocrite, she decided. Worse, he was keeping her away from

Manning Enterprises, the venture-capital company she'd nurtured from obscurity to *Wall Street Journal* recognition. That made him fair game.

An idea germinated and took root. She was a pro at harassing men. Maybe if she baited this guy into losing his cool, he'd expel her from the course and send her home. Yeah, that was the ticket. And if it didn't work, if he withstood her needling the entire two weeks, at least she would've had some fun. The question was, what to target first?

In a New York City boardroom his Boy Scout getup would've been the perfect bull's-eye. But in West Texas...

Casting a hesitant glance out the classroom windows, she shuddered. In the godforsaken Chihuahuan desert he'd blend in like a dropped contact lens. She might be wise to learn his weaknesses before shooting off her mouth.

"Hope Manning," a baritone voice boomed.

Her gaze jerked guiltily to the front.

"Hope Manning?" Jared repeated, looking up from his clipboard and scanning the first three rows. She sat by herself in the fifth.

Roll call. Of course. She lifted her hand and wiggled sheepish fingers.

His glasses flashed her way. "In the one-hundred-plus expeditions I've led, Hope, can you guess what caused the few student injuries on record?"

A pop quiz already? Twenty faces spanning a diverse range in age focused on her blank expression. She blinked.

"Inattention," Jared said meaningfully.

Twenty faces grinned as her cheeks grew hot. Examining one red-lacquered fingernail, she notched her arrow.

"If you want all eyes on the trail, Scout, I'd nix the shorts," she drawled, her native Texan accent rusty from disuse. "Your legs could sell Speedo swimsuits in the desert."

She peeked up through her lashes.

Jared's wire-rimmed glasses angled a bit, reflecting the room's rectangular windowpanes now. "In desert brush country we'll all be wearing pants. And even if we weren't, I doubt you'd notice my legs after carrying a thirty-five-pound backpack in ninety-degree heat for hours."

She flapped a dismissive hand. "Don't be so modest. Besides, I haven't even seen your tush yet. I'm sure it's worth a few stumbles over cactus." Twirling her index finger, she cocked her head. "Turn around and give us a peek."

Sensing a collective indrawn breath, she waited for the explosion.

He carefully removed his glasses and slipped them into his shirt pocket, then passed his clipboard to a plump blond woman sitting in the first row.

The man who looked up had heavy-lidded dark blue eyes and a vaguely familiar sneer. Flipping up the collar of his shirt with both hands, he smoothed back an imaginary pompadour with one palm and executed a lazy turn and straddle. His bump and grind, complete with whirling arm, was vintage Elvis Presley.

The group howled in appreciation.

Hope smothered her own startled laugh. She wouldn't underestimate the man—or his tush—again. Those khaki-covered buns of steel were worthy of a whole martini's description. Maybe two. Debbie, a second-generation Elvis groupie, would've swallowed her olive whole just watching this guy in action.

After a final pelvis thrust, Jared turned back around and curled his upper lip. "Thankyouverymuch."

Hope waited for the chuckles to fade, then inclined her head in tribute. "Definitely worth a few stumbles, Scout. I can see I'll have to watch my step around you."

His gaze sharpened, as piercing as any she'd met across a boardroom table. "Why are you here, Hope? What motivated you to join a MindBend Adventures expedition?"

Hoo-boy. "My...friend saw a feature story about your company on 'Good Morning America.' She was impressed with the executives who raved about their expedition experiences. She...suggested I take one of your Wilderness Leadership courses."

A hiatus, Debbie had called it, threatening to resign from Manning Enterprises unless Hope cooperated. She was not to come back until she'd completed the expedition and "chilled out." In the Texas desert, for heaven's sake!

"That's flattering," Jared said. "But what impressed *you* about our expeditions?"

The fact that people paid good money to join them, for starters. "The chance to get away from the office grind, for one thing. Plus the opportunity to meditate in one of the last unspoiled environments in the nation."

He seemed to want more.

"And, of course, I hope to make lifelong friends and grow as a person," she added.

His lips twitched once and stilled. "Very admirable. Many victims of corporate burnout feel rejuvenated after hiking ten days in Big Bend country."

Corporate burnout?

He leaned over and retrieved his clipboard from the matronly blonde in the first row. "Thank you...Karen, isn't it?"

"Yes, Karen Kent." She sounded surprised and flattered, as if her name tag hadn't been right in his face.

Jared put his glasses back on and smiled. "Why don't you tell us what you hope to get out of your experience, Karen?"

"We-ell. My husband and two sons love to camp in the summer, but I've never been very good at it, so I've always stayed at home."

Corporate burnout? A victim? Hope crossed her legs and bobbed her platform sandal hard enough to drive in nails.

"But I feel so left out," Karen admitted in a small voice. "And your catalog said you teach outdoor skills and wilderness self-sufficiency. Since the kids are visiting their grandparents for three weeks, Jim thought this would be a good time for me to join an expedition.''

"Your family must be proud of you."

I'm a victim of blackmail, dammit, not burnout! Hope fumed.

Karen didn't answer.

"Excuse me," Hope said loudly, capturing Jared's startled attention. Weeks of simmering resentment boiled to the surface. "I'll have you know I am not burned out. In fact, I love my job. I *need* stress in my life. Oh, I agree that not everybody's cut out for fourteen-hour workdays and pressure-cooker negotiations, but I happen to operate best under those conditions. And if I demand a lot from my employees, it's because I know they can meet my high standards. It is *not* because I am stressed out, maxed out or any of the other pat labels psychoanalysts stick on ambitious hardworking executives. I am *sick to death* of people making that assumption, and I resent the implication that peeing behind a rock or chanting under the moon is going to change me into a better per—"

A shrill bell cut off her tirade. She closed her mouth and looked around in dawning horror. Had that been her voice escalating in volume, ranting against a situation these people knew nothing about?

Twenty faces ranging in expression from shocked to morbidly fascinated told her it had been.

Jared broke the uneasy silence. "Sorry about the

interruption. When MindBend Adventures took over this old elementary school we left the bell system in place. It keeps us on schedule, but it takes a while to get used to.'' Studying Hope as if she were an X-ray revealing terminal cancer, he added, ''Why don't you take a deep long breath through your nose and count to five?''

Why don't you wipe that supercilious concern off your face? ''I'm fine.''

''Changing one's breathing pattern can bring instant stress relief for many people.''

''I'm not stressed,'' she said through clenched teeth.

''No?'' His gaze mocked her denial, then swept the entire group. ''This seems like an appropriate time to teach you a quick body-stress checkup. Starting at the top your head, I want you to scan your scalp, forehead and cheeks for muscle tension. Are you frowning? Are you grinding your teeth?''

Hope hastily relaxed her brows and jaw.

''Now try rolling your neck and shoulders.'' He demonstrated the technique, his obedient students following suit.

Eyeing them suspiciously, Hope tilted her head, lifted her shoulders—and winced at a sharp stab of pain.

''Do you notice any tightness or discomfort?'' Jared asked, sending her a knowing look.

She glared back, her chest rising and falling rapidly.

''Check your breathing now. Is it fast and shallow,

rather than regular and deep? What about your legs and toes? Do you feel any muscle tension or nervous spasms?''

Hope stopped bobbing her foot, lifted a hand and massaged the headache beginning to pulse at her temples. Her cool fingers brought instant relief.

"Finally, I want you to check the temperature of your hands. Are they abnormally cold? If your fingers are cooler than your neck, they probably are.''

Refusing to fondle her neck *or* meet Jared's eyes, she lowered her arm and sat very still.

"If you exhibited one or more of the symptoms I described, chances are your body is stressed. Throughout the first few days of this course you'll be learning how to reduce body stress, as well as how to survive in the wilderness—equally useful skills, I assure you. Now then, Hope, did you want to add anything to your earlier comments before we continue with roll call?''

And dig her grave deeper? "No thanks. I'll let Carol take back the floor.''

His gaze cooled noticeably, moved to the rumpled blonde and warmed back up to room temperature. "How about you, Karen? Is there anything you'd like to add to your reasons for joining a MindBend expedition?''

Karen?

The woman ducked her head and mumbled, "Not really.''

Karen, Carol—pretty damn close, if you asked Hope.

"Okay, let's get back on track." Jared referred to his clipboard again. "Bill Harper?"

"Here."

"Hank Thompson."

"Here."

Hope tuned out the remaining names, knowing she wouldn't remember them, anyway. While she never forgot a mathematical equation, people were another matter. Her analyst said she feared intimacy and the chance of rejection. Hope had her own theory. She simply didn't clutter her mind with unimportant details.

Roll call completed, Jared lowered his clipboard. Several people shifted in their chairs. "Why don't we take a short break? Rest rooms are on the right, vending machines on the left. Meet back here in ten minutes, and we'll go through some last orientation items."

Chairs scraped against linoleum. Chatter broke out as students turned to their neighbors with idle comments and headed for the door.

Uncrossing her leg, Hope stood and smoothed her oatmeal linen slacks, trying not to notice how many eyes avoided hers. So she wouldn't get voted most popular. Big deal. Once the UroTech sale went through, she'd have friends crawling from under every rock. All the world loved a millionaire.

"May I speak with you a minute, Hope?"

She turned and watched Jared close the gap between them. "Do I have a choice?"

He stopped at the end of her row. "Always. In everything."

The man was really getting on her nerves. "Your disciples are gone now," she said dryly. "You can drop the wise-guru act."

"All right, I'll be blunt. Are you certain you've given enough thought to joining a MindBend Adventures expedition? It really shouldn't be taken lightly."

She bumped past folding metal chairs and stood platform sandals to hiking boots, her head tilted back to accommodate his irritating height. "Just how should your little adventure be taken, Scout?"

"Not as a vacation. Not as therapy, either."

"Excuse me?"

"I just want to make sure you understand what the course entails. You were right that you'll have a chance to enjoy unspoiled nature. But it won't be any picnic. We won't cook for you, set up your tent or carry your gear. You'll do all that for yourself. The trail is strenuous, the heat is hellish, and your fellow students may not always be agreeable. You'll have to cope with that, too. Most importantly, you'll have to put the welfare of the group before your own."

He didn't think she could hack it. His expression clearly said so. "Are you telling me to quit now and go home?" Perversely, she was outraged.

"I'm *telling* you what to expect. I'm asking you to think carefully about your decision. If you're not up to the physical and mental demands of the expedition, you'll be a hazard to yourself and the group and I'll have to ask you to leave. There's no shame in changing your mind now. The company will refund your money, and you can hitch a ride to Alpine this afternoon on the grocery run.''

It was one thing to harass the teacher with the vague idea of getting expelled, quite another to actually *get* expelled—and before school had even started! "I don't want a refund, thankyouverymuch.''

"Are you telling me you're staying?''

"I'm telling you to expect trouble if you pursue this line of talk. Unless you can prove I'll endanger the expedition, you have no legal right to harass me into leaving.''

Their gazes locked. An invisible line was drawn.

When Jared sighed and looked away first, Hope allowed herself a small smile.

I won't endanger your precious group, Jared Austin. But nothing says I can't make your next two weeks a living hell.

JARED TURNED from the blackboard and watched the newest enrollees of MindBend Adventures straggle back into the room. True to human nature, everyone headed for the same chairs they'd occupied earlier.

Karen Kent reached her front-row seat and unzipped a mammoth canvas purse. Tucking several granola bars into it, she lowered her rump and rocked from side to side as if settling onto a clutch of eggs. Jared bounced the chalk in his palm and frowned. Hiking with a loaded backpack required considerable stamina. Karen's pretty plumpness would only increase the demands on her heart and lungs.

Looking beyond Karen, he focused on the group's other—and more serious—potential problem: Hope Manning.

The slim woman sat in a graceful slouch, one arm draped over the adjacent chair back, a bottled sports drink dangling from her fingers. Her expression was bored, her mahogany brown gaze restless. Taken one at a time, her features weren't knockout material. The mouth was a little too wide, the nose a little too narrow. Her chin was a little too square and tended to lift a *lot* too much. But that complexion...

A true magnolia white, Hope's skin was sensational against a riot of shoulder-length auburn curls. Recognizing his stir of interest as purely unprofessional, Jared looked away.

Hell, she'd burn faster than a marshmallow in a campfire under the intense April sun. What was she doing here so far out of her element? Pulled by a force he wanted to deny, his gaze returned to the back row.

She was studying the label of her bottle as if she'd never heard of electrolytes, much less sweated enough to need them. Shrugging, she unscrewed the cap, swigged a large mouthful and, cheeks bulging, cast frantic "Where can I spit?" glances around her chair. He knew the exact moment she swallowed from her shuddering grimace.

Whirling around to the blackboard, Jared disguised his laugh as a cough. She didn't respond well to being teased, he'd already learned. Lord knew what else she couldn't handle. He recognized the signs of extreme mental stress when he saw them.

Raising his chalk, he began writing the words by rote, freeing his mind to wander.

He should've checked Karen's and Hope's applications more carefully and spotted the red flags warranting a screening interview. But hell, he was spread so thin these days a quick glance was all he could manage. He hadn't even led a trail team in months. His guides now handled that task, allowing him to tackle the growing marketing and financial concerns of the company.

His hand paused and he stared blindly at a half-written word. *Since when have expedition members become a low priority, pal?*

Tightening his grip on the chalk, Jared completed the last sentence, tossed his chalk onto the blackboard ledge and turned around. "During the next two weeks we'll start every morning by saying this meditation out loud. By the end of the course you should have it memorized. For now, I'll give you a moment to read it silently."

Every pair of eyes fastened on the words that had changed his life:

What I am looking for is not "out there." It is in me.
The past has no power over me. Negative thoughts have no
power over me. I am the power in my world.

Today is a wonderful day and a new beginning.
I choose to make it so.

Jared noted the skeptical expressions without surprise. "I can see you're wondering what the heck
this has to do with a wilderness expedition. Granted,
a meditation won't carry your heavy backpack in the
desert or attend an important business meeting for
you in the city.

"But it can affect your mental attitude, your pre-
conceived beliefs in your own strengths or weaknesses. With repetition, it can help shape positive
future experiences, no matter what you attempt to
do."

"Shee-it!" The disgusted explosion came from a
balding man in the second row. As he fielded the
disapproving glances thrown from all sides, his scalp
turned sunset pink.

"I take it you don't agree—" Jared squinted at
the man's name tag "—Bill," he read, watching the
man thrust out his bearded jaw.

"I didn't buy up run-down grocery stores and turn
them into three hundred profitable Feast Markets by
meditating. I worked my ass off, just like that lady
said. You know, the one sitting in the back row."

Jared didn't need directions to know which lady
Bill meant. Against his better judgment, he looked
at Hope.

Supremely smug, she tossed her dark red curls,
licked one index fingertip and stroked an imaginary
point in the air.

"I thought we came here to learn hiking stuff," Bill groused. "When are we setting out?... Like, what day?...Hey, *earth to Jared.*"

Jared's attention snapped back to the irritated supermarket tycoon. "Huh? Oh—sorry."

"Inattention caused the few MindBend-expedition injuries on record," Hope reminded him sweetly. She licked a finger and air-stroked another point.

Priorities, pal, priorities. "Okay, Bill, let's go back to those two hundred grocery stores you built—"

"Three hundred," Hope called out.

Jared breathed in through his nose and counted to five. "Those three hundred stores you built—"

"He didn't build 'em, Scout. He bought up losers, gutted 'em, gave 'em a new look and, whammo! Feast Markets in every town at half the normal start-up cost."

Today is a wonderful day. I choose to make it so. Rolling his shoulders for good measure, Jared tried again. "Those three hundred stores you bought and gutted and whammoed into Feast Markets. Are you telling me that didn't take vision on your part?"

Bill picked at his graying beard. "Well...I didn't say or think no hocus-pocus crap, if that's what you mean."

"Fair enough. I suppose you could have worked hard and succeeded without really knowing where you wanted the business to wind up. Sounds like you were damn lucky."

"Luck had nothin' to do with it! I had goals, man.

Even in the beginning, I *always* knew where I wanted to be.'' Bill glanced around as if daring his peers to dispute him. "I *am* where I want to be."

Jared kept his expression carefully blank. "So you thought about your goals every day, you believed in your abilities, and now you're a huge success. Hmm...why does that concept sound so familiar?"

As the parallel with the meditation sank in, chuckles broke out among the students. Bill reddened, then much to Jared's relief, grinned sheepishly.

"I know you've all traveled a long way and must be tired," Jared addressed the group. "You'll have the afternoon free to explore and rest up. But bear with me here. I need to divide you into teams and introduce you to your trail leaders before letting you go."

Excited chatter broke out as he retrieved his clipboard from an empty chair and flipped pages. His guides were among the best-trained anywhere. These self-absorbed executives would return to corporate America more confident and aware of the big picture for having experienced very real hardships. He looked up and caught Karen's anxious gaze.

Ah, hell.

"Before I announce names, let me remind you that every member offers unique strengths to the team and is equally important to the expedition's success. Anyone who can't accept or get along with his or her teammates will be asked to leave the expedition. Any comments or questions before I move on?"

The weight of future responsibility created a pall of silence.

"I have a question," an all-too-familiar voice said.

Jared tensed, his gaze meeting wide brown eyes just oozing sincerity. "Yes, Hope?"

"Why don't the vending machines stock Diet Coke?"

There was an instant of startled silence. Karen giggled and clapped a hand over her mouth, setting off a chain reaction of nervous chuckles.

Rubbing his neck, Jared quickly removed his cold fingers and searched for inspiration. He found it in Hope's triumphant smirk.

"You know, people, this group is so much fun I've decided to change my plans and get some field-work in. The question is, who should I crack my whip over?" He scanned the eager faces and mentally made his remaining three selections. "Bill Harper, Karen Kent, Hank Thompson and...let me see..."

From the sick resignation on Hope's face, she was regretting her earlier flipness.

"Hope Manning," he finished, holding her resentful gaze. With deliberate movements and intense satisfaction, Jared licked his index fingertip and stroked the air.

CHAPTER TWO

HOPE STOOD in the doorway of the cabin she would share with three other women and contemplated murder. Nothing messy or painful, she decided. Just...permanent.

If she dumped sleeping pills in her VP's monogrammed coffee mug, then placed a carefully worded note next to Debbie's head on the desk—something about being unable to bear the guilt of blackmailing her boss—no cop in New York would suspect foul play.

Hope didn't know what she'd expected for her hefty MindBend Adventures enrollment fee, but it certainly wasn't this. Her disbelieving gaze swept the room a second time.

The bunk beds were still there.

They flanked a small moss green nightstand against the opposite knotty-pine wall. A round wooden table and four ladder-back chairs crowded one corner, a jumble of assorted luggage filled another. Orange-and-green-plaid curtains billowed at four screened windows, opened wide to let in an appallingly hot and unrefreshing breeze.

The promotional brochure had described a "comfortable private cabin.'' What comfort? What privacy? What a scam!

Just then Karen emerged from the bathroom, tugging down the hem of her long white T-shirt. Its heart-shaped red gingham appliqués matched her shorts. She looked up and caught Hope's glare.

''It's very…clean,'' she said, her tone apologetic. As if she was personally to blame for what the cabin wasn't.

Lifting the damp hair off her nape, Hope scowled. ''The school is air-conditioned. Why not the cabins? We should sue for misrepresentation.''

''Actually, the brochure explained all that. Don't you remember?''

Hope shook her head grimly. Debbie had provided a summary report of the brochure and filled out all forms for Hope's ''convenience.''

''Oh. Well. Most of our 'learning' time will be spent in the school, but our bodies need a chance to grow acclimated to the climate before we start the expedition. Sleeping here will help.''

''Excuse us,'' a loud voice announced from behind Hope, prompting her to step all the way inside.

A blond Barbie-doll woman wearing neon-pink running shorts and a black T-strap sports bra walked into the cabin, followed by a brunette about Hope's age dressed in designer ''cruise'' attire. Charlotte something or other and…Dara? Debra? It started with a *d*, Hope was pretty sure. Anyway, she did remember their occupations. Jared had forced short bios from everyone before releasing them for the afternoon.

"Hi, guys," the ponytailed blonde said, her perkiness undaunted by the room. "Looks like Dana and I are your roommates for the next few days."

Karen smiled. "Hi, Sherry."

Sherry, Charlotte—Dana, Dara—pretty damn close.

"Have you claimed a bed yet?" Sherry asked.

Karen shook her head. "It doesn't matter to me which bed I sleep in— I'm not picky—but..."

All three women stared pointedly at Hope.

"Hey, I'm not picky, either," she lied. "Stake your claim."

"Cool!" Bounding forward, Sherry swung up onto the left top mattress showing a curvy glimpse of what made her aerobics video, *Rock Bottom*, a best-seller with MTV couch potatoes. "This is just like summer camp. All we need is smuggled candy."

"I brought homemade brownies," Karen said.

"Tight! We can stay up late telling ghost stories."

Hope mentally switched the sleeping pills in Debbie's coffee to rat poison.

"I've got dibs on the other top bunk," Dana said, picking up a duffel bag almost as big as she was and heading for high country. The petite journalist's syndicated advice column appeared in newspapers desperate to attract younger readers. The shocking questions and her frank answers dealt with society as it was, not as it used to be.

Reaching her bunk, Dana tossed up her bag as if it weighed no more than a clutch purse.

"Good upper-body strength," Sherry complimented her.

Dana beamed. "Thanks. I've been working with a personal trainer for over six months to build my endurance. My editor went on a MindBend expedition last May and warned me that regular tennis wasn't enough."

Hope met Karen's cornflower blue eyes across the room and knew that Betty Crocker hadn't done a lick of exercise, either. Good. They'd be equally heavy ball-and-chains on the trail—one for each of Jared's ankles.

Dana stepped up onto the lower bunk mattress, unzipped her bag and rummaged through the contents. Karen wandered to the table and picked up a sheaf of papers—the promised schedules, no doubt— and read them over. Sherry began a series of stretching movements that defied gravity and human ligaments.

Hope sighed. Looked like she was stuck for the duration. She might as well get settled in. Her floral-tapestry suitcase, an elegant Mack truck among the Toyota-pickup luggage on the floor, held all the comforts of home she'd been able to stuff into it.

Eyeing Dana's body-size duffel bag on the top bunk, Hope raised her chin. Anything "Dear Abby" could do *she* could do better.

Rolling the suitcase forward on its nifty little wheels was easy. Wrestling the dead weight onto the foot of her mattress took a bit more doing. When the job was done, she turned and sat facing the nightstand, her feet braced on the floor, her forearms on her thighs, her breathing labored. She focused on the chipped green paint.

It hit her like a plunge in the Dow Jones.

"Where's the telephone?" she wheezed out.

Dana stepped down from her makeshift ladder, a stack of clothes topped by hiking boots in her arms. "Isn't it great? No phone, no TV, no distractions—"

"No, no, no-o-o," Hope moaned, opening the nightstand's single drawer as if a telephone might magically appear next to a room-service menu. The cellular phone in her purse was useless in this remote and sparsely populated area. God, she hated West Texas!

"There's a pay phone in the school." Sherry's voice floated down from the other upper bunk. "For emergencies," she added, a subtle reminder of Jared's instructions not to contact offices or family unless absolutely necessary.

Hope slammed the drawer shut. Forty-five investors had put their money and faith in Manning Enterprises and Hope's fund-management skills. The entrepreneurial companies she'd chosen to back were all worthy, in her educated opinion. But UroTech and its patents were the mother lode, the pot of gold, the venture-capital risk that would result in fifty-percent compounded returns for Manning Enterprises.

Johnson and Johnson, Houston Science Lab or any one of ten interested observers could get off the fence and make an offer for UroTech any day—despite the fact that its revolutionary incontinence-control implant was months away from FDA approval. One five-minute call to Leslie, the office secretary, would give Hope the updated scoop. She had to get to a phone!

Dana stooped over and peered into Hope's eyes. "You look a little flushed. Are you feeling okay?"

"Let me see," Sherry said. Her long tanned legs dangled into view, then she dropped to the floor. "You're right, her color's not good. And she's breathing too hard." Placing gentle fingertips against Hope's wrist, Sherry checked her own watch as she counted pulse beats. "A little high," she confirmed, exchanging a frowning glance with Dana.

A granola bar suddenly appeared under Hope's nose.

"I'll bet she's hungry," Karen said, crowding the others to get a peek in. "I get queasy on an empty stomach, and I noticed she didn't eat a snack earlier."

Hope blinked up at the three women, so different but for their identical expressions of concern. No one ever worried about her anymore. She'd clocked in through so many bouts of minor ailments that coworkers and friends assumed she never needed sympathy or comfort. Even Debbie had forced Hope to chill out solely for the good of the staff and the future of Manning Enterprises.

"What do you think we should do?" Karen asked, biting her lower lip.

"For one thing, quit talking like I'm not here," Hope snapped. She cleared the strange thickness from her voice. "For another, quit hovering. I'll be fine if you'll just give me room to breathe."

They backed away in unison, Sherry mumbling about ingratitude, Dana arching a brow and Karen looking like a kicked basset hound. Hope opened and closed her mouth. If there was one thing she'd learned, it was that softness could and usually did come back to bite her in the butt. She kept her apology to herself.

Dana headed for the bathroom. "I'm going to explore the compound after I change clothes. Anyone want to come along?"

"I'm in," Sherry said. "How about you?"

She wasn't looking at Hope.

But Karen was. "Well…"

Hope lay back on the bed and closed her eyes.

"Okay, I'll come," Karen said. "According to the schedule, we're supposed to meet for dinner at six o'clock in the cafeteria. Do you think we have time to see that elephant-shaped rock Jared told us about?"

"Oh, cool idea! He said it's an easy walk, about forty-five minutes round trip. We'd better wear boots, though."

Hearing a flurry of activity, Hope sorted through the sounds. Luggage zipped open and closed. Boots clattered against the floor. Something clicked, then a battery-assisted whir—ah, film advanced in a camera. She caught a whiff of tanning lotion and sensed the giddy first-day-of-vacation mood. The bathroom door opened, then the front door. Dana said, "Let's go."

And Hope was alone.

The silence was oppressive. She opened her eyes and stared at the spillage from half-closed luggage, glad her roommates were gone. She had better things to do than look at a stupid rock shaped like an elephant. She wouldn't have walked with them across the room to see such a ridiculous thing.

Even if they had asked.

ONE HOUR LATER Hope pressed the pay phone to her ear and searched the school hallway for eavesdroppers. No one in sight. Apparently no one at her office, either. Four rings and counting.

Five rings.

On the sixth ring someone picked up. "Manning Enterprises."

"For God's sake, Leslie, how many times have I said you never get a second chance to make a first impression? I could have been a prospective investor and decided to hang up."

"Ms. Manning? Is that you?"

"Of course it's me. Have you heard—"

"But Ms. Stone said you were out in the middle of the desert somewhere and wouldn't be able to contact us for at least ten days. Would you like to speak to her? She's standing right—"

"No, wait!" At the sound of a fumbling exchange, Hope squeezed her eyes shut. "Leslie?"

"You wish," Debbie said dryly. "Hello, boss. Fancy hearing from you so soon."

Debbie's wide blue eyes would be innocent of all sarcasm, Hope knew. But she'd also known the woman since their freshman year at Wharton School of Finance. She braced herself.

"I'm sure you have a perfectly good reason for breaking your promise and calling on your very first day away from the office. Something that has nothing to do with the UroTech sale. Because you know that since I haven't called *you* with significant news— which I told you I would do if anything important came up—well, then, there's nothing new to report. So...why am I talking to you, Hope?"

Damn. "This isn't the Home Shopping Network?"

"Pretty lame. Try again."

"I wanted your martini recipe?"

"I do make a mean martini," Debbie admitted in that husky contralto voice men loved. "But yours are better. Keep trying."

Hope leaned one shoulder against the wall and put some thought into it. "Okay, here's the deal. I'm holding Betty Crocker, Malibu Barbie and Dear Abby hostage in a summer camp twilight zone. Fed Ex an air conditioner and a case of Diet Coke in an unmarked bag overnight, or I'll be forced to drown them one at a time in my sweat."

A reluctant chuckle warmed the line. "I'm a feminist. That's supposed to be a threat?"

"Did I mention that Elvis Presley is bound and

gagged, too?'' Hope could picture the antennae rising from Debbie's cap of short blond hair.

"Elvis, as in black leather lean? Or Elvis, as in white polyester bloated?''

An image of Jared's bump-and-grind antics released Hope's grin. "Oh, definitely lean. Best buns I've seen in a long time. Great shoulders, too…'' She trailed off, remembering exactly how good Elvis had looked for his age.

"Why, Hope Manning. Has the infamous Nutcracker finally met her dream shell?''

Hope groaned at the reference to the nickname her male colleagues bandied among themselves.

"Who *is* this Elvis character?'' Debbie persisted.

"No one.''

"Don't pull that on me. You know I can tell when you're lying. Is he a rich handsome executive?''

"No.''

"A studly wilderness guide?''

"No.''

"He's a studly wilderness guide! But could it be *the* guide? The boss guide? The man who's going to save you from a nervous breakdown and me from interviewing hell?''

How did she *do* that? "No.''

"This is great!'' Debbie hooted. "Is he as cute as he looked on 'Good Morning America'? Why do you call him Elvis? Any chance he'll love you tender before the course is over?''

"You're blowing this way out of proportion. Besides, I'm not exactly the teacher's pet.''

"Okay, forget tender. Settle for a hunka hunka burnin' love and enjoy it. C'mon, boss, tell Aunt Debbie all about him."

Hope would never hear the end of it if she didn't nip this thing now. "If you must know, Jared Austin is an overgrown Boy Scout who quotes meditations one minute and cracks a whip the next. He doesn't like me any more than I like him, because a strong woman obviously threatens his authority and masculinity, and he has a short supply of both. Now, is there anything else you'd like to know, or does that about cover it?"

Pushing off the wall, she ran agitated fingers through her hair and turned.

Jared stood three feet away, his arms folded and his gaze unreadable. "I'd say that about covers it."

"Who was that?" Debbie asked sharply.

Hope couldn't have answered had Johnson and Johnson been on the line.

"Oh, my Lord, it's *him*, isn't it?"

"I've got to go now, Debbie. Call me if anything develops on the UroTech sale. And don't make any major decisions while I'm gone. If something comes up, stall until I get back."

"Wait! Call me as soon as you get rid of him. Forget what I said earlier. You're hereby released from your promise not to contact—"

Hope hung up. Meeting the steely blue glint in Jared's eyes, she hugged the flutter in her stomach and smiled weakly. "Hi, there."

He nodded with no change in expression.

"I, um, guess you're wondering what I'm doing making a phone call."

"No. I know exactly what you're doing. You're flagrantly disregarding one of the guidelines this course recommends its students respect."

"'Recommends' is the key word, Jared. Last I heard there was freedom of choice in this country. I simply chose not to follow one teeny guideline." His silent regard made her feel childish, goading her to act the part. "So what are you gonna do, Scout— send me to the principal's office?"

Emotion flared and died behind his round wire-rimmed lenses. "The van leaves for Alpine in fifteen minutes. You can still get on it," he said evenly.

As much as Hope wanted to hightail it back to civilization, she sensed he wanted her gone even more. Her chin came up. "It was an important phone call. You can't expect us to ignore the rest of the world just because we're here."

"I can and I do, because this is a place for you to concentrate on *you*. Not a pending negotiation, not a stock report, not your phone messages or staff problems or piled-up mail. There's just you out here, along with something so much bigger even a narrow-sighted worshipper of the almighty dollar should be able to see and feel it."

Unbelievable! She took a step forward and tossed her head. "Where do you come off judging anybody, Scout? For your information you don't *know* anything about me or my values. So get down off that pedestal you've climbed on before I kick it out from under your feet in front of all those adoring students you've managed to fool."

The jerk had the gall to grin.

"You don't think I can do it?" she asked, her glare obstructed by a corkscrew curl dangling over one eye. "Watch me. You'll be flailing on your back like a flipped turtle by tomorrow night. The view from down there won't be quite so funny, I'll bet."

Unfolding his arms, he stepped forward, forcing her to tip her head back. A tickle of feminine awareness stirred deep inside Hope as an acre of khaki shirt filled her vision.

"You're dead wrong, Hope. I know a lot about you. I know you work fourteen-hour days under tremendous pressure to perform. I know you expect your employees to work the same long hours, probably for considerably less money than you either make now or have the potential to make in the future."

Okay, so he'd listened carefully to her earlier outburst. Big deal.

"I know you're not very comfortable making friends and you're either divorced or you break off relationships with any man who won't take a backseat to Manning Enterprises for your attention. I know that business—that making a deal and outwitting the competition—is more exciting to you than sex, more gratifying than friendship and a helluva lot safer than trusting people. For someone looking down from a pedestal, I know you pretty damn well, Hope Manning."

Seconds ticked by as she stared up into eyes that saw far too much. Absentmindedly she swept back her stray curl, uncaring when it slithered down again.

"On the other hand," he continued, "you don't have the faintest clue about me."

Her gaze faltered and fell to a safer level. "You can't deny that you quote meditations."

"No," he agreed, his lips thin, but well shaped and sharply defined. A woman would feel the outline of that mouth wherever it pressed.

Frowning, she focused on his chin. "And you *did* threaten to crack a whip over us, didn't you?"

"Yes," he agreed, the shadow of a cleft making her fingertip itch to poke for depth. "I have great buns and shoulders, too, according to reliable sources."

Her gaze jerked to his. She blew up a puff of breath to dislodge the hair stubbornly draping one eye. "Then you also agree that you don't like your authority challenged, especially by a strong woman."

He moved a step closer, into that skin-prickling zone just inches from contact with her breasts.

"Now see, that's where you're wrong. I like a strong woman, even when she challenges my authority. Give me Wonder Woman over Betty Crocker any day."

His scent wrapped around her, a mixture of shaving cologne and desert sand and warm male safety. She held herself rigid to keep from leaning into his heat.

"As for threatening my short supply of masculinity…well, I know you do *something* to it, honey. Anytime you want to test your theory, let me know. We'll see how I measure up.'' His voice had dropped two octaves, his navy blue eyes darkened to near black. He reached out now and untangled the wispy curl from her eyelashes, threaded it behind her ear, trailed a scratchy thumb pad down her cheek.

''Magnolias,'' he murmured, cradling her jaw in his large palm.

The gentle touch was at odds with the sudden intensity of his gaze, the violent pounding of her heart. She grew very still beneath the fingers stroking her neck.

''I can feel your pulse going off the stress chart, Hope. Deep breathing is just one way to alleviate tension. Would you like me to show you another technique?'' His gaze lowered to her mouth and lingered.

Hoo-boy…

Technique?

She jerked back her head from his light grip and put some space between them. ''I don't know how many past students have agreed to your extracurricular tutoring,'' she managed, proud when her voice came out steadier than she felt. ''But I won't be added to the list. Keep your hands and your amateur psychoanalysis to yourself from now on, or 'Good Morning America' will get a follow-up scoop on MindBend Adventures that'll send its ratings through the roof and your reputation down the toilet.''

Without waiting for an answer she fled down the

hall toward the front entrance, Jared's hooded gaze burning a spot between her shoulder blades. She hit the doors at a near run and burst into blinding sunshine and furnace heat. Swaying, relief and disappointment battling for dominance of her swirling emotions, she wished that just this once she'd obeyed the stupid rules.

Then maybe ghost stories would be the only thing haunting her sleep tonight.

JARED STARED at the empty hallway in dazed confusion. What in hell had happened just now?

Twenty minutes ago he'd been working at his office desk when Hope had walked past his window, her stealthy movements arousing his suspicions. He'd followed her to the school and known instantly she was headed for the phone. Slipping in a side entrance, he'd watched her from around a corner like some damn peeping pervert. And when she'd finally turned her back, he'd made his move.

He'd intended to spook her, not eavesdrop on her conversation. But her remark about his buns had made him greedy to hear more. He'd gotten an earful, all right.

That woman's tongue should be registered as a weapon.

His stinging ego had demanded payback, proof that he could make her think of him as a man, instead of a flipped turtle. He'd made one fatal error, though. He hadn't considered his own response to her as a woman. Still...

How could he have known her worldly brown eyes would go soft and innocent while focusing on his lips, that her sassy pink mouth would part in unconscious invitation? How could he have known that her skin would feel like the magnolia blossom it resembled? Velvety. Supple. So fine-textured he'd wondered how the tenderest parts of her body could possibly feel any smoother....

He muttered an explosive curse. She'd been right to back away and rip him apart. He'd crossed the line between professional and personal big time. He wouldn't repeat the mistake, he vowed, walking slowly past abandoned classrooms on his way outside.

That wasn't to say he wouldn't keep pushing her buttons on the issue of business. He'd created MindBend Adventures for people just like her. Just like he'd once been himself.

Just like he was becoming again.

Jared stopped in midstride, scrubbed his face with both palms and looked up, the truth suddenly clear. Hope Manning was a blessing in disguise, his opportunity to recommit to ethical values while opening up her mind and heart to the same. He would give "Good Morning America" a story that would renew people's faith in one another and the capitalist system. He would show that hothouse magnolia a world that shrank urgent and important phone calls down to size.

And, if he exercised every bit of discipline at his disposal, he might even manage to do it all and keep his goddamn hands to himself!

CHAPTER THREE

"RISE AND SHINE, Hope! Breakfast is in fifteen minutes."

Hope swam up from the depths of a comatose sleep and swatted the hand shaking her shoulder.

"C'mon, grumpy head. You'll be mad at yourself later when your stomach starts growling."

I'll show you growling. Opening bleary eyes, Hope made a sound closer to a groan. It was barely dawn. And she was still in the twilight zone.

"Not a morning person, huh?" Sherry asked, grinning.

Eyeing the girl's bikini briefs, ribbed knit undershirt and depressing absence of cellulite, Hope grabbed her blanket and pulled it over her head. Blessed privacy. A chance to grab more z's. Her biological rhythm didn't catch the beat of a day until well past noon, didn't rock and roll until at least eight at night. She'd stayed awake last night long after the final maniac-versus-baby-sitter story had been whispered in the dark.

Jared's haunting presence had ensured that. Even now, as she closed her eyes, she could see the heated blue gaze that had startled her into awareness, made

her heart go pitter-patter with equal parts thrill and
fear—

The blanket was yanked from her loosening fists
and settled on her feet. Cool air nipped across her
sheet-clad body. Shivering, she slowly opened her
eyes.

"Go away, or I'll have to hurt you," she said suc-
cinctly.

Sherry laughed and pulled out her suitcase from
under the bed. "I woke up three grouchy brothers
and got them off to school every morning until they
left for college. I doubt there's anything you could
try that they didn't."

"Bet your brothers didn't have these," Hope
purred, curling her fingers and raking the air with
acrylic red claws.

"Bet Jared makes you cut 'em," Dana countered
on her way to the bathroom, looking like an impish
ten-year-old in her baby-doll pajamas. She shut the
door on Hope's indignant frown.

"Jim likes long fingernails, but I bite mine to the
quick."

Hope turned toward the apologetic voice. Karen
sat on the edge of the opposite lower mattress, her
hands buried in her pink flannel lap, her honey-blond
hair puffed up in odd places. The sadness tinging her
features seemed a little drastic for the crime.

"Hope's nails are definitely fine," Sherry said, re-
capturing center stage. Lifting a black scrap of material from her suitcase, she stepped into shorts that

were marginally larger than her bikini underwear. "'Course, it doesn't hurt to have great hands."

Hope glanced down at her hands skeptically.

"You've got those long fingers like my girlfriend Catherine. She makes big bucks modeling—get this—her hands. If you want, I can find out who her agent is."

Hope shook her head. "My schedule's booked solid, but...thanks."

"You're welcome." Sherry smiled and flashed two dimples—the only ones on her magnificent body—then pulled on a white sports bra.

Despite such strong justification, Hope couldn't maintain her irritation. It would have been like shunning a friendly puppy.

"Next!" Dana called, emerging from the bathroom wearing white Keds, red shorts and a navy T-shirt. "I cleared us each a shelf in the towel cabinet for personal items. My stuff's on the bottom, and I'm warning you, if I find any hair in my brush that isn't brown—" she gave her ash-blond, honey-blond and red-haired roommates a meaningful look "—I'll know who you are."

Sherry sidled past the smaller woman, slipped into the bathroom and cast a cheerful smile beyond Hope. "I'll be out in a sec."

"Darn," Karen muttered, her bedsprings squeaking as she sat back down.

Dana opened the cabin door. The whoosh of incoming air, crisp and tangy with unfamiliar scents, blew away the last of Hope's drowsiness.

"Sorry not to wait for you guys, but I'm *starving*," Dana explained. "I'll try to save you seats at my table."

Slam!

Hope turned to the opposite bunk. "Correct me if I'm wrong, but isn't that the same starving waif who scarfed down about a half-dozen brownies last night during story time?"

"Seven," Karen corrected. "Eight, if you count the one I gave her right after dinner. Sherry had five."

The two women exchanged baffled and increasingly irritated looks.

"Want me to short-sheet their beds?" Hope asked.

"No, let me. I bite my nails to the quick, anyway, so there's nothing to break." Lively golden lights animated Karen's blue eyes.

Hope found herself wanting to keep the lights dancing. "I used to bite my nails, too, before I discovered that the glue-on kind are tougher than teeth," she admitted. "Great way to break the habit. Now I can't risk irritating my manicurist *or* my dentist."

"Those are fake?"

Hope covered her teeth with one hand. "Do they look fake?" she mumbled.

Karen laughed. "Not your teeth, silly, your fingernails."

"These?" Hope extended wiggling fingers and huffed. "I'll have you know these babies are gen-u-ine acrylic."

Leaning forward, Karen admired the polished ovals. "They look so real. I've always wanted to try them myself."

"Why haven't you?"

"Oh, they're terribly expensive, I've heard. I barely manage groceries on my monthly allowance as it is."

Allowance? Hope quickly hid her distaste at the thought of being doled out money as if she were a child. "If Jim likes pretty nails so much, he'll spring for an occasional manicure, I bet. After all, he paid for you to take this Wilderness Leadership course, didn't he?"

The shadows crept back into Karen's eyes. She lifted one hand and fingered the top button of her nightgown. "Yes, but this isn't frivolous. This is an investment in his career," she said, as if that explained everything.

"I don't follow you."

"Oh, I'm sorry. Jim is director of marketing for twenty-two SportsArama stores in the Houston area. Mr. Coteras, the company owner, well, he and his wife are really into hiking. They've already asked us several times to join them on weekend trips, and Jim is running out of excuses to say no."

Hope clambered up into a sitting position and frowned. "Why say no in the first place?"

Karen's laugh was soft and humorless. "I'm the world's biggest klutz. If I went hiking with the boss, Jim knows I'd slow the group down—not to mention make a fool of myself."

"I doubt—"

"Don't doubt it. If there's one thing I'm good at, it's embarrassing Jim."

Jimbo was really starting to bug Hope. "So let him go alone."

"I can't." The fingertips twisting Karen's night-gown button revealed glimpses of torn cuticles, as well as ragged nails.

Hope sighed, knowing she would regret this. "Why not?"

"Jim thinks he's being considered for a promotion. Both of the company's vice presidents cor.fided that right before they were promoted Mr. Coteras invited them—and their wives—on hiking trips. Jim says we have to make a good impression or he'll be passed over."

Hope opened and closed her mouth. It was none of her damn business what kind of marriage this woman had.

"No, go ahead and say it, Hope. You don't think this course will do any good, do you? You think I'm wasting Jim's money."

For an instant Hope could only gape. "Why in the world would I think that? And what the hell do you mean *Jim's* money? Who made him keeper of the family treasure chest?"

During her postgraduate years as a financial planner, she'd seen too many wives allow their husbands complete control of all financial decisions only to become devastated later by divorce or widowhood.

"You don't understand."

"I understand that it's okay for you to spend money as long as it ultimately benefits Jim, but that a lousy manicure is 'frivolous.' Karen," she said urgently, "Texas is a community-property state. Whatever belongs to Jim belongs to you, and vice versa—including the household income."

"You don't understand," Karen repeated, her distress bordering on desperate. "Jim is a generous man. But he works too hard for his money for me to—"

"There you go again with that 'his' money crap. Sure he works hard, but so do you, right?"

In answer, Karen stopped torturing her nightgown button and gnawed on two fingernails, instead.

"Your boys are—what—seven and nine years old?" At the other woman's wide-eyed nod, Hope panicked. She had no experience with little boys or suburban lifestyles. "Then you cook and clean and...I don't know, break up fights and comfort hurt feelings."

Welcome snippets of "Home Improvement" reruns surfaced in her memory. "I'll bet you help them with homework and schlep them to team practices and lessons and...well, who knows what all I've left out. I'd like to see ol' Jim walk in your shoes for a day, then tell you to your face that you don't work as hard as he does.''

Karen removed her abused fingers from her mouth and smiled sadly. "Can you tell me to my face that I work harder than you do?"

For one of the few times in Hope's life, she was speechless. Her cheeks stung with sudden heat.

"I didn't think so."

"Whoa, wait a minute. I can't say you work harder than me because, quite frankly, not many people do. But that doesn't mean—"

"It's okay, Hope. I'm sorry I embarrassed you, but now maybe you won't think so harshly of Jim. If I can learn some wilderness skills, I'll help his career, be able to go on family camping trips and make everyone happy."

Someplace deep within Hope throbbed in shared pain. She'd spent the first eighteen years of her life battling low self-esteem, trying to "make everyone happy," and had only scars to show for it.

"What about you, Karen? What about your needs, your happiness? Isn't that important, too?"

Surprise, confusion, wariness—the emotions rolled across Karen's expressive face with the turbulence of thunderclouds.

Hope gentled her voice. "Feed the kids macaroni-and-cheese two nights a month and go get yourself a manicure. You've earned it."

"Next!" Sherry called, walking out of the bathroom wearing full war paint and a bouncing ponytail.

Karen scrambled to her feet, her eyes welling rapidly. "I'll just go—" She stopped and cleared her throat, then, shaking her head, gathered the folds of her nightgown and nearly ran into the bathroom.

Staring at the closed door, Hope wondered how much subtle condescension Karen received from other "working" women—not to mention from a husband who sounded like a jerk. The probable answer made Hope squirm at her own arrogance. She knew what it felt like to be low man on the family totem pole.

Yet at her most vulnerable, Hope had at least had her grandmother to champion her square-peg eccentricity. Karen seemed to have no one.

Sherry gazed from the bathroom to Hope. "What's wrong with *her*?"

"Mm? Oh...nothing." Nothing, Hope mentally corrected, that a little vacation from a round hole wouldn't cure.

ONE HOUR LATER Stan Lawler hoisted his backpack and suitcase into the trunk and slammed it shut. His satisfied gaze swept the white Lincoln Continental, tinged pink by the rosy morning sky.

"Enjoy your vacation, señor," the rental-car attendant said, handing over the keys. "The hill country has many good places for hiking, no?"

"That's what I've heard. I think I'm going to like it here."

"San Antonio *es muy bonito,* very pretty. You travel from Chicago, *verdad?*"

The luggage tags. Eagerness had made him careless. Nodding, he headed for the driver's side of the car.

The stocky attendant opened the door and eyed Stan curiously. "*Pero* you are not living there long, *verdad?*" He smiled at Stan's sharp glance. "You have the accent like President Clinton." He pronounced the Arkansas politician's name "cleentone."

"You have the accent like Ricky Ricardo, but that don't make you Cuban." Damn nosy Mexican. Forcing his features to relax, Stan slid behind the wheel and held up a ten-dollar bill. "Tell me how to get to Highway 281, and this is yours."

As intended, the man's black eyes locked onto the money. "*Es demasiado,* too much."

Stan shrugged and started to withdraw his hand.

Snatching the bill, the attendant closed the car door, then leaned through the open window to point out highways on a map clipped to the windshield visor. Not that Stan listened. He'd memorized his route on the long flight from O'Hare Airport. At last the attendant finished his directions and backed away from the car. "*Gracias, amigo. Vaya con Dios.*"

"Yeah, whatever," Stan said, rolling up the window and driving off.

Frigging foreigners were taking over the whole goddamn country. He knew enough Mexican lingo to recognize the word Dios, and he didn't want any part of the SOB. If God did exist, He'd let things happen to a little kid no man should have to remember.

Stan trusted no one but himself, answered to no one but himself, depended on no one but himself. The arrangement made him available to anyone who could pay, and his fees had risen along with the risk of the job. For a dumb-ass cracker runt—the last name his daddy'd ever called him—Stan was doing mighty fine. And about to do better.

Shifting his large frame in the roomy bucket seat, he inhaled the smell of new car. The Lincoln had been reserved as promised under the alias he'd supplied. Two weeks' rental had been paid in advance. These people were class!

Excitement burned in his gut, different from the adrenaline rush he got from his work, but no less intense. The button man had been unusually interested in Stan's two-year stint with an Ozark survivalist group. He figured that was why he'd gotten lucky—this time.

But if he completed the job with his usual anonymity and skill—which he *would*—and if his self-polishing paid off at his lunch meeting today—and it *would*—his fees would take a giant leap. The ability to blend into a cosmopolitan setting, as well as the wilderness, would open new doors. At age thirty, he'd be right up there with a handful of independent professionals driving their own luxury cars, instead of rentals.

He almost wished his daddy'd lived to know it.

Pulling directions from his suit-coat pocket, he checked them against the signs, entered the right lane and barely made the Commerce Street exit. He passed a sign for the Alamo and made a mental note of the street. Maybe he could get in a few sights before leaving the city. He always tried to catch a museum or theater show when he traveled. High-class people were into that.

A snazzy mall on the right alerted him that he was close to his destination. When he entered a circular drive and stopped in front of a palatial hotel, his fingers tightened on the wheel.

A valet promptly opened the driver's door. "Welcome to the Marriott River Center, sir. Do you have any bags to check in?"

Nodding, Stan popped open the trunk and unfolded from the car, trying not to stare like a dumbass cracker from Arkansas at the five-star hotel. Oh, yeah, he could get used to this.

He *would* get used to this.

JARED STOOD in front of the main classroom blackboard and watched his students file inside. He'd eaten his meals alone and hadn't seen the group since last evening. Today they chatted more, laughed more easily, sat according to new friendships sparked the day before.

Now that he'd committed to leading a trail team, anticipation sharpened his senses. His pleasure in teaching increased, he realized, with the knowledge that he would see these students practice what they learned. With luck, they would apply some of it in the business world when they returned home.

After he'd smiled or nodded at nineteen faces, when he couldn't resist the pull one second longer, he allowed himself to look at Hope.

She'd abandoned the fifth row to sit in the third between Sherry and Karen. Her black sleeveless turtleneck was a striking contrast to the curls of living flame around her face and shoulders, curls he knew were as soft as thistledown. She became suddenly too interested in her neighbor's conversation, too animated in her responses.

Look at me, Hope. Let's get this over with.

She grew still, then turned her head.

He wasn't prepared. Although he'd lectured himself the whole night through, her soft dark eyes packed the wallop of a mule's iron-shod kick. From her dazed expression, Hope had caught a hoof in the stomach, too.

She blinked, and her aloofness was back. But not before he'd seen that she wasn't nearly as disgusted with his lack of professionalism as she'd like him to think.

"Good morning," he said cheerfully, offering his first genuine smile of the day.

"Good morning," everyone parroted.

"Mr. Austin," a singsong voice added.

Jared chuckled along with the others at Hope's perfect imitation of school kid answering the teacher. "I hope you rested well, because we have a lot of material to cover today. As we will each day, let's start things off by saying the course meditation out loud."

With his back to the blackboard, Jared began reciting from memory what the others read from the slate.

"What I am looking for is not 'out there.' It is in me. The past has no power over me."

Jared paused. "Come on now, I'm dyin' up here. Help me out and put some conviction behind it."

He continued slowly and relaxed as more voices joined in. "Negative thoughts have no power over me. I am the power in my world. Today is a wonderful day and a new beginning. I choose to make it so."

By the final line, the volume of voices had swelled enough to produce a satisfying reverberation through the room. Although Hope's lips hadn't moved, he'd noticed her gaze moving across the blackboard.

"Great job. And it'll get easier every day, you'll see. Now let's get on with the next order of business." He walked to a utility table set up nearby and dragged it front and center for easier viewing. "I have here what is known by climbers and hikers as the Ten Essentials. Some of these we asked you to bring with you, others will be provided by MindBend

Adventures. All items will be carried in a fanny bag around your waist, separate from your backpack.''

He lowered his glasses to the end of his nose and directed a dire look at the class. ''*Don't leave home without it.* This is not a vacation. If you lose it, the consequences might be a little more serious than eating burgers instead of French cuisine.''

He reached for a lightweight sweater and small plastic package and held them high. ''Item one—extra clothing. Spring temperatures here range from one extreme to the other, and storms can blow up in an hour. An additional sweater can feel pretty good when the sun goes down. And if it rains, this sheet of polyethylene can prevent the wet clothes and boots that lead to chafing and blisters.''

''Not to mention the worst wedgie of your life,'' Hope said, earning snorts and giggles.

So they were back to square one, were they?

Without deigning to respond, Jared picked up a can of fruit-nut pemmican, a granola bar and a box of raisins. ''Item two—extra food.'' He caught Bill's grimace and raised an eyebrow. ''You'd be surprised how good this stuff tastes after waiting ten hours for a rescue party, God forbid.''

''Amen,'' Hope echoed with revival-meeting fervor.

Plodding resolutely forward, Jared said, ''Item three—sunglasses.'' He held up a pair. ''I trust you all brought the kind that screen both ultraviolet and infrared rays?'' At their nods of agreement and

Hope's blessed silence, he moved on to a familiar red shape. "Item four—a knife. We provide the Swiss Army brand, and I can vouch that it opens cans, whittles wood and picks teeth with the best of 'em. It even has a pair of tweezers—" he pulled out the tiny versatile tool "—for those nasty encounters with a cactus."

"Or a really *bad* eyebrow day," Hope added solemnly.

If his smile was a bit grim, he gave himself credit for not demonstrating a more violent use of the knife. "Item five—fire starter. You'll be glad to know I don't mean striking flint or rubbing two sticks together, which wouldn't work, anyway, if the kindling was wet. In an emergency, without a gas stove, there are more effective means of starting a cook or signal fire." He extended a palmful of oval objects. "Can anyone guess what these are?"

Everyone turned to Hope.

"Beans?" she offered, shrugging when their expressions remained blank. "Well, it worked in *Blazing Saddles.*"

Groans and guffaws broke out as the connection was made, and chaos followed as those in the know described the campfire scene to neighbors who'd missed that fine moment in cinematic history. Throughout it all, Hope grinned unrepentantly.

"Hey, what *are* those things?" Hank Thompson asked.

The youngest basketball coach in the NBA, Hank

knew the importance of team discipline and had drawn everyone's focus back to the table. Jared could've kissed him.

"Hydrocarbon fuel tablets," he answered, trickling the tablets onto the table. He decided to speed through the rest of the essentials without undue elaboration.

"Item six—waterproof/windproof matches to light the tablets. Pretty self-explanatory. Item seven—first-aid kit, which we'll discuss at length tomorrow." So far, so good. "Item eight—flashlight, for traveling at night, if necessary, without stepping off the path and into a gully or a black bear."

"We'll see bears?" Karen squeaked, growing pink when several men turned to smile at her indulgently.

"Probably not before they hear or smell us first and run away, but we could see one. There are still a few left in the area. Also coyotes, mountain lions, javelinas, mule and white-tailed deer, lizards, snakes—we could see them all before the expedition is over."

"We could go to the zoo for a lot less money and sweat," Hope muttered.

Her disruptive private battle with him had to stop. He held her flippant gaze. "Yes, you could've paid your five bucks and seen fiberglass boulders and roadrunners under heat lamps. You could've stopped at the concession stand for a Diet Coke and then gone home to your air-conditioned apartment.

"But you missed the van to Alpine, didn't you,

Hope? Your choice, not ours. So kindly keep your comments to yourself and let the rest of us learn from the land—even if you can't.''

Ignoring his twinge of regret at her stricken expression, he held up the last two articles on the table. ''Items nine and ten—a map of the area and a compass. We'll go over our expedition route in more detail later. For now just remember that getting to a designated rendezvous point if you get separated from your team can save the rest of us hours of worry and rescue mobilization.''

''Can we add anything to our emergency pack,'' Dana asked. ''Or should we stick with the ten essentials?''

''Don't take anything out of course. There might be room for one or two other important items. Stuff like sunscreen, insect repellent, prescription medicine—''

''Deodorant, toothbrush…'' Hope met his exasperated gaze with wide-eyed innocence. ''They're important,'' she insisted. ''If I'm spending ten days in the wilderness with you, I sure hope you think so, too.''

She was bound and determined to make him lose his temper, but why? He saw a hand go up and turned to Karen.

She waited for his nod before speaking. ''Has any student ever actually used his emergency pack? I mean, been separated from his trail team and backpack for a long time?''

The room grew conspicuously quiet. Apparently even Hope was interested in his answer.

"Not during a MindBend Adventures expedition," he assured the group, unable to prevent the touch of pride in his tone. "If our luck holds out and you listen to your trail guide, you'll live day to day from your main backpack and never unzip your emergency pack."

"Will our backpacks look like that?" Hank asked, pointing to the loaded Gregory internal-frame model leaning against a side wall.

The idea came to Jared out of nowhere, evil and irresistible. He really shouldn't consider it.

Dragging his gaze back to Hank, Jared shook his head. "Yours will be a little smaller and an external-frame model. But you'll pack in enough supplies between the entire team to last ten days."

"And what will you pack in, Scout?" Hope asked. "The bullwhip?"

Ah, well. Sainthood was overrated. "As a matter of fact, I can show you exactly what I'll carry." Walking to the Ferrari of backpacks, Jared lifted the seventy-pound weight by one shoulder strap and returned to the front of the room. "Before I unpack this, come on up here, Hope, and help me demonstrate the proper way to put on one of these."

While Sherry prodded Hope's shoulder and the others called out encouragement, she eyed him warily. He maintained his best trustworthy-guide smile until his arm muscles trembled with strain and his facial muscles ached. At last she rose and moved with the speed of petrifying wood to his side.

His flagging smile revived. He held open the shoulder straps as if the backpack were a mink coat. "Okay, Hope, this is real simple. Put your arms right through here."

She slanted up a suspicious glance. "I thought *you* were going to put it on."

"No, no, if you can handle this bigger pack, everyone will know the smaller ones won't be difficult. Come on. Put your arms through here. Right through here." He jiggled the straps invitingly. "Right here."

Still looking unconvinced, she slipped her arms where he indicated while he supported most of the weight from behind.

Jared restrained his urge to chortle. "Now then, that's not so bad, is it?"

"No." She sounded surprised and relieved. "No, it's really not."

"How about now?" he asked, releasing the straps and allowing the full dead weight to jerk her shoulders without benefit of a hip belt.

Arms flailing and spine arched, she hit the ground backpack first and blinked in obvious shock.

Amid the gasps and cries of concern, while she thrashed to be free of the pack, Jared sat on his heels beside her.

"Who's the flipped turtle now, Hope?" he murmured for her ears alone.

CHAPTER FOUR

HOPE BIT SAVAGELY into her apple and imagined it was a piece of Jared's hide. He wouldn't get away with humiliating her this morning. Somehow, someway, she would get even.

Crunching steadily, she leaned back against the school's cement-block wall, stretched out her legs and wished the ground boasted more grass than sand. Damn, it was hot! Even on the shady side of the building, with a mesquite tree blocking the high-noon sun, the temperature had to be in the nineties. If she hadn't needed this time to herself so desperately, she would've stayed in the air-conditioned cafeteria or gone on to her cabin with the others. But she couldn't stomach the amused—or worse—pitying glances of her classmates one second longer.

She'd tried so hard to make him lose control in front of the class, to put a crack in that Boy Scout facade...

Squirming, Hope relived the helplessness of staring up into Jared's sardonic gaze, knowing he'd bested her at her own game. If her arms had been free, she would've tested the indestructibility of gen-u-ine acrylic nails and gladly risked damaging a perfect set. He must have seen the bloodlust in her eyes, because he'd allowed Hank the honor of untangling her from the heavy backpack.

She cast a resentful glance now at a small adobe structure in the distance. Jared's house, she'd learned from Matt, one of the guides. A few subtle questions, and Matt's natural friendliness had provided just enough information to pique Hope's curiosity.

The house and surrounding acreage had belonged to a native American called Ben Running Bear, who'd died and left Jared the whole shebang. Matt didn't know who'd built the school or why it had been abandoned, only that the old man had acted as the building's custodian for many years.

Despite little knowledge of his employer's background, Matt had nothing but praise for Jared's accomplishments during recent years. From the guide's expression and tone, the founder of MindBend Adventures was Daniel Boone, Gandhi and Steven Forbes rolled into one. Ha!

Sanctimonious know-it-all, lecturing her about learning from the land. She knew all she wanted to know.

The land obsessed entire communities, so that nothing outside of weather, crops and livestock had value—certainly not a skinny red-haired girl inept at everything but math. Her father's mood and the very roof over her head had depended on Jared's precious Mother Earth, and one thing was clear. The land was something to be hated, not appreciated.

Hope chomped off a last bite of apple and hurled the core, wishing it were an aluminum can. "Take *that*, Mother—"

"Good thing that's biodegradable," a deep voice interrupted mildly.

She clapped a hand over her pounding heart and craned her neck. Jared loomed above her not ten feet away. The building's shade had prevented his warning shadow, but she hadn't heard a sound.

"Stop *doing* that," she snapped.

"Doing what?"

"Sneaking up on me. Unless of course you want to add a coronary to your record of student injuries."

He thrust his hands into his pockets. "Sorry. I didn't mean to scare you."

This from the man who'd tricked the turtle into a top-heavy shell. "What did you mean to do?"

"Apologize."

She narrowed her gaze. He looked serious, but his aviator style sunglasses hid his eyes. Hmm. Drawing in her legs, she pointedly ignored the helping hand he extended and scrambled to her feet.

"Apologize," she repeated, peering through his sunglasses at the shadowy gleam of his eyes. She couldn't be sure, but...

Glancing down at herself, she grimaced and swiped at the layer of sand and fine pebbles dusting her kneecaps, then did the same to the backs of her calves and thighs. She was slapping debris from her butt when she froze, her torso twisted, and glanced up at his dark lenses.

The set of his mouth, the predatory stillness of his body told her exactly where his gaze was now.

Heat suffused her face. With as much dignity as she could muster, she straightened and stared at his chin. "No apology necessary," she assured him, moving blindly toward her cabin.

He stepped into her path. "I think it is."

The bass resonance in that formidable chest sent her stumbling back a step.

"I shouldn't have let you fall earlier," he continued. "No matter...well, no matter how much you provoked me. I knew the backpack would cushion your impact, but I still shouldn't have chanced your getting hurt."

She crossed her arms and raised a brow. "So you admit it was a trick?"

"Yes."

No prevarication, no blustering excuses. Fascinating. "A low-down dirty one," she persisted.

He hesitated the briefest second. "Yes."

Grudging respect tempered her anger. She studied him closely, searching for a crack in his sincerity.

His sports sunglasses, framed in purple with a lime green safety cord, were a startling change from his usual round wire-rimmed lenses. They added an intriguing dash of recklessness to his pleasant but unexceptional features. Her gaze lowered to his sculpted mouth, the lips thin but well formed. Entirely and indisputably male.

Maybe unexceptional wasn't quite the right word....

"So am I forgiven?" Jared asked, his voice as gritty as the ground.

"That depends." She peeked up through her lashes, his height suddenly not so irritating. "How provoking was I?"

He snorted. "I wanted to wring your beautiful neck, and you know it."

A startled thrill hitched her breath at the word *beautiful*. "You got me back pretty good," she managed. "I still can't believe I bought that demonstration schtick."

"And I still can't believe I rigged a student demonstration." He broke into a slow grin, white and reckless and more appealing than she had any business thinking. "So...I guess that makes us even, huh?"

"Even?"

"Squared, ready to call a friendly truce. We both behaved pretty badly back there in the classroom. If you can forgive my dirty trick, I'll forget your childish disruptions and wipe the record clean."

"How...adult of you," she said, dismissing her fleeting idea as unworthy and manipulative.

"Yes, well, once we're out on the trail, you'll have to grow up fast."

Then again, manipulation had its uses.

"That didn't come out quite the right way," Jared said, backpedaling too late. "All I meant was..." He hesitated as Hope stepped forward.

"That you think of me as a child," she finished for him, her fingers first flattening, then fluttering against thin khaki fabric. Heavens, what a chest! She slid her palm over a slab of concrete muscle and heard his indrawn hiss of breath. "What will it take for me to change your mind, Jared?"

His hand shot up and gripped her wrist, his fingers overlapping at least an inch. "Don't play games with me, Hope."

Raising her free hand, she cupped the back of his head. "Life is a game, Scout. Winner takes all."

Spearing her nails through his hair, she sighed. No stingy precision cut this, but a profusion of coarse silk. Hope burrowed her fingers deeply, hit scalp and massaged in slow lazy circles.

"Do you like that?" she whispered, a languid warmth invading her limbs.

A muscle bulged in his jaw. "Yes."

Honest, gruff. Incredibly arousing. She tugged her manacled wrist free from his grip, glided her palm up and kneaded the bunched muscles of his shoulders. The new position lifted her breasts closer to his chest. "You seem awfully tense to me. I know a better way than massage to alleviate tension. Want me to show you?"

"No."

She leaned into the wall of his chest, watching the

cords of his neck snap taut, the sheen of perspiration bead on his bronzed skin. Her excitement heightened. He was letting her take the lead, as if unwilling to initiate more touching but helpless to resist. She pulled on the back of his head, lowering that fascinating mouth closer...closer...until their lips were a mere whisper apart.

''Liar,'' she murmured, settling her trembling mouth over his.

Hot pleasure spilled through her veins. She forgot about revenge, forgot about everything but imprinting the shape and texture of his firm lips into her softer yielding flesh. The contact was light, the connection moist and erotic despite their closed mouths. The sound of his strangled groan filled her with power and drained her of strength.

Kiss me back, she ordered silently, pressing flush against his body.

Damp skin and fabric meshed, molded, steamed. At last, at last, at last, his passive hands crept around her hips and snugged them closer; his tongue probed the seam of her lips and pushed inside.

Her knees buckled. Held up by his cradling hands, her body a melting wax taper, she fought to regain control, regain *herself.* Only her finely honed instincts of self-preservation enabled her to push hard against his chest, wrench free from his arms, stumble back and stand panting and dazed, frightened and triumphant.

Waiting until she had Jared's full shocked attention, Hope lifted her chin. "*Now* we're even."

STANDING IN A SEMICIRCLE with Hank and Karen, Hope watched Bill unpack the first of two compact bags. After lunch, Jared had led each trail team to a separate classroom and instructed them to unload the tents, set them up—complete with rain fly—then paint and seal the seams. He would be back within the hour to check on their progress.

Great. As if her nerves weren't already shot. She'd done some stupid things in her life, but kissing Jared to go one up on the man topped the list. All she'd proved was that he could turn her into warm willing mush without halfway trying.

What would it feel like to have his unforced and *willing* participation?

She fanned herself with the tent instruction booklet and noticed the others looking at her strangely. Striving for nonchalance, she gestured at the paraphernalia Bill had spread over the floor.

"Anybody ever put up one of these things?" she asked.

Hank shrugged. "I've seen one already assembled in the store. Without the rain fly," he added dispiritedly.

Bill scowled and looked up. "Why do we need a fly, anyway?"

Hope snorted. "Because it's more work for us, and that makes Scout a happy camper."

"Jared explained why before the lunch break." Karen colored at their startled glances. "Weren't y'all listening?"

"I don't concentrate well on a growling stomach," Hank admitted.

Bill said nothing, and Hope wasn't about to confess she'd been preoccupied with plotting revenge. "Refresh our memories," she suggested.

"Each of us will exhale as much as a pint of water at night. We'd wake up in a swamp if the inner tent material didn't 'breathe.' The rain fly is there to keep out hard drizzle and rain."

Bill sat on his heels and studied the tent's skin and bones as if about to begin surgery. The bald crown of his head shone pink beneath the long thin strands he'd combed from an unnaturally low part.

"Humph. It can't be that hard to set up," he pronounced. "I'll give 'er a try."

Hope flipped through the instruction booklet. "The directions seem pretty clear. Want to take a look?"

He waved aside her offer. "This sucker has fewer pieces than a point-of-purchase display. Instructions will only screw me up."

Hope leaned over and rapped her knuckles on his skull. "Hello in there. Anybody home?" Straightening, she splayed one hand on her hip. "That's the most ridiculous statement I've ever heard. Tell him how ridiculous it is, Hank."

"I don't know, Hope. The last instructions I followed left me with two extra brackets and three unidentified bolts. Turned out my model C bookcases came with a model A diagram.''

"You see?'' Bill crowed.

"I've helped put up a tent,'' Karen said quietly.

Hope barely heard, she was so disgusted. "I promise I won't tell Jared that the big strong men resorted to intelligence to complete a task.'' She shoved the booklet under Bill's nose. "Spare me your macho pride and follow the instructions.''

He cast up a killing glance.

"Okay, I'll skip the big words and read it to you.'' She snapped open the booklet and ran her finger down the page.

Karen cleared her throat. "I've helped put up a tent,'' she repeated more loudly.

Bill rose and faced Hope, his bearded jaw thrust out almost as far as his substantial stomach. "Your panties have been in a wad ever since we got back from lunch. If all you're gonna do is bitch, then *you* put up one of these dudes, and Hank and I'll set up the other. We'll see who finishes first.''

"Fine, I will! Losers kiss the winners' feet in front of all the other teams. Get ready to pucker up, pal.''

"I've helped put up a tent," Karen bellowed in a voice worthy of the stock-exchange floor.

Hope was impressed.

"SportsArama sells a lot of freestanding tents. Jim owns two of them,'' Karen explained in a near whisper.

Hank cocked his head, his expression curious but not unkind. "You know how to assemble a tent?"

"I've...helped."

Well, whaddaya know? Hope smiled.

"No fair," Bill protested. "The bet was with you, Hope."

She huffed. "Oh, that's real fair. You were okay when the odds were two against one, but now that they're even you're whining. What's the matter, hotshot—afraid the girls will beat you?"

Hope saw Karen stiffen beneath Bill's insultingly dismissive glance and kicked herself. She'd been as guilty as the men of assuming that the timid woman couldn't contribute to the assignment.

Bill bent over and examined the items on the floor once more. "Go ahead and knock yourselves out," he said over his shoulder. "We'll polish our boots for your dainty lips, right, Coach?"

Hank rubbed the back of his neck, the length from his jutting freckled elbow to his bony shoulder only slightly shorter than Hope's entire arm. Her respect for his intelligence rose when he didn't answer.

Picking up two pieces of metal tubing, Bill started to fit them together.

"Ah-ah-ah," Hope warned, wagging her finger. "Nobody opened the starting gate yet. Put those down until we unload our stuff." Carrying the second bag to the opposite side of the room, she turned to her partner and sent her an encouraging smile.

"Well don't just stand there, girlfriend, come on over here and let's show these monkeys a few tricks."

When Karen's face lit with gratitude, Hope vowed to set her expectations for help as high as her teammate deserved. Working together, they spread the makings of a dome tent on the dingy linoleum floor.

"This stuff doesn't look very familiar," Karen admitted once everything was unloaded.

"It'll come back to you when we get started. I mean, it's probably like riding a bike, right?" When silence met her question, Hope quelled a rush of irritation.

"All right, girls," Bill called out, crossing his arms and rocking back on his heels. "Time to put up or shut up. On the count of three, the starting gates open. One...two...three!"

The men sat on their heels and began fitting pole sections together. Hope studied the instruction booklet with intense concentration. In a matter of minutes she had the diagram down cold. Child's play for someone who'd aced high-school geometry at age ten. It was the "easy" stuff like home economics and volleyball that she'd struggled to master. Shaking off the memory, she checked on her partner's progress.

Karen was kneeling on the floor staring at an expanse of sturdy nylon fabric. She looked up vacantly. "I...can't do this."

"What's wrong? Aren't you feeling well?"

"I lied to you." Misery showed stark in her eyes.

"I'm a clumsy cow, a stupid moron. I didn't really help Jim set up a tent. I mean I *tried*, but..."

He called you those terrible names, Hope mentally finished the sentence. She struggled to mask her anger at Jimbo the Jerk.

"Who said you have to do this alone? We're in this bet together." Flicking a glance at the mens' activities, Hope spoke in a confidential whisper. "They're doing it wrong. Follow my directions and we'll whip their tails." She squeezed and released Karen's shoulder, then explained what to do.

Karen fumbled the first task as if her fingers were frostbitten.

Every competitive instinct Hope possessed clawed for release. Conscious of the tent rising across the room, she had to force herself not to shove her teammate aside and take over. From Karen's nervous glance, that was what she expected.

Hope merely repeated the instructions and watched Karen oh-so-slowly connect the first frame section.

She botched the second step and checked Hope's reaction again. Repeating directions without interfering was one of the hardest things Hope had ever done.

After that Karen began to relax, move faster, grasp directions the first time. Eventually Hope pitched in and helped with the assembly. Their tent rose with amazing speed. Only one more rain fly clip—

"We won!" Bill shouted from across the room. Grinning in the face of both women's glares, he pounded a gorilla drumbeat on his chest in time to "Hroo-hroo-hroo-hroo."

"Don't mind King Kong," Hope said underneath her breath. "Remember, Fay Wray was still kickin' when Banana Breath bit the dust. Go ahead and fasten that last clip—we ain't down yet."

Nodding, Karen finished the job and rose to follow Hope to the enemy camp.

"Good job, ladies," Hank praised, his hazel eyes warm. "You gave us a very close race."

Bill cackled. "Close, but no bananas."

"There goes your afternoon snack," Hope muttered.

Laughing, Karen looked years younger and startlingly pretty. If the expression on Hank's face was any indication, Hope wasn't alone in her opinion.

The men had thrown the tent together without instructions. There had to be an "unidentified bolt" leftover somewhere. Walking around the dome-shaped tent, she lifted, poked and prodded at various intervals. She reached the front flap again, got down on her hands and knees and crawled halfway through the opening.

"Aha!" she yelled, spotting victory. "We win, doofus. You missed a sleeve here along the flooring."

"Like hell we did," Bill's muffled voice argued. "I'll tell you what, though. Why don't we let Jared decide who won the bet?"

Hope frowned in the dim interior. "Fat chance. I

don't trust that man as far as I can throw his backpack. Now get in here and I'll show you where you
screwed up.''

"Hope?" Karen sounded anxious. "I think you'd
better—''

"I'm not going to let them get away with this,
Karen. C'mon, Bill, quit stalling and get your tail in
here.''

"I'd suggest you move your own tail out of the
way, honey.'' The deep voice spoke from directly
behind Hope. "Because I'm comin' in.''

Frozen in position on her hands and knees, Hope
squeezed her eyes shut.

"Move it,'' Jared prompted.

Yes, but which direction? Opening her eyes, she
peered around the tent. The cozy two-person tent.
She imagined herself inside with Jared, then backed
up carefully, connecting with his crotch like a mesh-
ing gear.

Her mind took a second to assimilate the heat,
shape and feel of him before screaming a warning.

Plunging forward, she crawled all the way into the
tent and raised shaky hands to her hot face. Perfect.
Just what she needed.

"Why don't you all take a break and return here
in ten minutes?" Jared suggested.

That lecherous chuckle had to be Bill. "Sure you
don't need more time?''

"C'mon, doofus.'' Hank sounded disgusted.
"Let's go find you a banana.''

"All right, all right. But I hate bananas. And what the hell is a doofus, anyway?"

"Buddy—" a backslap punctuated the word "—if you have to ask, you *are* one. Let's go grab a drink and…"

Hank's voice faded as he and Bill left the room. Karen no doubt trailed behind them like a good little woman.

Hope stared at the green tent walls and strained to hear anything beyond the amplified sound of her own breathing. The cloying scent of new nylon permeated the air. What was Jared doing?

"I'll wait for Hope," Karen volunteered.

Well, whaddaya know?

"Hope will be fine, don't worry."

"But—"

"Trust me." A long pause followed, heavy with unseen communication.

Be strong, girlfriend. He's a wolf in Boy Scout's clothing.

"I'll be back in ten minutes," Karen said.

Hope's stomach dipped just short of queasiness. She was on her own as usual. But there was no one she trusted more. The sound of the closing classroom door straightened her backbone.

"The hell with this," she muttered.

Hope scrambled toward the entrance just as the tent flap lifted and Jared ducked through.

CHAPTER FIVE

HOPE'S FOREHEAD collided with Jared's with an audible thud. Recoiling, she fell back on her rump and moaned.

"Are you hurt?" Jared asked sharply.

"What am I? A bighorn sheep? Of course I'm hurt."

His bass chuckle vibrated around her, through her, within her, quickening her pulse, stealing her air. His shoulders spanned wall-to-wall as he crawled forward and she hastily scooted back.

Her spine hit a barrier and she stopped. The tent now smelled of sunshine and dusty male, a combination far more unsettling to her stomach than new nylon. He hadn't been pursuing her, Hope realized, but simply hauling his big carcass to sit where the domed roof was highest.

"Oh, you're definitely not a sheep," he said wryly, stretching out one treaded boot to rest near her hip, drawing in the other close to his body. He hooked an elbow around his upraised knee. "You like to lead, not follow. Win, not lose."

She dragged her gaze from his muscular calf. "And the problem with that would be...?"

His teeth gleamed pale in the dusky light. "Nothing, unless it turns into a power trip. Like that little episode you staged before lunch—that kiss." His blunt-tipped dangling fingers casually dusted off his boot toe, adjusted his sock. "Do you always use sex as a weapon?"

She blinked, then stifled a laugh. Wouldn't Debbie howl at that one? "Do you always kiss your female students?" she countered.

"I never have before. MindBend Adventures is as important to me as Manning Enterprises is to you. Don't pull a stunt like that again, Hope. I won't jeopardize my company's reputation for the sake of a temporary thrill."

"Do I thrill you?" The instant the words were out, Hope wanted to snatch them back.

He frowned and looked away.

To cover her embarrassment, she maneuvered around on her knees, leaned down and probed where the tent floor met the wall. "Bill and Hank will be back any minute," she told the mountain looming beside her. "I know it's here somewhere."

"What?"

"The spot they missed. Karen and I won the bet."

"It doesn't matter."

Hope stilled, sighed, then continued probing. "It matters to me. No more lectures please. So you dance to the beat of tom-toms, and I like Ludwig snares. You said yourself that every team member offers

unique strengths and that we should all get along—
Aha! Here it is.'' She glanced over her shoulder.

Jared wasn't looking at the exposed metal frame.

A flush bathed her skin from fingers to toes. She
knew what he was remembering. The same thing she
was—the moment she'd backed into his lap; a perfect
intimate fit. Hoo-boy.

"Do you see where they missed the sleeve?" she
croaked.

"Isn't it enough that *you* know they missed it? Is
a public win that important to you?"

Her primed body made the switch to high temper
in an instant. She pushed up and sat on her heels,
close enough to slap the disapproval from his face if
she'd dared. "Yes, Father Austin, a public win is that
important. And if your eyes had been on the tent
frame and not on *me,* I might be more inclined to
hear your sermon. So you listen to a story of mine,
instead.

"I know a doctor who's worked years developing
an implant for incontinent women. It's been tested in
France and Sweden and it works! Better than any
option currently available. Better than a competitive
device crawling through the FDA-approval process
as we speak. Better than thousands of housebound
women let themselves hope for during their lifetimes.
Can you understand what that means to them, Jared?

"It means regaining a normal active life—regaining dignity, for heaven's sake. But only if I push and
demand and shove my silent hero's product into the

public eye and onto the market. Only if I *win*, dammit. Loudly. Publicly.''

He was watching her with an odd expression, as if she'd surprised but not exactly pleased him.

''If that labels me the Nutcracker, I can live with the title. Silent heroes can't change the world by themselves, Jared. They need people like me to speed things along.'' Her steady gaze issued a challenge. ''Will you verify that Bill and Hank missed a section inside this tent?''

''It's really not necessary.''

Hope flinched, only that instant realizing how much his opinion mattered, how desperately she wished it didn't. She scrambled toward the tent entrance, away from this man who'd turned her inside out and discarded what he'd found. Would she *never* learn?

A steely hand clamped around her ankle.

She kicked and tugged to no avail, his strength as infuriating as it was humiliating. ''Let go of me,'' she ordered, horrified at the tremble in her voice.

He relinquished her foot, grasped her waist with both hands and deposited her effortlessly to face him. Her protest died from lack of oxygen as he leaned forward to mere inches from her nose.

''It's not necessary to show me what you found in here, Hope, because I already saw a mistake outside. The rain fly's not rigged properly.''

Her attention latched onto the thumbs stirring upward on her rib cage. They grazed the undersides of her breasts, detonating twin sunbursts of heat. If she shifted ever so slightly, those big palms would be exactly where her aching flesh needed them.

"Did you hear what I said?"

"Something about the rain fly?" she managed, appreciating its function for the first time. Without fabric that "breathed" the inner tent would be a swamp at the rate she was exhaling.

The indulgent gleam in his eyes said he knew exactly what he was doing to her—and enjoyed the knowledge. "That's right, Hope. Congratulations. You win."

The sweet words finally registered. She tightened her grip on brawny forearms and stared up at his face. An extremely handsome face, she finally admitted, her triumph mingling with the pleasure of simply looking at him until she couldn't have said which gave her more satisfaction.

"You don't play fair, Hope Manning." His voice had gone sandy and deep, his eyes smoky and intense.

"All's fair in..." Hoo-boy.

One corner of his mouth lifted. "Now you see my problem. We can't be lovers...and I really don't want to be your enemy or a competition that you win or lose. I guess that leaves only one thing."

Uncharted territory, that was what. Friendship with someone not connected to her business or easily controlled.

The classroom door opened. Lumbering footsteps

neared the tent. "Jeez, are you guys still in there?" Bill whined. "So who did you decide wins the bet, Jared?"

"Hang on, we're coming out. I have an announcement to make," Jared said. "A *public* one," he added, a smile starting in his eyes and spreading fast.

Helpless to do anything else, Hope smiled back and took her first shaky step into the unknown.

IN THE QUIET HOUR before dawn, Jared sipped a cup of coffee at his small kitchen table and cursed his promise of the day before. What had he been thinking, telling Hope that she could accept her bet payoff following this morning's meditation? The answer was that he hadn't—been thinking, that is. He'd been too busy feeling.

Too busy coping with the volatile emotions Hope provoked. Too busy touching the supple body he'd already memorized, a body so vibrant with feminine energy he'd wanted to bury himself deep and feel her hum around him. It'd been a helluva long night.

It was going to be a helluva lot longer expedition.

Lifting his glasses with a knuckle, he massaged gritty eyelids and sighed. If only Ben were standing at the clunky old stove, serving up a batch of fry bread along with sage advice and wisecracks. The Apache would know what Jared should do. God, he missed that old man.

He let his glasses drop and snugged up the wire frames, then briskly raised his mug. Coffee squeezed past the thickness in his throat and landed audibly in his empty stomach. He lowered the mug to one thigh and blinked hard, his gaze following a curl of steam over the Formica-topped table to a coiled shallow corn basket in the center.

The handiwork of Ben's mother, Jared knew, as were the beaded deerskin moccasins next to Jared's running shoes on the pine floor. The cutwork-leather saddlebag displayed like a painting on one adobe wall was a legacy from Ben's great-grandmother. Noting his own sleek inner-frame backpack leaning against the same wall, Jared smiled briefly.

The Dallas art gallery his father had once owned would've called the juxtaposition profound. And damned if it wasn't. He could appreciate the blend of modern technology and ancient craftsmanship—now.

Yet when he'd first wandered into Big Bend country six years ago, penniless and soul-sick, he'd rejected everything that had reminded him of his former fast-track lifestyle. It was Ben who'd shown him how to achieve a balance, embrace the best of both Native American and contemporary white man's culture, heal his spirit and strive to make each day a new beginning.

Draining the last of his coffee, he rose and moved to the rusting sink, filled with stacked dishes, a chore he'd put off too long. The hot water sputtered along with his frustrated thoughts.

His attraction to Hope was dangerous and inconvenient, a cursed itch he couldn't scratch. Which of course made him itch more. He hadn't been so hip-deep in poison ivy since his randy teenage years.

Scowling, Jared scrubbed the shine off a glazed stoneware plate and wished that Hope was the money-hungry capitalist he'd first thought.

But he'd stood outside the classroom door, knowing how important winning was to her, and seen her patience with Karen's initial clumsy efforts to set up the tent—efforts that could've lost the wager. Hope's "silent hero" story had rung true, also. And the vulnerability he'd glimpsed behind her need to win hadn't been faked. Someone in her past had really done a number on her self-esteem.

He didn't want to feel protective, dammit! His protection wasn't worth a bucket of sand.

A fist of memory blindsided him: Beth, as she'd looked when he'd broken their engagement, her hair and clothes rumpled, her beautiful eyes hungry, her fingers reaching as greedily for the bottle as they'd once reached for him.

Jared gripped the edge of the counter and bowed his head. Air. He needed some that didn't stink of whiskey, didn't echo with foul language.

Thrusting away from the sink, he headed for the front door, threw it wide and started walking, kept walking until his lungs felt clean and a soothing balm of silence penetrated his guilt. Awareness followed and he stopped.

The Chihuahuan desert loomed ahead. Vast. Calming. An irregular silhouette against a star-spangled violet backdrop. He checked the sky, adjusted his stance and waited for the show that beat a Vegas extravaganza hands down.

The curtain opened on a golden mist rising slowly from the eastern horizon, softly eliminating the violet night in delicate airbrushed sweeps. The higher the light climbed, the hotter its base glowed, first pink-gold, then strawberry-gold.

Only the brightest stars glimmered now, and they were fading fast.

And suddenly the headliner hit the stage. A rim of wavering molten orange pushing up...up...exploding spears of sunlight in all directions.

Humbled, Jared watched the shadowy desert cactus awaken in the dawn, their thorns tipped in gold. Hardy plants to survive a harsh land—one he'd grown to love as much as respect. He couldn't imagine living anywhere else, couldn't believe he'd once needed his corner office, his sexy car, his high-rise apartment, his party every night. Feeding his hungers of the flesh had nearly starved his spirit to death.

It had drowned Beth's in a sea of booze.

"No!" he shouted to the desert, shattering the quiet and his crippling thoughts.

He hadn't been able to save his fiancée, true. But by the grace of God and Ben, he'd made a productive new life for himself. These memories were a warning to get his act together, to remember the lessons he'd learned. All he had to do was keep his priorities straight, rein in his libido, and his hard-won peace would return. He could do that. He *would* do that.

But it was going to be one helluva long expedition.

"HOLD STILL," Hope ordered one hour later, waiting for the bare foot propped in her lap to stop fidgeting. The instant it did, she uncapped her nail polish.

"This is so embarrassing," Karen murmured from the edge of her bunk bed. She tugged down the hem of her glittering T-shirt for the third time in as many minutes. "Why can't I just keep my shoes on?"

"Because this will be a beautiful moment in women's history. Your feet should be beautiful, too."

"We're going to be late for breakfast."

Hope completed a shiny red stroke and glanced up sternly. "Where's your pride? Where's your sense of style?" She returned to her task and frowned. "Where's your little toenail, for heaven's sake? It doesn't even show. I've never seen a toe shaped quite like that."

Sherry and Dana leaned over from their perch on Hope's bunk.

"Oh, cool! It looks like a deformed turnip my grandma once grew. I kept it in a jar until it rotted."

"It looks like my editor's nose."

"It looks like a penis," Karen pronounced, attracting three startled gazes. "I've always thought so. At least, ever since I knew what one looked like."

Fascinated, Hope studied the toe in question more closely. *Well, whaddaya know?* Her mouth twitched.

Dana snorted.

Sherry giggled.

And all pretense of dignity crumbled. When the bawdy laughter subsided, Hope gazed down fondly. "We should give it a name. Men do that, you know. Name their little friends, I mean. Want to know why?" Having baited the hook, she carefully polished a second toenail.

Dana bit first. "Why?"

Hope erased her smile and looked up. "Because they don't want a complete stranger making ninety percent of their decisions for them."

Sputters dissolved into adolescent whoops and snickers. Sherry suddenly bounced on the mattress and flapped both hands. "Oh! Oh! Here's a good one." She paused, her bright ponytail swaying, her dimples deepening. "What's the difference between a man and E.T.?"

Hope wondered if she'd ever been that young, that...happy.

"E.T. phones home."

Sherry's belly-deep giggles were funnier than the joke. Or maybe it was nerves doing their laughing. They hit the trail tomorrow, and pressure to hold their own against the men was high.

"Okay, here's another one." Dana raised a finger for silence. "What does a man call 'helping with the housework'?" She waited the appropriate moment, then said, "Lifting his legs so you can vacuum underneath."

Chuckling, Hope recapped the nail polish and set it on the floor. It was time to separate the women from the girls.

"What's the difference between a man and a government bond?" she asked, her authoritative tone gaining their attention. "Bonds mature. What's the difference between men and parking spots?" This was almost too easy. "None. The good ones are taken and the rest are disabled. What do you call a man with half a brain?" The groans were escalating in volume now. "Gifted. How do you save a drowning man?"

"Don't tell us," Dana pleaded.

"Take your foot off his head," Hope told them, and grinned shamelessly. A white missile whizzed past close to her ear.

Dana reached for her second sock on the bunk and balled it up.

"Don't shoot!" Hope laughed and raised her palms. "I'm out of ammo."

Dana lowered her arm, unwadded her weapon and pulled the sock over one dainty foot. "That was without a doubt some of the lowest man-bashing I've ever heard."

"Thank you," Hope said modestly. "But actually I kept it pretty tame compared with some of the faxes I've received."

"Women fax you man-hater jokes?" Karen sounded incredulous.

"Man-*bashing* jokes, please. There's a big difference. And we don't hate men. We're just tired of the good-ol'-boy mentality a lot of them hang on to." Uncapping the bottle of polish again, Hope went back to work on Karen's toenails. "Women in my field—especially successful women—get so much chauvinistic flak we tend to collect and trade jokes to keep up morale. You should see the file my VP's collected."

Hope looked up, a smile tugging at her mouth. "Debbie considers it her feminist duty to fight fire with fire. The man who tells *her* a dumb-blonde joke gets torched in return."

"That is so rad!" Sherry tossed back her very blond ponytail, focused her very wide blue eyes on some inner vision that hardened her features. "I'd sure love to get my hands on that file."

"Me, too," Dana seconded, shaking a small fist in the air. "Then the next man who calls me 'little girl' would be toast."

Karen remained conspicuously quiet.

"I'll send all of you copies when I get home," Hope promised, and listened for the one thank-you she didn't get. Frowning, she continued polishing Karen's fourth toenail.

Sherry slid off the bunk bed and moved into Hope's peripheral vision. A sock arced through the air and bounced on the mattress next to Dana.

"Hey, little girl, want some candy?" Sherry asked in a dirty-old-man voice. "Put your shoes on and let's go eat."

"Sure, babe, I'm starved," Dana answered, her voice a dirty-young-man-on-the-make's. "And I don't mean for food, if you know what I mean."

Hope chuckled and spoke without looking up. "Okay already, I'll send your copies overnight mail. Sheesh."

"What a gal! So are you guys coming with us to breakfast?" Dana sounded flatteringly hopeful.

Karen's propped foot stirred.

Hope pressed her free hand down on the arch. "We'll grab a granola bar later, thanks." A sigh drifted over her head, but the toes in her lap stayed put.

Minutes later Sherry opened the cabin door and paused on the threshold. "We'll be sitting front row center in the classroom. I'm taking my camera."

Dana prodded her roommate outside, reached for the doorknob and added, "I'm sending a print to Bill's wife." The door closed on her evil laughter.

Grinning, Hope lifted the little toe that had created such hoopla and painted the tiny hidden nail. "This foot is ready for homage now. The other should go much faster without distractions. Give it here, please."

Karen absently obliged, her light blue gaze riveted on the toes of her deserving foot. She seemed enchanted with the fanned display.

Hope hid her smile and polished a naked toenail. "Aren't they pretty? When you go home and get that manicure we talked about, be sure to arrange for a pedicure, too." The long silence brought her head up.

All trace of delight had vanished from Karen's plump face. She tugged down the hem of her glittering T-shirt and bit her lower lip.

"You're not going to get a manicure, are you?" Hope already knew the answer.

"Please don't get mad. I'm not like you, Hope. I guess I have no pride, no sense of style. But the kids don't care what my nails look like, and I'd just ruin a manicure, anyway, scrubbing the bathtub or washing dishes. Besides, Jim... Well, it would be a silly waste of money."

Masking her irritation, Hope wielded her nail-polish brush again. "And your budget won't allow for waste, right?"

"That's right. I'm glad you understand."

She'd gotten a fair picture the other day. "I don't mean to pry, but I get the feeling you don't know as much about your family finances as maybe you should."

"I think I manage pretty darn well to make each penny count," Karen said stiffly, her nonexistent pride making a welcome appearance.

"I *know* you do. But that's not what I mean." Hope's experiences as a financial counselor kicked in to help her explain. "Let me put it this way. If

Jim were to suddenly die or fall seriously ill, or if he moved out of the house and wanted a divorce, would you know how to get your hands on the family money?''

''We have a joint checking account.''

There was no kind way to do this, so she plunged right in. ''What are your debts and your credit rating? Are your assets held in savings accounts, real estate, stocks—what? How much insurance do you have and what kind? How much money does Jim spend each month, Karen? He expects an accounting from you. Don't you think it's fair to see what kind of budget he's put himself on?''

''I never pretended to be as smart as you.''

Hope glanced up at the trembling mouth, the welling eyes, and ruthlessly hardened her heart. ''The 'poor pitiful me' stuff won't wash, Karen. Anyone who can manage a budget like you do is smart. What you *aren't* is informed, and you can change that by demanding some answers when you get home.''

''Jim doesn't want a divorce, and he's in perfect health.'' The first tear spilled. ''Why are you being so mean?''

''You want to hear mean? Mean is the husband who canceled all credit cards—the ones Mrs. Rangel was authorized to sign also—and then opened new accounts in his name. Mean is the husband who wiped out Mrs. Pothier's joint checking account, then asked her for a divorce. Mean is the husband who hid income from both Mrs. Tucker and the government. When they divorced, she received a settlement based on his understated tax returns.

"I've counseled women who were totally victimized by widowhood or divorce, simply because they didn't take the time or responsibility for learning about their husband's money." The cases had reinforced Hope's belief that she was right to trust only herself, to take control of her own destiny. That way she could never be made to feel lacking or inadequate by someone else.

"Um, Hope?"

Shaking off her thoughts, Hope met Karen's gaze, which was dry now, but wary.

"The, um, nail polish is drying on the brush."

Realizing she was scowling fiercely, Hope relaxed her mouth and looked down. "So it is. Thanks."

She peeled off a rubbery layer of polish, dipped the brush for a fresh application and set to work, painting quickly and steadily. A bittersweet twinge of regret stilled her hand as it poised above Karen's little toe. She'd ruined their earlier camaraderie, but she'd done the ethical thing. It wasn't right that Karen should remain dependent and vulnerable if Hope could help change that status.

She finished the tiny toenail, recapped the bottle and lifted the newly polished foot from her lap to the floor. "There you go, beautiful. Give it ten minutes to dry and you'll be all set. Want me to get your sandals for you?"

Karen pulled her gaze from her matching set of

toes and nodded. "They're in the side compartment of my suitcase."

Hope dragged out the case, removed the white flat sandals and shoved the luggage back. Funny how quickly she'd gotten used to living in Camp Twilight Zone. She would almost miss the cabin when they left for Mexico tomorrow. For sure she'd miss Dana and Sherry. Go figure.

Standing up for a joint-popping stretch, Hope dropped the sandals at Karen's feet.

"Thank you," Karen said, her gaze making it clear she wasn't talking about sandals.

Hope's heart gave a happy little lurch. "You're welcome. Now, let's go rub some noses in it!"

CHAPTER SIX

FROM HIS FRONT-ROW SEAT, Jared didn't know whether to laugh or frown. He'd turned over his classroom floor as promised, but damned if he'd known they wanted his utility table, too.

Hope and Karen sat side by side on the square surface, their bare feet dangling, their expressions comically haughty. Hank and Bill stood off to the side, their expressions comically grim.

Hope unrolled a scroll of legal-pad paper and held it like a royal proclamation. "Hank Thompson and Bill Harper, we hereby demand that you pay proper respect to the superiority of female logic and instruction-book literacy by honoring the terms of our bet."

As she lowered the paper, two right feet stretched out as one, like the Queen Mother's royal knuckles.

Whistles and applause broke out among the women students, laughing groans from the men. Dana and Sherry had spread word of the bet at breakfast, and the class knew what was coming.

Hank lowered to his knees first and yanked Bill down beside him. When they each pressed lips against fluttering red-tipped toes, a camera flashed blindingly from the front row. Hope gave a thumbs-up sign and the camera flashed again.

Her cinnamon brown eyes sparkled, her wide mouth laughed, her rich auburn curls caught the light and tossed it back. Dressed in a rainbow tie-dyed T-shirt and cuffed denim shorts, she was a prism in a sunny window flashing color and life and joy.

The woman behind Hope's veneer of sarcasm and distrust was nothing short of dazzling. Jared couldn't look away.

He let the rowdiness go on a few more minutes, knowing that some of it was due to tomorrow's departure for the trailhead. Spirits were high. Nerves were edgy. His own felt like Mexican jumping beans. When he finally tore his gaze from Hope, he noted Karen's uninhibited participation with interest.

This Karen was a far cry from the timid creature he'd worried about leading into the backcountry. Hope had obviously taken the blond woman under her wing. The tough lady executive who didn't need anyone responded compassionately to someone who needed *her*, and the result was impressive.

Deciding it was time to move on, Jared rose and reclaimed his table. When the four flushed teammates were settled once again in their chairs, he faced a more relaxed and attentive group than he had fifteen minutes earlier. Hope had actually done him a favor by releasing the students' pent-up tension.

Too bad she'd tied the teacher's guts in a double square reef knot.

THEY'D GLOSSED OVER this part of the program in the MindBend Adventures literature, Hope realized. After an hour of listening to Jared, she could understand why. If she'd known the dangers of backcountry camping included diarrhea, she might've let Debbie resign as VP and taken a chance on finding a comparable replacement.

From her front-row seat, Hope studied the first-aid items on the table and shuddered at the possibility of using them. Moleskin for foot blisters. Ace bandages for sprained joint ligaments. Antibiotic cream for minor abrasions and "inevitable" cactus punctures. Antidiarrhea medicine in case proper cooking sanitation wasn't observed.

She made a mental note to watchdog the assigned trail-team chef, then moved on. Gauze pads and tape for bleeding wounds—not to panic. Prescription painkiller for, in Jared's words, "more serious injuries." Since the other ailments had sounded pretty serious to her, she dreaded to learn what he meant.

She'd been feeling so good about things, too. So...well, good. She glanced sideways and warmed at Karen's quick smile. The foot-kissing ceremony had brought out a playful side to her nature that Hope suspected Jimbo the Jerk didn't approve of one bit. Now, if only she could work on Karen's fragile self-esteem.

Jared had dragged the card table back several feet and was replacing it with a television and VCR unit from the rear of the room. He rolled the squeaky stand to prime viewing position, tossed the coiled cord toward a wall plug and said, "Get that for me, will you, Hank?"

As the tall lanky man appeared in Hope's line of vision, she remembered the moment he'd wrapped hands big enough to span a basketball around Karen's ample waist and lifted her onto the table. They'd stared into each other's eyes in a way that made Hope delighted—and uneasy.

After all, her friend was a happily...well, she was married, anyway. Learning self-reliance should be Karen's priority. She did *not* need complications like Hank before then.

Against Hope's will, her gaze strayed to her own complication.

Jared fussed with the VCR, looking capable and absorbed and amazingly comforting after only two short days of acquaintanceship. Hoo-boy.

She didn't depend on people; it was the other way around. Her employees, her investors, her few friends, the various entrepreneurs who were going to set the world on fire but needed her to light the match—they all looked to her for guidance and support. She was strong because she'd broken off every relationship that threatened to make her emotionally vulnerable. Jared had guessed the truth of that right away.

Had he also guessed how lonely she was?

The overhead lights flicked off, and with them, her

confused thoughts. She gazed at the TV screen where the title "Dealing with Accidents" faded in and out.

The audio and video quality of the tape was terrible. Wannabe actors delivered their lines with painful woodenness. Without the production values of "Rescue 911," the reenactments bordered on laughable.

She leaned over to Karen and muttered, "Forget accident. This tape is a national disaster."

From her teammate's fixed stare on the screen, Hope gathered she wasn't amused. In fact, she appeared to be extremely involved in the action.

Turning back to the TV, Hope decided to be a good little girl and watch quietly. The fractured-wrist segment was kind of interesting. Actors placed the victim's arm in a sling and immobilized it against his chest. When shock set in, they elevated his legs and tipped water down his throat. She could do that. Maybe.

Uh-oh, what was this? Didn't grown men know better than to play with sharp knives? The idiot on screen was whittling small fire-starter shavings from a piece of wood, his supporting hand smack in the path of the blade. Oops! Yu-uck.

She groaned along with the class. The copious flow of blood certainly stained the man's shirt and dripped like the real thing. The gruesome sight held her spellbound. Something swayed into her peripheral vision.

Hope reached out, grabbed air and stared at the woman lying facedown on the floor.

Well, hell, the tape hadn't covered anything about fainting.

HOPE SAT ON THE EDGE of Jared's king-size mattress and held the patient's limp hand. Karen had protested as he'd carried her to his house, but his large bed and air-conditioning window unit beat the hot cabin bunk bed, hands down. She still looked too pale for Hope's liking.

"C'mon, girlfriend, open your eyes and talk. You're scaring me." Hope brushed flyaway strands of hair back from Karen's sweet face. "I am *not* going to be the only woman on a trail team with Bill, do you hear me?"

Long golden lashes fluttered, then lifted. Understanding chased confusion across widening eyes, leaving a gaze as clear and blue as the West Texas sky. "I made a huge fool of myself, didn't I? Are they going to send me home?"

Jared's sudden bedside appearance prevented the need for Hope's response. She hadn't heard him approach, but then, she never did.

Studying Karen as if she were his clipboard, he seemed reassured. "Well, I see you decided to rejoin us." He set a glass of water on the nightstand, then draped a wet washcloth across Karen's forehead.

The action pulled his khaki shorts and shirt tight and did similar things to Hope's stomach muscles.

"I've gotta hand it to you, Karen. I thought Hope knew how to stage a dramatic scene, but you could give her lessons." He tweaked her nose before straightening.

Two splashes of pink stained Karen's cheeks. "I'm sorry I caused so much trouble. I feel better now, really." She struggled to sit up.

He pressed her gently back against the pillow. "Relax."

"But...who's teaching your class?"

"Matt took over the lesson. Don't worry, he's a pro. They won't even know I'm gone."

"But—" she looked wildly around the room "—I'm in your bed. I can't impose like this."

"Karen, Karen, Karen." Jared pushed up his glasses, his slow arrogant grin as far from nerdy as it got. "The time a pretty woman in my bed is an imposition is the day I take a dirt nap. Now hush up and stay put. I want to check your heart rate." He sat on the edge of the mattress and sank deep into the springs.

Releasing Karen's hand, Hope fought gravity— and lost.

It was like rolling into a boulder. Her breast, hip and thigh flattened against his granite frame and came away imprinted with a new area of his body. She was learning the feel of him one muscle group at a time, Hope realized hysterically as she scooted to the foot of the bed. And her Silly Putty imitations left him totally unaffected, the pig.

While she waited for her heartbeat to slow, he counted Karen's and checked his watch.

"Good. You're doing fine. Can you drink some water now?"

When she nodded, he supported her shoulders, held the glass against her lips until she finished, then guided her back down.

A fierce pang of longing gripped Hope. What would it be like to let someone else do the worrying? Someone with shoulders strong and broad enough to bear problems and a woman's head with equal ease?

"All right, Karen, I want you to tell me the truth here. Is there a medical condition you didn't write down on your application? High blood pressure? Pregnancy? Some reason you fainted in class that I need to know about?"

"Well…"

Hope tensed in alarm.

"Don't be embarrassed," Jared soothed. "Whatever you say will stay in this room. Right, Hope?"

"Of course." She scooted closer and stretched out her hand.

Karen grasped it eagerly. "All right, there *is* a condition you should probably know about. I have a major case of…weenie-itis."

The air-conditioning unit hummed in the silence.

Hope twisted to stare at Karen's little toes.

"No, no," Karen said on a groaning laugh. "It has nothing to do with Thing One and Thing Two."

Thing One and Thing Two? Hope's gaze leaped

up to meet mischievous blue eyes. "When did you name them?"

"Somewhere between 'blisters' and 'diarrhea.' What do you think?"

Hope thought the vacation from a round hole was doing her friend a world of good. "Hmm, easy to remember. Descriptive." Her lips curved. "I like it."

"What the *hell* are you two talking about?" Jared asked. "No, never mind, I have a feeling even Dr. Seuss wouldn't want to know. Just tell me what you mean by weenie-itis, Karen, and leave it at that."

A cloud passed over the blue West Texas sky. "It means having no guts. Jim made up the term. You know, the boss who vetoes an aggressive marketing strategy has weenie-itis. The seven-year-old son who can't pull the trigger of a deer rifle has weenie-itis. The wife who faints at the first sight of blood—who lies on her kitchen floor while her son needs help— that wife has a *major* case of weenie-itis.

"It means that if anyone on the expedition has the bad manners to bleed, I'll be totally useless to the team." She offered Jared a rueful smile. "I'll understand if you send me home."

Hope opened and closed her mouth. Her protest would have had no clout.

"Do you faint often?" Jared asked carefully.

"Just the one time before today, but that was a doozy."

"What happened?"

Karen turned away, her gaze growing unfocused.

"Lee was still at school and I was making a meat loaf for dinner. I told Tommy—he was five at the time—to go outside and play. He'd never touched his father's hunting gear before, but he did this particular day. He sneaked a skinning knife right past me and went outside just like I'd told him. If I'd checked, I would have seen him cutting tree branches in the backyard. But I didn't." Her mouth twisted. "Heaven forbid I not have Jim's meat loaf out of the oven by six. When Tommy burst in later, I took one look at his finger—" She stopped. Remembered horror thickened her voice. "It was dangling by a piece of skin. Blood was everywhere, and he started screaming..."

Hope's own fingers were being squeezed numb, but her heart ached more.

"So he was scared," Jared prodded. A statement, not a question.

Karen's head turned, her eyes blazing with self-contempt. "He was terrified. But did I calm my little boy's fear? Did I try to stop the bleeding or in any way deal with his accident? Not the gutless wonder. No, I passed out cold, hit my head on the counter and woke up in an ambulance. Tommy called 911 himself and then ran next door. If Mica hadn't been home...well, Tommy retained limited use of his finger, thanks to her."

Jared gave her story the long moment of consideration it deserved. Then he reached for the washcloth on Karen's forehead, shook it out and fanned it in the air. "I could tell you that seeing someone you love in pain was a traumatic shock to your own system. Or that three-hundred-pound linebackers have fainted watching their wives deliver a baby." He refolded the cooled cloth and laid it gently back on her forehead. "I could tell you that you can be proud of teaching a five-year-old what to do in an emergency. Or that Jim should have his butt kicked for adding to your guilt about Tommy's accident. I could tell you all that—but I know it wouldn't help, because you're not ready to believe me yet."

Hope found her brow furrowing along with Karen's.

His lips quirked. "*The past has no power over me. Negative thoughts have no power over me. I am the power in my world.* Funny how if you say those words often enough and stop to think about what you're saying, one day they really are true." He patted Karen's knee and rose swiftly. "I want you to rest about fifteen more minutes, then we'll head over to the school and start learning some navigational skills."

Hope's fingers had regained their circulation. She slipped her hand free and stood.

"Do you need anything else right now?" Jared asked Karen from the bedroom door.

She shook her head. "Does this mean I'm still on the team?"

"Are you kidding? I am *not* going to be on a trail

team with Hope as the only woman.'' He grinned and ducked out of sight.

Hope stuck out her tongue at the empty doorway.

''You like him,'' Karen said.

''Do not.''

''Do, too.''

Hope thought of his compassionate response to Karen's guilt and tried for a casual shrug. ''Quit talking and rest, enjoy the air conditioner, roll around in all that space. You'll be squeezed in a tent with me soon enough.'' She headed for the bedroom door.

''Hope?''

She turned around.

''Do, too.''

Shutting the door on the sight of Karen's goofy grin, Hope knew that her own was a close match. She spun around, took a step and pulled up short.

''You're a good influence on her,'' Jared said quietly.

He sat at a small table off the small kitchen, his sprawled form dwarfing a small chair. Uncrossing his clunky hiking boots, he shoved one rubber sole against a second chair and sent it scraping back from the table.

''Join me?''

On a scale of one to ten, the invitation rated about a two. She shook her head and started forward.

He flowed up from the chair with the speed of a blink and moved to block her path. ''Bet I know how to change your mind.'' His voice was low, taunting, with a definite sexual growl.

For the life of her she couldn't speak, couldn't unlock her muscles as he reached out and gripped her shoulders. Her nerves leapt beneath his hands, her pulse joined the erratic rhythm, so that it was seconds before she realized he'd turned her toward the kitchen.

His warm fingers at her nape guided her forward, then to a stop. Yanking open the door of an ancient refrigerator, he rummaged inside, withdrew his hand and grinned.

"Still want to go?" he asked, waving something in her face.

She focused on the Diet Coke and blinked.

"I love you," she said, meaning it, then stroked the can to make sure it wasn't a mirage.

Chuckling, he nudged the door shut with his hip, returned to the table and sat in his original sprawl. She followed the can and stood staring at the white-and-red logo.

"Join me?" he asked again.

She dropped readily into the second chair.

"I finally find the secret to making you pliant and obedient, and I only have one Diet Coke on the premises."

"Give it to me." She reached out.

He pulled the can against his body. "Say please."

"Give it to me…please."

"Say it nicely."

"Give it to me please, or I'll take your bottom lip, stretch it up over your head and pull it down to your tailbone," she said nicely.

"Well, okay, that's better." He leaned forward and offered her the can.

She snatched it and fumbled to pop the top without breaking a nail.

"Here," he said disgustedly, performing the simple task for her. "You're going to have to cut those before we hit the trail tomorrow."

Intent on one thing only, she raised the can and gulped. Cold fizzy heaven. After five or six swallows she was forced to stop and breathe. "No way," she managed.

"Think again."

She thought a second. "No friggin' way." Six gulps later she plunked down the empty can.

"You would've enjoyed that more if you hadn't been in such a hurry."

Annoyance laced her delicate burp. "Do you always have to analyze everything?"

"Do you always have to challenge authority?"

"Do you always have to answer a question with a question?"

"What?"

"Do you always have—" Hope stopped, clued in by the unholy amusement in his eyes, and allowed herself a grudging smile.

She enjoyed sparring with a worthy opponent, and this man was one of the most aggravating and intriguing she'd ever met. Her gaze wandered curiously around the room. Details she'd missed earlier in her concern for Karen claimed her attention now. Hope's visual tour ended at the shallow basket sitting in the middle of the table.

Hesitantly, reverently, she fingered the woven black-and-wheat-colored fibers. "This basket—the moccasins, the saddlebags, that feathered hat-looking thing over the sofa—all of them are real, aren't they?"

"If you mean they were crafted by Apache hands, instead of a machine, then yes, they're real. And that feathered hat-looking thing over the sofa is a feathered hat. You're very observant." He grinned as she narrowed her eyes. "Owl feathers, to be exact. The basket you're touching is about 150 years old."

Hope jerked her fingers away.

"Don't worry, it's made of yucca and Desert Claw, so it's tougher than you think. One day I'll donate everything to the Museum of The Big Bend at Sul Ross University. Joel—he's the curator— would be hounding me now if he knew about this stuff, but—" he reached out and idly traced the basket's black-diamond pattern "—as selfish as it sounds, I'm not quite ready to let go of it all yet."

As he'd had to let go of the old Indian Matt had told her about. "Mr. Loping Wolf trusted you to take good care of his things, or he wouldn't have willed them to you."

Jared looked startled, then gave a bark of laughter.

"Running Bear," he corrected. "And I can see I'll need to have a little chat with Motor-Mouth Matt about fraternizing with the students. Especially our nosy beautiful ones."

She grabbed the Diet Coke and tipped it to her mouth, knowing the can was empty, yet needing to do something to cover her confusion. This was the second time he'd called her beautiful. It wasn't a name men used in connection with the Nutcracker.

"You're a lot like the old coot. Ben, I mean," Jared said, a reminiscent smile tugging at his lips. "Stubborn. Smart-mouthed."

So much for being beautiful.

"Constantly challenging what I say and think I know. You two would've hit it off."

"He sounds like my kinda guy," she admitted. "You really miss him, don't you?"

"More than my own father."

"Oh—I'm sorry."

"Don't be. My father's not dead."

"Oh." Now what? "Well, that's good."

His smile held no trace of humor. "He might disagree. He's serving a twelve-year sentence for racketeering, fraud and conspiracy. My father is Charles Austin, of Loan Star Savings and Loan. You may remember him?"

She tried to control her expression. Charles Austin had been among the worst swindlers leading to the collapse and government seizure of countless S and L's during the eighties. By investing the Texas S and

L's insured deposits in high-risk land, hotels and se-
curities deals—deals that went sour—he'd cost tax
payers over three billion.

"Ah, I see you do remember." Jared's eyelids
lowered, but not quickly enough to screen a flash of
vulnerability.

"You're not responsible for what your father did.
No one judges you for his crimes."

"*Everyone* judged me, including the federal
courts. I worked for my father's holding company
and lived like a damn prince, so it's no wonder they
suspected me of conspiracy, too."

"You weren't convicted."

"I didn't spend time in jail, no. But what with
legal fees for Dad and me...well, I hit rock bottom.
Financially *and* emotionally—" He broke off and
frowned, as if regretting the confession.

He'd hit rock bottom but wound up establishing a
successful new venture, one designed as much to
help executives get their heads on straight as to earn
a profit. Her respect for Jared rose another notch.

"What about your mother?" Hope asked gently.
"Where does she live?"

"Why don't you ask Matt?"

She lifted the empty can and sucked air again. Jared couldn't know that normally she didn't ask nosy
questions. Normally she flat out didn't care.

"Hey, I'm only teasing. My mother died the year
I graduated from UT. There's an uncle still in Dallas
where I was raised, an aunt in Detroit. No brothers

or sisters. Probably a few distant relatives somewhere if I bothered to do the research. How about you?'' he asked, bringing her head up. ''Any more Hope clones out there terrorizing the financial world?''

Turnabout was fair play. ''I'm an only child, too. But I have about a zillion relatives whose idea of a stock market is the monthly cattle auction in Hopeful, Texas.''

''Hopeful?'' Without moving from his slouch, he perked up.

'''Fraid so. And yes, I was named for the town, which is as apple pie good ol' country as it sounds. My parents run a small ranch ten miles outside of town. I lived there until I was eighteen.''

He shook his head, slanted up a disbelieving glance, shook his head once more and grinned. ''Hopeful, huh? I have a hard time picturing you from a small town. I'll bet Bill could get a lot of mileage out of that.''

Not if he didn't know about it. She arched a warning brow. ''Museum of The Big Bend, huh? What was that curator's name again?''

''Okay,'' he said with a chuckle, ''I won't squeal if you won't. But I don't know what the big deal is. There's no shame in being small-town born and bred.''

''I agree. I'm not the one who's ashamed.''

''So who is? Ashamed, that is.''

Good going, brainiac. ''It's not important.'' Checking her watch, she slapped both palms on her knees. "Well, thanks for the Diet Coke. I really enjoyed—"

"Whoa, whoa, whoa. Back up a minute. I have a feeling it *is* important."

"Wrong again, for the first time in your life."

"Then why not answer the question?"

"And you called *me* nosy?" She huffed. "Why should I tell you anything?"

"Because you don't trust me."

"Oh, that makes sense."

"Because you are the power in your world, and whatever I think, whatever I say has no influence over you unless you choose to let it."

She flung up her hands in disgust. "Good grief, Jared, do you really believe that New Age bunk?"

"That 'New Age bunk' was a part of Native American spirituality before our ancestors built Stonehenge."

His quiet response triggered a blast of righteous anger. How many times had she heard that same tone of disappointment in other lectures? "I don't care who takes credit for the concept, it's still bunk. A child has no power in an adult world. *I* sure didn't." She winced at his startled expression but blundered on. "You want to know who's ashamed in good ol' Hopeful, Texas? My parents, that's who. But they're ashamed of me, not the town."

Jared removed his glasses, pulled up some shirt slack and began cleaning his lenses. "You take active responsibility for the operational decisions, successes and disasters of— How many ventures are in the Manning Enterprises fund?''

It took her a second to switch gears. ''Seven.''

''Seven entrepreneurial companies, not to mention deciding where, when and how much of your investors' money to sink into each operation for a profitable return. There are only about five hundred respected venture capitalists in the entire United States, and you're one of them.'' He looked up and met her gaze. ''I doubt your parents are ashamed of you.''

His familiarity with her world stunned her—almost as much as the unobstructed beauty of his dark blue eyes.

Three sharp knocks prevented her from having to answer. He rose swiftly and opened the door.

Hank stood with his hands on his hips, his expression anxious. ''Matt's finished with the class now. I said I'd come tell you.'' His hazel gaze searched the room beyond Jared. ''How's Karen?''

''She's fine and resting comfortably. In fact, would you mind getting her, Hope?''

She was already out of her chair.

''We'll continue our talk another time,'' Jared told her pointedly. ''I'd like to hear more about your family.''

''Sure thing, Scout.''

When the Chihuahuan desert freezes over.

CHAPTER SEVEN

AT THREE O'CLOCK the next afternoon, Hope stared after the dust billowing behind three vans going the wrong direction. Although rusty, jouncing and without air-conditioning, they represented the last of civilization as she knew it. When they were distant glints beneath the broiling sun, she turned to the sign that read Cabeza de Sendero.

Trailhead her fanny. Typical MindBend Adventures propaganda. If the desert beyond contained a legitimate path of any kind, it hadn't been trod by human feet.

Crossing the Rio Grande that morning near Terlingua had been light-years from her one and only trip years ago to Nuevo Laredo, Mexico. This time there'd been no bridge traffic, no bridge guards, no *bridge,* period. Jared had prearranged for the group to be rowed across the river, where three decrepit vans waited to take them from here to the trailhead.

The Mexican landscape shimmered with heat waves, bristled with low clumps of hostile-looking vegetation. A ridge of hazy blue mountains, the Sierra del Carmen, beckoned on the eastern horizon. She scowled at the lack of trees in the immediate vicinity, her concern having more to do with the huge quantity of water she'd been instructed to drink than with diminishing desert flora.

Underlying her cynicism, a current of nervous excitement hummed steadily. This was the destination she'd traveled thousands of miles to reach, the moment she'd spent the past three days preparing to confront.

Backpacks rested beside students dressed for desert brush country—long pants, light fabrics and colors, assorted styles of hats and sunglasses. Four trail guides huddled around Jared for mysterious last-minute orders. This must be a little how untested soldiers felt before entering a battle, Hope thought. Would they return as heroes or as cowards? She really didn't want to humiliate herself or the female race.

Jared broke from the huddle and fiddled with his backpack. He'd left his Boy Scout uniform back at the school, opting, instead, for a body-hugging white T-shirt, multipocketed olive green pants, a baseball cap in the same range of green and his purple-framed sunglasses. When he straightened and flashed a smile as white as his shirt, Hope heard the woman next to her sigh.

Go find your own trail leader, Hope thought uncharitably.

He raised his hand for attention. "Okay, everybody, listen up. This first leg of the expedition is our only full group hike, and we'll be spread horizontally for minimum impact on the desert surface. That means we're more likely to disturb animals and reptiles out of their routines, so remember to walk softly, observe quietly and keep your distance.''

No problem.

''The first few miles I want you to pay attention to your body. If your backpack needs adjusting or your feet are bothering you in any way, don't hesitate to speak up. Adjustments today can save you from a lot of nuisance pain farther down the road.''

No problem.

''If you absolutely positively have to answer your own call of nature before a scheduled rest stop, let your trail leader know. He'll stay close and then make sure you catch up with the others.''

Hoo-boy.

''Finally, I want to say how pleased I am with your progress over the past few days. Each one of you is ready and able to pass through this special ecosystem as an integral and natural part of nature.'' He paused to sweep his approving gaze over the students. ''I'm sure you'll be a credit to MindBend Adventures.''

All around Hope, chests swelled with a desire to hike this one for the Gipper. Jared was good, she admitted. Damn good. He'd even taken the edge off her resentment. She glanced down at her amputated fingernails and grimaced. *Some* of the edge.

''All right, then.'' Jared clapped his palms together

once. "I guess it's time to find your trail buddy and gear up."

Karen stood gnawing a fingernail as if it were her last meal. Walking close, Hope tugged the brim of her trail buddy's jaunty straw safari hat.

"Stop ruining your dinner and put on your sunglasses."

The hand came down. Karen patted one camp-shirt pocket and pulled out a tube of zinc oxide, patted the other and struck pay dirt. Slipping on the huge round frames, she smeared opaque white cream on her nose and offered the tube to Hope, who shook her head.

"Did you put on plenty of sunscreen?" Karen asked.

"Yeah. But if you ask me, this beach stinks. No towel boys, no bar service—and the tide is *really* low."

Groaning, Karen reached out and yanked the bill of Hope's No Fear baseball cap down over her grin.

Resetting her cap, Hope hoisted up her friend's external frame backpack and held it at the ready. When Karen was strapped and buckled in, they walked to Hope's backpack and repeated the process.

They'd organized the contents so that the heaviest items were high and close to the body. The shoulder straps absorbed about twenty percent of the weight with the rest centered in the hip belt. Much easier on the back, Jared had assured them, than earlier beltless versions.

As thirty-five pounds of supplies made itself known, Hope thought fleetingly of those pioneer hikers. Martyrs, that was what they'd been. Stupid ones, at that.

"Hiya, girls. Need any help?"

Hope was amazed to feel a smidgen of affection for Bill as he approached, followed by Hank, who merited her sincere smile. "No thanks, I think it's under control."

By now most of the students had clustered into trail teams, instinctively wanting to start the journey with those who would see them through to the end. Jared moved to the trailhead sign and faced the restless group.

"Is everybody ready now?" The silence crackled with anticipation. "All right then, people...let's do it!"

Hope moved forward on a surge of adrenaline. They fanned out approximately six feet apart and settled into an uneven horizontal line facing the mountains. Bill and a few others charged ahead as if running a footrace. She snorted and began the rhythmic breathing Jared had recommended. Three steps while inhaling, the same for exhaling. Unnatural but manageable. It felt weird to concentrate on something like breathing.

In fact, everything felt weird. The bulky aluminum-frame backpack, the pull of her padded hip belt, the ankle-high boots she'd twisted this way and that in front of the shoe-store mirror. She'd complained they made her feet look like sperm whales. Thank goodness her salesperson had insisted their durability and fit were better than the funky red pair she'd favored. These brown clodhoppers were awkward enough as it was.

Up ahead, she saw Jared gaining on the four front-runners, his walk fluid, yet odd in a way she couldn't pinpoint. He spoke to each man individually, said something they all laughed at, then positioned them as they fell back in line.

She dodged a prickly pear cactus, skirted a spiky unidentified plant, sent a spray of pebbles skipping over the sandy ground. Shifting her right shoulder, she eased the strap a half inch to the left. Was it supposed to pinch like that? Tickles scurried like insect legs down her neck, her back, between her breasts. She was only slightly less repulsed to know they were rivulets of sweat, not centipedes.

The last time she'd endured the sensation she'd been eighteen, standing over her mother's stove helping can summer vegetables. Never again, she'd vowed to herself in the hot steamy kitchen. No more endless chores that earned only sweat and criticism. No more of the Texas heat that had sapped the life from her grandmother, freeing Hope to leave.

She only visited her parents now in the winter, a few weekends at the most. They refused to travel to New York. Too dirty, too big, too filled with punks who'd as soon mug you as say hello. Uncle Eddy and Aunt Michelle had been to the Big Apple and had passed the word. Never mind that the daughter who lived there said differently. Hope thought that pretty much summed up how she rated with her parents.

"Why the grim face? Are you hurting?" Jared had moved soundlessly up beside her.

It took her two seconds to realize he meant physically, another three to scan her body for the answer. There was a spot on her heel... "No, I'm fine. A little thirsty, though."

Never breaking stride, she unsnapped the canteen from her waist and sensed him watch her swallow, watch her wipe self-consciously at a dribble, watch her recap the container. She groped for the snap loop at her belt, her hands clumsy because he watched. He found the loop for her and she stumbled, pressing his hand into her belly in a desperate grab for balance. A heat to rival the desert floor spread from the point of contact. She helplessly met his eyes.

They were screened by dark lenses, but they watched her. They wanted her.

Hoo-boy.

She straightened and found her stride, an awkward shuffling thing compared with Jared's smooth motion. Seizing the distraction, she gestured to his feet.

"There's something different about the way you walk, but I can't quite put my finger on it."

"You mean the fox walk. It was one of the first things Ben taught me after I met him." His glance seemed to gauge her level of interest before he continued. "Most people walk on the insides of their feet, heels first, heads down, bodies leaning slightly forward. That's okay for pavement and level floors, but it can be noisy and clumsy out here. Boots can do a lot of damage to plant life and terrain."

As if on cue, her boot toe hit a partially submerged rock and she lurched forward. Regaining her balance, she threw him a wry smile. "Point taken. So why didn't you cover how to walk properly in class?"

He shrugged. "For short courses I concentrate on the essentials. Advanced-course students get into the finer points. They usually have a deep commitment to preserving our wilderness resources."

An irrational spurt of jealousy thinned Hope's mouth. Anything an advanced-course student could do, she could do better. "Show me this fox walk...please."

"Or I'll be using my bottom lip for an umbrella?"

She didn't smile. "No. But I'd still like to learn. Would you teach me?"

Her interest stemmed from more than competitiveness, she realized when he agreed. Everything important to him had become fascinating to her. So obvious. So stupid. So totally beyond her control. She pushed aside her sudden panic and concentrated on his instructions.

"Roll from the outside to the inside of your foot," he told her. "Keep your body and head erect, your eyes on the horizon, instead of the ground."

She made it five steps before cheating. "It feels so unnatural. I'll trip if I can't look down."

"No, you're much *less* likely to trip. Try it again and sense what you're doing. The fox walk forces you to use your thigh and buttock muscles, rather than your calves. That puts the emphasis on lifting, rather than sliding your feet."

And solves the buns-of-steel mystery.

"Also, your boot comes down more softly, and you're more alert to changes in the terrain or danger up ahead."

"It's the cactus in front of me I'm worried about," she muttered, but moved into the awkward walk again.

"There, you see? You passed right over that rock without looking down. Your peripheral vision picked up on it and guided your feet. I guarantee that by standing erect you have better balance than the others. Take Bill, for instance."

She waited a beat. "You couldn't pay me enough."

Jared's deep chuckle buoyed her steps. "Take a *look* at him, wiseguy." He gazed past Hope and sobered. "Not only is he wasting valuable energy, at the rate he's going, he's headed for a nasty fall."

Hope peered at the third hiker on her left. Shoulders hunched, head down, stocky body leaning forward, Bill reminded her of a bull charging a red cape. He approached the act of walking with the get-out-of-my-way attitude that had created a three-hundred-grocery-store chain. If he fell, it wouldn't be pretty.

"So...this fox-walk thing is our little secret, right?" she asked, then raised her palms at Jared's frowning glance. "Just kidding. Go clue him in, Scout. I think I've got the hang of this dance now."

She didn't, of course, but his departing grin of approval kept her practicing the uncomfortable gait for long stretches of desert. In her private fantasy Jared halted the line of hikers, praised Hope's perseverance and had her demonstrate her skill to the others.

In reality he moved up and down the line asking and answering questions and, in general, ignored Hope completely.

Not that she cared, she lied to herself at four o'clock. If she'd thought earlier that the man behind those purple-framed glasses had watched her, had wanted to throw her down and ravish her among the cacti, she'd obviously been hallucinating.

Not that she cared, she assured herself more truthfully at five o'clock. Despite a recent rest break and the cooling temperature, her shoulders hurt, her legs ached, and that spot on her heel felt raw. As her mood shifted, so did her fantasy. Jared still halted the line of hikers and praised her perseverance, but now, instead of asking her to demonstrate walking, he gave her a full body massage.

By six o'clock the only fantasy penetrating her haze of abject misery was the vision of strangling

Jared with one bare hand and Debbie with the other until their tongues turned black.

"Look! A peregrine falcon!" the avid birder on her immediate left exclaimed.

Hope glared upward at the black speck gliding in the sky. She was heartily suspicious of Brett's frequent sightings. He'd named at least ten feathered species since leaving the trailhead, some of them so far away he couldn't possibly have identified features.

"Men have trained peregrines to hunt for centuries," he continued self-importantly. "They're very smart, you know."

No, du-uh. "Yes, Brett—"

"Brent."

Whatever. "Yes, Brent, I do know. In fact, considering that the peregrine's up there and we're down here, I'd say he's a damn genius."

Brent chuckled and wisely shut up.

The worst part of walking in a sandy skillet, Hope realized, was that she'd actually paid good money for the privilege. The rip-off deeply offended her nature, made her ashamed of lecturing Karen on matters of fiscal responsibility. Speaking of Karen...she hadn't looked too great the last time Hope had checked. Staggering ahead of the line, she searched to her right.

Karen looked even worse now. Her dragging stride was neither charging bull nor stealthy fox nor anything in between. It was more like the walk of the living dead. She turned a zombie face toward Hope and they exchanged a long-suffering look.

Hang in there, Hope communicated silently before melding back into position.

"We're almost at the campsite," Jared said to her, no longer surprising her with his soundless approach. "How are you holding up?"

If they didn't stop soon, she'd crash harder than the market of 1987. "Just call me the Energizer bunny."

The wry cant of his mouth said he wasn't fooled. "Glad to hear it, since there's plenty of work ahead of you. By the way, thanks for keeping an eye on Karen. Your encouragement seems to motivate her better than mine."

Now he'd surprised her.

"Oh, and before I forget, I could use your help tonight. You picked up the fox walk like a pro. Would you mind demonstrating it to the others after dinner?"

With tremendous effort she managed a careless shrug. "No problem."

Nodding, he veered away and left her mulling over the fact that he hadn't ignored her at all.

Suddenly her spirits lifted along with her fox-walk steps. Her gaze leveled on the horizon. A small bird moving within a cluster of thorny vegetation caught her eye.

"Look, Brent!" she shouted, pointing. "There's

a...brown-crested..." A name, she needed a name. "Merrill finch," she finished triumphantly.

"Really? Where!" Brent walked closer to her and peered ahead, apparently as unfamiliar with brokerage firms as he was with legitimate birds.

"Right there, straight ahead. It's beating around the bush. They do that, you know."

"Yes, I know."

Hope suppressed a yelp of laughter. "I thought you would," she said gravely.

How far would this guy go? Giving Brent her concentrated attention, she settled down to have some fun. "So tell me, Brent, have you sighted any merrill finches in your home state?"

MILES AWAY on the San Antonio Riverwalk, Stan Lawler sipped a frozen margarita beneath an umbrella table and ignored the elbow-to-elbow crowd streaming past. Aw, yeah, this was the life. A ballsy negotiation behind him, a fat wallet in his pocket, a classy broad joining him at eight in the hotel lobby bar. He was going to like living like this.

Glancing up, he met the wide eyes of a kid riding her mother's hip. The little girl blinked, her face crumpled, and she started to squall. Her mother crooned words of comfort as they rushed past his table.

Sniveling brat was at least four years old—too old to be clinging to Mama. Shit, by that age he'd been practically on his own, as wild as the woods he roamed. Remembering how he'd scavenged like the squirrels, like the tenant farm's rooting pigs, his mood soured further. He'd eaten things that he knew now would make polite people puke up their guts.

But back then...back then he'd only known hunger. And piss-in-your-britches fear.

Stan took a sip of frozen drink and flicked the salt from his lips. The social workers who'd made sure he went to school had let him go home to hell. But he'd survived. And grown. And learned more than reading, writing and arithmetic. He'd learned that hunters invading his woods left extra guns and knives unattended in parked trucks. He'd learned he never had to be hungry—or scared—again.

Eyeing a passing teen's carefully ripped jeans and T-shirt, a cigarette hanging from his lip, Stan sneered. You didn't buy toughness at a mall or convenience-store counter. By age fourteen he could make other kids piss in their britches with a single look, by age sixteen ram a blade deep in his daddy's quivering belly and rip upward.

Recalling the godlike power of that moment, Stan shivered pleasantly now.

He'd buried the carcass in the woods and never looked back. Folks just assumed the Lawler white trash had finally moved on, and good riddance. No kill since then had been as sweet. But he'd always taken pride in the planning, ridden high for days afterward. Then days became a single day. And then a few hours.

His last spurt of power had been as brief as a hand job, and he'd known it was time for the second phase of his career.

Finishing his drink, Stan tossed a bill onto the table and merged into the flowing crowd. Lush palms, colorful flowers and noisy restaurant patios lined both sides of the winding canal. Arched walkways spanned the water at regular intervals. A boat loaded with camera-snapping tourists chugged by, and he discarded the idea of getting on at the next landing. He was too pumped from his lunch meeting the day before to sit.

He'd used the right forks, chosen the right wine, presented the right credentials and plan. All those hours of private study had paid off. He was in the major leagues now.

The hit would go down in the remotest area of the expedition route, with a chopper taking him in and out. That gave him a couple of days before leaving for his assignment to get used to the role of big shot.

The blonde meeting him tonight after her management seminar was a definite step up from his usual women. And she'd put out, he knew. He'd seen it in her fearful fascinated gaze.

Clearing the contempt from his throat, Stan spat into the canal. White trash or classy manager, they were all the same.

Little girls grew up to like what they saw in his eyes.

WHEN HOPE REACHED the "campsite," she was bitterly disappointed. She hadn't expected coconut palms around a shimmering pond, but except for a wimpy stand of mesquite trees, the area looked exactly like the miles of scrubby desert they'd just crossed.

Jared called for attention and instructed each trail team to set up cooking and sleeping equipment ten to thirty yards apart. That minimum-impact thing again. Humph. If you asked her, the ground was more likely to damage *them* than vice versa, but she kept her mouth shut. She'd rubbed Brent and her feet the wrong way once too often.

All three had wised up and refused to walk with her mouth another step.

Her male teammates ambled close and slipped off their backpacks. Bill pressed one fist against the small of his back and groaned. "Man, are you lucky you don't have to carry forty-five pounds."

She'd been thinking the same thing until he said so. "Give me five pounds of your gear to carry tomorrow and we'll be even."

"Nah, I wouldn't want to mess up your hormones or nothin'." He referred to Jared's warning that rigorous hiking upset the menstrual cycle of some women.

"Make that ten pounds, why don't you?" Hope snapped. "I can handle it."

Bill blew out a peeved breath. "Feminists. You're all nothin' but headaches."

She arched a brow. "Chauvinists. You're all nothin' but pigs. And with aspirin *I'll* be human. What's your cure?" Hank's gentle grip on her shoulder stopped her from saying more.

He nodded toward something in the distance.

Thirty yards away, Karen stood slumped in the midst of three hikers as if unaware they weren't members of her trail team. Hope frowned and waved at her to come over without success.

Bill cupped his palms to his mouth. "Yo, Karen, look alive!"

Her straw hat lifted, exposing round dark glasses resembling eerie hollow eye sockets, a complexion as pasty as the zinc oxide on her nose. She shuffled forward woodenly, her boots impacting the hell out of everything in her path.

Worry galvanized Hope into action. She rushed to meet the exhausted woman. "Hey, girlfriend, you're scaring me again. Do you feel faint?"

"I passed the point of feeling a long time ago."

"I hear you. Hold on a little longer and I promise you can relax." Squeezing Karen's arm in sympathy, Hope led her to Hank and Bill, who'd started unloading their tent.

Hank sprang up and helped Karen unbuckle and shrug out of her backpack. Her heartfelt groan could have been agony or ecstasy. She took the canteen he held out and sipped deeply.

By the time Hank turned to Hope, she'd already struggled halfway out of her gear. "No, no, I can do it myself...but thanks. It's nice to know chivalry's not dead with *some* men.''

Bill raised his head, his salt-and-pepper eyebrows drawing together above mirrored sunglasses. "Thanks for letting Hank help you, Karen. It's nice to know chivalry's not called chauvinism by *some* women.''

Good comeback, Hope admitted. Before she could think of a worthy response, their team leader approached, unbuckling his hip belt as he walked. Bill rose and closed ranks with the others.

"How's everybody doing here?" Jared asked, slipping out of his shoulder straps in one easy movement. He lowered the sleek backpack to the ground, his sweat-dampened T-shirt hinting at six-pack stomach ridges, his biceps bulging like veined cue balls.

"Fine."

"Good."

"Great."

Hope prayed her involuntary whimper got buried beneath the other's answers.

Jared chuckled. "You lying dogs. Right now you're wondering why you ever signed up for this course. But you'll change your minds once you have a nice hot meal in your bellies and the stars come out. They're unbelievable this far into the desert.''

Hunkering down, he unzipped one section of his pack and pulled out a bulky "stuff bag" containing the trail team's stove. Next came gallon jugs of cooking and cleaning water for the group, as well as a CB radio and assorted cookware.

Hope stared in awe at the growing pile. He'd hauled all that and more? Her own muscles ached as if she'd carried Dumbo piggyback up a mountain. "Exactly how much does your backpack weigh, Jared?"

One side of his mouth curved up. "With or without the bullwhip?"

Bill cackled obnoxiously.

Jared resumed his busywork and shrugged. "About sixty-five, maybe seventy pounds."

Seventy. "As in, twenty-five more pounds than forty-five pounds?" It was Hope's turn to cackle. "Why don't you let Bill share some of that weight with you tomorrow?"

Jared set down a plastic bag of noodles, wiped his hands on his thighs and stood up. "We're not in a contest here. Everybody will pull their own weight in one way or another, starting right now. Karen, what are the three priorities in setting up a camp?"

Hope was glad to see a little color tinge her friend's cheeks.

"Shelter, latrine and kitchen?"

"Right. I'll find a suitable kitchen site. Matt's team is digging a latrine behind the mesquite stand in the east. That leaves shelter." He lowered his sunglasses and gave them each a meaningful look.

They got the message and hustled. At least, Hope tried to move quickly. Of the two women, she had a tiny reserve of energy left, but a crippling blister on her right foot. And she was damn tired of sweating. Deciding the sun wouldn't fry her skin now, she stripped down to her tank top, tossed the outer loose-weave shirt over her backpack and sighed. Too bad she couldn't ditch the pants, as well.

Limping in circles, she searched the uneven ground for a clear site. Five minutes later she realized Karen hadn't moved from a dead stop in front of a cactus patch. Hope didn't have the heart to make her partner walk around the obstacle.

When the men were halfway finished erecting their tent, Hope finally sighted an area that looked relatively free of flesh-jabbing rocks and vegetation. The rotting mesquite log lying where the tent floor would rest should be easy enough to move.

She reached down to grab the silvery gray wood.

"Hope, *no!*"

CHAPTER EIGHT

JARED WATCHED HOPE stumble backward, one hand pressed to her heart, her gaze riveted on the log. He hadn't meant to frighten her or the other team members. All three had dogged his heels to Hope's side.

"Don't move that," Jared warned again.

Hope nodded. "What did you see?"

"You were about to re-landscape the campsite for your own convenience."

"Yeah. What did you see?"

"You weren't adjusting your tent location to the existing terrain."

She gaped. "That's it? No rattlesnake? No nest of scorpions? No rare hand-eating lizard?"

He blew out a breath and folded his arms. "Insects thrive in that decaying wood. Small animals eat the insects, reptiles eat the small animals—the food chain is a delicate balance. Move the log and you'll affect a fragile interdependent community."

Hank shifted and rubbed his neck. "It's pretty hard to find a clear piece of ground out here, Jared." His tone held mild reproach.

Jared scanned the surrounding desert floor and relaxed his standards a bit. "If you have to chuck a few small rocks out of the way, that's okay. But try to remember where they were so you can put them back when we break camp.''

"Put them back when we break camp," Hope repeated. "The rocks." She made a scoffing sound. "Get real, Scout. Conservation is one thing, but that crosses the line to fanatical."

"As much as it kills me to say this, she's got a good point," Bill said. When everyone turned to stare, he angled his bearded jaw. "Well, she does. If a javelina hog kicked a few rocks outta his way and settled down to sleep, nobody'd give a damn. But we do it and we're messin' up the environment? That's a lotta bull."

Jared found himself looking at Hank.

The tall man shrugged almost apologetically. "It does seem a little extreme."

Preempting any question, Karen raised a fingernail to her mouth and gnawed.

Jared noted the bustle of surrounding campsites and realized that he hadn't covered this topic in class as thoroughly as usual. Hell, *nothing* about this particular course had proceeded as usual. He glanced up at the sun, then back at his team. "Look, I understand what you're all saying, and I'll try to explain where I'm coming from later. But if we don't get this camp set up soon, we'll be working by flashlight. Why don't we save this discussion until after dinner, fair enough?"

One by one they nodded and turned to leave.

"Hope, could I talk to you a minute?" Jared asked.

She paused, backlit by the setting sun, and for a second he couldn't think, much less talk.

Her long shapely legs were revealed in window-shade silhouette through thin beige pants. The gauze shirt he'd worked so hard all day not to stare at was gone, revealing what he'd tried so hard all day not to imagine. Creamy shoulders. A small rib cage narrowing to a slender girlish waist. Nice womanly breasts. *Very* nice. His knowledgeable gaze traced the scalloped edge of her bra beneath clingy beige material. Front clasp, he decided. A one-hand job, easy.

"You wanted to talk to me?" Hope prompted.

He started guiltily. Thank God he wore sunglasses. Thrusting a hand into his pocket, he fingered the folded knife he always carried. "I'm scratching you from the fox-walk demonstration tonight."

She seemed disappointed. "Why? Oh, the limp."

"Yeah, the limp. I want to see that blister before you turn in for bed."

"Don't worry. I'll take care of it."

"No, *I* will. I'd hate to cut short the others' expedition because your foot got infected. You should've told me the minute it started bothering you."

"You're right, I should've."

"What?" He banged the heel of his palm above one ear. "I could've sworn you said I was right."

She laughed, a bubbling brook of sound flowing clear and feminine sweet.

He suddenly wished he could see the eyes sparkling behind her dark glasses. "That's the first time I've heard you laugh like that."

Still smiling, she flipped off her baseball cap and fluffed up her smashed curls. "Like what?"

"Like..." He trailed off, mesmerized by the crackling red fire of her sun-burnished hair.

"Like an idiot? Like a hyena?" She paused. "You can correct me any time here."

His answer came with the strength of truth. "Like you're happy."

Her smile collapsed into a dark scowl. "For your information, I *am* happy. People are sick and tired of hearing my gay happy laughter. The fact that *you* haven't heard it ought to tell you something, Scout." Jamming her cap down low, she turned and limped away in a dramatic huff.

Jared walked slowly back toward the flat rock he'd selected for a kitchen site. He'd touched a raw nerve in Hope, that was for sure. The same one he'd scraped that first day when he'd called her "burned out." That she was both unhappy and burned out was a given, but most people recognized that in themselves and sought solutions. Hope was in denial.

Kneeling, he checked to make sure that the women had found a tent site. They had, and like the men's it was far enough from the "kitchen" to be safe from stray sparks.

As an added precaution, he'd topped off the stove fuel tank and spirit cup in another location. Spilled fuel on the ground could and sometimes did ignite. He'd once seen a buddy's pants go up in flames that way. He'd never cut corners on safety after that.

Hank walked up asking for his and Bill's ration of bathing water. Jared handed over two jugs and asked Hank to deliver one to the women with the instructions to share.

"I'll do it," Hank agreed. "But you owe me one."

Grinning, Jared set the stove on his makeshift kitchen counter, carefully lit the spirit cup and waited for the generator to warm. His thoughts returned to Hope—an all-too-common occurrence since she'd erupted into his life.

He recognized so much of his former self in her competitive controlling nature. Always looking "out there" for happiness when the answers were within. He couldn't tell her what those answers were any more than Ben had been able to provide them for Jared. The old man had simply said, "Everyone has a path. The search—that's part of the path. Each traveler has to find his own way."

Remembering the dark terrible days immediately following his father's trial, Jared expelled a sympathetic breath. He wouldn't wish his own path on anyone and didn't envy Hope hers. She was as prickly as a cholla cactus, but he admired her determination and spirit. He'd discovered, in fact, that he liked the

woman as much as he was attracted to her. He was
still getting used to the idea.

The wailing coo of a mourning dove penetrated
his musing. The generator had long since warmed
enough to vaporize the fuel. He opened the safety
valve, struck a match and lit the burner. The white-
noise roar he associated with food had his stomach
rumbling for some action. A chicken noodle casserole ought to do the trick.

Dumping all utensils and two cooking pans into
one large sterilizing pot, he left the water to boil and
rose to check on his team's activities.

Hank and Bill had unpacked the gear they would
need for the night and morning into neat separate
piles. Their tent faced properly into the wind, and
both men had washed some of the day's grime from
their skin. Praising their efforts, Jared promised them
a meal soon and headed for the second shelter.

The strengthening sunset breeze struck the tent
broadside, he saw immediately. Not a problem now
since Karen appeared to be inside acting as an an-
chor. But freestanding tents were known to go
bouncing off into a cactus patch when unoccupied.

Hope sat outside the zipped front flap staring at a
clear plastic bag in her lap. He smiled down at her
baseball cap, then identified a bottle of shampoo, a
bar of soap and miscellaneous jars and tubes in the
bag. When she looked up, he clamped down on a
powerful urge to laugh.

She'd removed her sunglasses, but a bandit's mask

of smudged mascara encircled her bleak eyes. "Why not just shoot me and get it over with?"

"What's the problem? Your foot?"

"Worse. I can deal with a blister."

He waited.

She twisted around, scooped up the jug of bathing water next to her backpack and held it aloft. "This is criminal."

"Tomorrow we'll camp near a water source," he promised.

"You don't seem to understand. I'll die *tonight* if I can't wash my hair."

Good grief. "You'll live. And trust me, you can take a decent bath with half of that jug of water."

"I can't even brush my *teeth* decently with half of that water. I'm a very clean person," she said in a prissy tone that implied he wasn't.

"You sound like a very wasteful person to me." He frowned at the zipped tent. "How's Karen doing?"

"You killed her, not that you care."

"I care a great deal about the condition of my students," he said tightly.

"Your students are filthy. They need to wash their hair. They need more water, dammit."

The last lingering trace of his good humor fled. He shoved one hand into his pocket and rubbed the folded knife inside like a worry stone. "I'm tempted to give you tomorrow's allotment of drinking water and let you suffer through the day, but then you'd have the satisfaction of dying on me.''

"Dear me, we couldn't have that. What would you do with the body? It might affect the fragile inter-dependent food chain.''

He thumbed the knife in his pocket and breathed in slowly through his nose.

"I mean, I'd hate to think that gorging on me would keep some coyote from controlling the rabbit popu—'' A gust of wind flipped off Hope's cap.

Jared grabbed for it, missed and watched the No Fear logo scud across the sandy ground and flatten against a lechuguilla century plant about thirty yards away.

"No, no, I'll get it,'' Hope said when he started to retrieve the cap. "Go make dinner. All that talk about food has made me hungry.'' Rising, she dusted off her sassy butt and gave him an eyeful walking away.

He'd never wanted to throttle a woman and kiss her at the same time—until he'd met Hope.

Turning to head back to the stove, he paused. His highly sensitive inner alarm hummed like a tapped tuning fork. He scanned the campsite and found nothing out of place, but…the humming grew louder. Without hesitation he closed his eyes and opened himself to the spirit-that-moves-through-all-things.

Wind, whistling through thorns, lifting the feathers of a dove flying low. Sand, shifting as it cooled.

Heartbeats—human and free of fear. The rasp of a snake's belly...

His eyes opened and zeroed in on the danger slithering toward the lechuguilla and a probable underground lair. Hope was about five yards from her cap now.

"Hope, *no*," he yelled, a noose of panic choking the words.

"Oh, right," she called over her shoulder without breaking stride. "Like I'm falling for that again."

She reached down at the same time the six-foot diamondback rattlesnake saw her boots blocking his bedroom door. The snake coiled instantly and commenced one of the most dreaded sounds in the western hemisphere.

Hope froze.

Good girl, Jared thought, his body crouched low, his feet already lifting high in the stalker's walk of a hunter sighting prey. He moved silently, smoothly, grateful now for the hours he'd spent practicing under Ben's demanding eye. So slowly as to be almost undetectable, he reached into his pocket, unfolded his knife and pulled it free.

The snake seemed increasingly agitated. Hope was threatening its safety and stood well within striking range. Jared didn't have much time. Ten yards from the target, he was close enough.

He rose and threw in one fluid movement, the knife an extension of his hand and eye.

And Ms. No Fear screamed bloody murder.

HOPE SAT CROSS-LEGGED with her trail team around a glowing candle lantern and forced down a mouthful of chicken noodle casserole. Staring into the wedge-shaped face of death had put a definite crimp in her appetite.

Never as long as she lived would she forget those eternal minutes. The cold reptilian eyes. The flickering black tongue. The powerful coiled body thicker than her arm. And of course, that sound. A sinister maraca percussion that increased in volume with her rising blood pressure.

She'd known that the snake would strike; known, too—with deep instinctive conviction—that Jared would try to help. Still, the sight of his blade slicing through flesh and bone had shocked her to the core. She might've held on to her dignity if the damn head hadn't fallen near her feet and proceeded to yawn open and closed while the body writhed five feet away.

A small hand squeezed her arm, and Hope blinked back to the present. Even wearing a light sweater, she shivered.

"You've got to eat more," Karen said gently.

Realizing she'd laid her fork down after the first swallow, Hope picked up the utensil and tried again.

"Hey, if you don't want yours, I'll eat it," Bill said before shoveling a huge bite into his mouth. "This is great, Jared. I'd always heard that rattlesnake tastes like chicken. Guess everyone was right."

Hope dropped her fork with a clatter.

Bill's bray of laughter turned into a yelp. "Dammit, Hank, I was only joking! I think you broke my rib."

"I think your rib broke my elbow," Hank groused. The men exchanged glares and rubbed their bruised bones.

Jared caught and held Hope's gaze. "There's nothing in here but canned chicken," he assured her. "You really should try to clean your plate. You burned a lot of calories today."

Smiling weakly, she nodded and reached for her fork.

"So Jared—" Bill leaned forward as eagerly as a six year-old "—do you think maybe I could have the rattle you took off that sucker? The guys back home won't believe what you did without proof."

Hope choked down a mouthful of noodles.

"I'll think about it. Right now let's change the subject."

"What about rocks?" Hope blurted. Anything to get off rattlesnakes. "You said you'd explain why you had a cow about us moving rocks from the campsite."

Jared sent her a wry look. "I don't think that's quite what I said, but okay, I'll try to justify my reaction. First—would anyone like some coffee?"

There were nods all around.

"I'll serve," Karen offered quietly, and scrambled to her feet. Earlier, she'd filled plates and passed them around as if it were her duty. As if she'd been *trained.*

Hope frowned. "I'll help."

"Stay," Jared ordered. "Eat." He rose and joined Karen at the edge of the candlelight.

Speaking of trained, Hope thought, too weary to be irritated. Clanking cups and companionable murmurs lulled her tense muscles into relaxing. Her next bite of food actually tasted better than sand. The strong coffee Karen delivered soon after was nirvana.

Once everyone had settled down with a cup, Jared stared into the flickering light and began talking.

"If I seem fanatical about minimum-impact camping, it's because I've seen what happens when it's not practiced. Entire lakes polluted. Fragile vegetation crushed beyond recovery. Toilet paper decorating the bushes. Animals driven away or forced to starve because the natural food chain has been destroyed.

"Here in Mexico we're virtually alone, and abuse is not a problem. But there's a serious chance that thousands of acres around us—my vacation home, if you will—is going to join with Big Bend National Park in the next few years to form a huge international park. When that happens, Americans will flood into this area."

Bill's legs stirred and he shook his head. "That don't make sense. Why would they come here when there are prettier places a helluva lot easier to get to in the States?"

"First of all, wait until the expedition is over before judging the beauty of this land. Secondly, both governments will improve access roads to a joint park. Thirdly, it wouldn't matter if access didn't improve. Americans would still come in droves." Jared took a sip from his cup, rubbed a thumb over the rim, sipped again. He didn't seem inclined to elaborate.

"Why?" Karen prodded, earning Hope's gratitude. If anyone else had asked, he might not have felt obligated to answer.

"Why have any of you taken time out from your hectic lives to carry a backpack, pitch a tent, brave rattlesnakes and dirty hair?"

He shared a private smile with Hope that warmed her more than the coffee.

His sobering expression was all the more riveting by contrast. "Over *three hundred million* people visit our national parks each year, and that number keeps rising. People will flood this area, all right, because true wilderness in America is disappearing. We're destroying it acre by acre."

Jared had replaced his sunglasses with the familiar wire-rimmed frames. The candlelight reflected in his clear lenses made it difficult to read his eyes, but Hope could hear the emotion in his voice.

MindBend Adventures wasn't just the latest operation to hop on the "executive retreat" bandwagon. Jared really did care passionately about his work and this godforsaken land. In that sense he was very much like her parents.

Hank broke the unsettled silence. ''I had no idea national parks were so popular. Can't the government regulate the number of visitors?''

''Lock the gates and hand out limited tickets? That's one option. But it goes against another characteristic Americans share—some of us more than others,'' he said, again sending an intimate smile Hope's way. ''Self-reliance. We don't like staying on the beaten path or restrictions on our behavior or bureaucratic regulations.''

''And the second option?'' Hank asked.

''The second option is learning how to regulate ourselves. By using minimum-impact techniques, not only can we make sure that those following us don't have to pick up our mess, we make sure that they *don't even know we were there.* The good news is that MindBend Adventures students and graduates of similar schools are slowly spreading the word. We don't move logs or stones, we don't trample trails like cattle, we pack up all trash, we return the campsite landscape as closely as possible to its original condition...well, you know the routine.''

''We act like courteous houseguests,'' Karen concluded thoughtfully, surprising them all.

''Exactly!''

If Jared ever beamed at Hope like that, she'd serve the man like a slave, too.

He started to say more, then seemed to change his

mind. "But enough with the lecturing already. Why don't you folks go enjoy this beautiful night? Lights out in an hour." Rising, he waved aside offers to help clean the dishes and set to work in his usual efficient manner.

As Hope limped with her trail buddy to their tent, she tilted back her head and gasped. Her absorption with Jared had prevented her from noticing the awesome spectacle above.

"I know," Karen said. "Have you ever seen such a sky? It looks like a planetarium show."

In New York, Hope never bothered looking up except to check for rain. Even Hopeful, Texas, hadn't boasted so many stars. "It puts Times Square to shame," she admitted, lapsing into thought.

How was Manning Enterprises faring without her? Had Debbie reminded Dr. Hiller that Hope needed his latest test-patient statistics on her desk when she returned? Had Leslie copied UroTech's board of directors on the last letter she'd sent to the FDA?

Her worrying was cut short when they reached the tent. Lighting their own candle lantern, the women agreed to take turns behind the far side of the shelter making use of the bathing water. Hope went first.

Thank heavens she'd tucked unauthorized packets of magnolia-scented moist towelettes into her backpack. She managed a fairly decent job of maintaining her reputation as a "very clean person." In fact, she was feeling downright smug—until she lifted her hand mirror.

"A-a-a-ck!" She was going to sue La Belle cosmetics when she got home. Nonsmudge mascara her heinie.

"What's wrong?" Karen asked sharply from inside the tent.

"I look like a raccoon, that's what's wrong. Why didn't you *tell* me?" Hope rubbed the mess off with cold cream and a tissue.

"I...didn't want to upset you more after the snake incident," Karen said, too smart to pretend ignorance. "It's not so bad. Really."

Hope grimaced. Just what she wanted to hear after staring at Jared for the past hour. The man had eyes. Unless he got off on the Lone Ranger, she'd grossly misinterpreted his intimate smiles.

Finishing her facial-repair job with astringent followed by night cream, she gathered her stuff and ducked into the tent. "I'm surprised Bill restrained himself. Did he feel sorry for me, too?"

Karen scooped up a small bag and crawled toward the flap. "The only thing Bill felt was Hank's elbow." She grinned over her shoulder, then disappeared into the night.

By the time she returned, Hope had changed into her favorite sleepwear and was rummaging in her limited first-aid items. The blister on her heel stung like the devil, and there was a spot on her toe that threatened to turn nasty.

Karen moved the lantern closer and peered down.

"Oh, wow, you should've told Jared you were hurting."

I should've hitched a van ride back to Terlingua.

"Look, I'm going to visit the mesquite stand now, but I'll help with your feet when I get back. Love your pajamas, by the way," Karen added, referring to Hope's faded pink T-shirt and green plaid boxers overprinted with pink pigs.

Probing the tender skin of her heel, Hope smiled. "I thought I might lend them to Bill. What do you think?"

"I think I want to see his face when you offer them."

"Hope, are you decent?" Jared's canyon-deep voice rumbled outside the tent.

Hope's head snapped up. Her heartbeat stalled, then jumped into overdrive.

"I need to take a look at that foot for a minute," he said.

Karen smiled coyly, then pulled a small flashlight from her bag. "Then again, maybe I'll stay out there and commune with the stars for a while."

Ignoring Hope's fierce-eyed but silent demand to stay, Karen scooted outside the tent. "Hi, Jared. Go on in, she's decent—but the foot looks pretty bad."

Thanks, trail buddy, Hope thought.

And then Jared's muscular body was crawling inside, lifting the hair on her arms as if he were electrically charged. She flared her nostrils at the scent of kerosene and casserole and dried sweat and dusty man, a mixture that should have been unpleasant but made her want to bury her nose between his bronzed neck and powerful shoulder, breathe deeply and count to five. Or ten.

The thought made her skin tight and shivery, her insides hot.

He laid down a first-aid kit, positioned himself on one knee proposal-style and patted his upraised thigh.

"Put your foot up here where I can see it, Hope."

CHAPTER NINE

ALTHOUGH JARED AVOIDED looking at Hope, unfortunately he had to breathe. Her clean flowery fragrance went straight to his head, the underlying scent of woman straight to his loins. He'd never gotten so hard so fast in his life.

"Put your foot up here," he repeated, wanting to get this torture over with as quickly as possible.

Her legs whispered against the Ensolite sleeping pad in a restless movement. "Saving my life is enough thoughtfulness for one day. Leave the kit here and I'll return it when I'm finished."

He ground his molars hard enough to crack acorns. "Must you *always* make things harder than they should be?" His erection pulsed in agreement.

"Excuse me, but I'm trying to make things easier on you."

"When Karen fainted, you missed Matt's demonstration using molefoam. Now give me your damn foot so I can get the hell out of here!"

"Yes, *sir,* leader, *sir.*" She thrust her glossy red toenails into his view, propped her heel on his thigh and hissed as if in pain.

Clamping a hand around her ankle, he lifted her

injury to eye level and bit back his own hiss. During the foot-kissing ceremony in class, Hope's face had captured most of his attention. No such luck now.

Small and white, delicately boned and prettily arched, Hope's foot was one the most erotic pieces of feminine anatomy he'd ever seen. The pressure against his zipper increased as he pictured himself suckling each toe, nipping the underside of her arch, watching that same arch slide over his—

"Is it that bad?" Hope asked.

Jared choked back a laugh. He ached to the point of pain, but knew she referred to the blister on her heel. "The skin hasn't broken yet, no thanks to your stubbornness. You should be able to walk tomorrow without too much discomfort." Pressing her sole against his inner thigh, he twisted to reach the first-aid kit.

"Hold still," he ordered, removing antibiotic cream, scissors and two molefoam pads. "I know you're a very clean person, but did you wash this foot thoroughly, including the hot spot?"

"Of course I washed it thoroughly. I don't do anything halfway."

His imagination instantly defined "anything" in very specific detail. Desperate for a distraction, he finally looked at Hope.

She'd scrubbed her face clean and piled most of her hair into a messy topknot. The rest spilled in charming tendrils more suited to a girl from Hopeful, Texas, than a lady executive from New York. He liked her this way. Liked her too damn much. His lips could almost feel that petal-soft skin, the fluttering fan of her silky lashes—

"Do I have toothpaste on my nose or something?"

He checked and shook his head.

"That's a joke, Jared. It means stop staring. You're making me nervous."

Nervous, huh? He hid a satisfied smile. "Sorry. I promise not to stare again."

Squeezing out a dab of cream, Jared rubbed her heel in a slow circular motion. He spotted a red area on her middle toe and massaged cream there, as well. Her foot looked as delicate as a white dove in his large sun-darkened hand. She was trembling, he realized with a start, and gentled his fingers in response.

How many people were deceived by the force of Hope's personality into thinking she was larger, stronger, tougher than other women? She wasn't any of those things, though she'd like him to think so. She'd like him to think she was immune to his touch, also. But she wasn't. Not by a long shot.

His macho surge of triumph ebbed all too soon, leaving the ache of sexual frustration.

"How's your other foot?" he asked, his husky tone a dead giveaway to his condition.

"Okay," she said breathily, more Marilyn Monroe than Hope, and his condition went from serious to critical.

Capping the tube of cream, he listened to the

sound of her increasingly rapid breathing and felt his own speed up in return. The air grew more humid by the second, the scent of magnolia blossoms more dizzying, the unmistakable musk of arousal more maddening. The desert tent became a sultry southern garden lush with intimate possibilities.

Praying that his hands wouldn't shake, he cut a small hole in the center of a molefoam pad, unpeeled the adhesive backing and somehow dredged up his voice. ''The idea is to build a barrier around the hot spot and protect it from friction, but leave the tender skin open to air.'' He applied the molefoam to her heel, cut a second smaller square and pressed it against her toe. ''That should do the trick.''

Let go of her foot, his mind ordered. But his hands still gripped her toes, his thumbs massaging her sole with long slow strokes. The roar in his ears rivaled the camp-stove burner, yet he heard her throaty moan. He turned to look.

And he was lost.

She'd fallen back onto her elbows, her opposite leg stretched out full length on the floor, her flannel boxer shorts gaping around her upraised thigh. His unrepentant gaze traveled inside plaid fabric to the beginning sweet curve of her buttock.

A primitive rumble started deep in his chest, a growl of caged lust rattling the bars of common sense. One of his hands abandoned her foot and kneaded a firm shapely calf, a smooth satiny thigh.

At the hem of her shorts his fingers paused, restrained by a slender thread of sanity.

He pulled his gaze out of danger to meet drowsy brown eyes, passion dark and as lethal as a loaded gun. His focus moved out of the cross hairs to the gravest peril yet: the thin pink T-shirt molding her chest.

He tried to drag his gaze to safer territory, God knew he did. But the full uptilted breasts beckoned to everything male in him. He could no more resist the challenging peaks than he could get pregnant.

Lifting his hand from her thigh, he reached for a soft swell of pink.

"You don't play fair, Jared Austin," she accused, verbally smacking his knuckles.

He lowered his hand at the phrase he'd used himself a short time ago. The insulation of passion dissolved into guilt. He'd almost felt up a student! Worse, he still wanted to, despite the fact that she'd pulled her foot from his grip and now hugged her knees protectively against her chest. Wouldn't "Good Morning America" have a field day with this first-aid lesson?

"Hope, I'm..." What? Sorry she'd turned him on as no other woman ever had? He settled for a half-truth. "I'm sorry I didn't take your advice and leave the kit here. I should've realized that no matter how detached I'd like to be, I'm as susceptible to certain stimuli as any healthy male. But I guess you understood that."

Her eyes flickered, then grew scornful. She lifted an indifferent shoulder. "Sure, Scout, I understand. It's that Pavlov's dog reaction. See a female breast— *any* breast, bare or not—and males automatically salivate and seek oral gratification."

The image that analogy conjured up made him swallow hard. Twice. He rallied for his honor's sake. "I wouldn't say that exactly. I've seen hundreds of breasts in my time and managed to control my baser instincts."

"Hundreds, is it?" Her tone feigned awe. She lowered her knees and sat cross-legged. "Would that be hundreds of *bare* breasts?"

He should have known better than to try to defend himself.

"And if so, is that hundreds of *pairs,* or should I divide by two?"

"Hope…" he warned, in no mood for sarcasm.

"I'm a numbers person, Jared. Accuracy is vital in my line of work. What if I went around telling investors I was buying hundreds of shares of stock when I was really buying hundreds of *pairs?* Of shares, that is."

"Don't push me, Hope. I mean it."

Her wide-eyed innocence vanished. "What's the matter, tough guy? I'm in no danger here. You've got control of your baser instincts, and anger is as base as it gets."

"It gets baser," he promised darkly, letting his

gaze caress her thinly covered chest, feeling his tenuous thread of control stretch gossamer thin.

She stiffened, then flapped a wrist. "Shoot, you've seen hundreds of breasts, maybe *twice* that amount, without salivating."

"Hundreds of breasts don't affect me. Yours do."

Arching a skeptical brow, she reached out and tilted his chin this way and that, her fingers branding his jaw. "No drool in sight," she concluded, releasing him with a snort. "You're all bluff, Scout."

The thread snapped.

He braced a palm on the floor on either side of her hips and leaned forward as she shrank back. "You think I'm bluffing, Hope? You must be one sorry poker player. Your breasts make me salivate, all right. I'm a goddamn Saint Bernard when I look at your breasts. As for seeking oral gratification..." He studied her wide pretty mouth, her dewy flushed cheeks, her graceful white throat with the pulse beating nearly as fast as his own. Her choppy breath fanned his face in soft arousing puffs.

"With you I want every kind of gratification there is," he crooned, his mouth hovering inches above hers. "And I know them all, honey, make no mistake. I'm no Boy Scout, whatever you'd like to think. In fact, I'm feeling meaner by the minute. Too mean to be your friend. So do us both a favor and don't call my bluff again." He stared into her dilated brown eyes and battled the wildness inside him. When he could speak without snarling, he gave his last warning. "The next time the choice is between being your lover or your enemy, you can bet the family ranch which one I'll choose."

Wrenching himself away from her drained the last of his reserve stock of willpower. He snatched the first-aid kit from the floor and plunged outside into the welcome darkness.

When he finally came to a halt, Jared had no idea how long he'd been gone. He drew a ragged breath and noted the diffused glow of light within several distant tents. A good ten-minute hike from where he stood, and he still had to set up his bivouac sack and rinse the sand, kerosene and scent of magnolia from his skin.

Damn, he wished they'd camped next to a water source. Half a jug of water was plenty to bathe with, but it wouldn't come close to dousing the fire in his blood.

"RISE AND WHINE, girls! It's time to get up," Bill called cheerily from outside the tent.

Hope cracked open her lids in the dim light and noted Karen's bleary gaze. They both groaned and closed their eyes at the same time.

"The last team to break camp has to restore the latrine site to its original condition," Hank added in a sympathetic voice. "Breakfast in ten minutes."

As Karen stirred and sat up, Hope kept her eyes stubbornly closed. She'd had maybe four hours of sleep, thanks to Jared's first-aid treatment the night before. If only she'd known then what she knew now. She would've gladly walked with blisters, rather than learn the full bone-melting power of his attraction.

"I feel like doo-doo," Karen said, her tone confirming the words. "Just leave me here and swing back by on your way home. I'll be the white blob lying next to the mesquite log. You have my permission to pick me up and move me from the site."

Hope quit playing opossum and chuckled. "You'll feel better once your blood gets moving—" She stopped, sniffed once and met Karen's eyes.

"*Coffeeee,*" they said in blissful unison.

That and the threat of latrine duty was incentive enough to prod Hope into a vertical position. She scooted out of the way of jabbing elbows and jerking legs as her tent mate struggled into a pair of khaki pants.

Karen fell back onto her sleeping bag, zipped the final inch and lay panting. "I don't understand," she said to the ceiling. "I know I lost at least fifty pounds yesterday."

"Well, of course you did. It's those darn dry cleaners, not you. When *will* they learn not to shrink our stuff?"

As intended, Karen's despairing expression faded to a grin. She sat up and shook out her shirt.

Hope eyed her own stack of clean clothes and tapped her chin. "Let's see...should I wear the beige shirt and the beige pants, or the beige pants and the beige shirt?''

A tousled blond head popped through the neck of a beige T-shirt. ''Oh, be a fashion rebel and go with the beige,'' Karen said, finding the armholes and tugging down her shirt hem. ''It's definitely your color…and mine, and Dana's and Hank's and Bill's and— Hey!'' She grabbed the rolled socks that had just bounced off her shoulder and threw them back at Hope.

Resisting the urge to have a sock fight, Hope dressed hurriedly. If Bill asked for a second cup of coffee—which of course he would, the selfish lout— there wouldn't be enough to go around. She didn't waste time putting on makeup. Jared had already seen the face she'd been born with and hadn't run screaming from the tent. On the contrary… *Whoa, girl.*

Reining in the line of thought that had kept her up most of the night, Hope crammed her sleeping bag one fistful at a time into her stuff bag as she'd been shown. The task proved harder than Jared had made it look. But then, he made everything look easy, from beheading a snake with Jim Bowie finesse to whipping up a chicken casserole worthy of Julia Child.

Hope had nicknamed the man ''Scout'' in self-denial, but last night's episode had forced her to face the truth. Everything about Jared made her drool worse than Pavlov's dog and a Saint Bernard combined. His bad-boy virility attracted her as much as his inner peace and formidable will. The Nutcracker had finally met her match.

And Hope couldn't have him. At least, not and protect her heart, too. Even if he wanted to explore this...*thing* that was between them, some deep feminine instinct told her that a temporary fling with Jared now would make her miserable in the long run.

Memory of his final murmured warning sent a thrill skittering up her spine. Helpless to resist, her mind drifted into fantasy....

...Jared hovered above her, his eyes glittering shards of sapphire, his arms powerful columns flanking her hips, his mouth so close she could almost taste the salty sweet heat she'd sampled once before. She stared at his lips and willed him silently, desperately to close the gap between them, instead of pull away. And, oh, praise the heavens, he did, pressing her down onto the sleeping bag and gratifying them both with that wickedly beautiful mouth—

"Um, Hope?"

She blinked into awareness and realized she clutched her sleeping bag in a way no manufacturer had intended. Hoo-boy.

Other than the heightened pink in Karen's cheeks, she pretended not to notice. "I'm going to grab some breakfast. Want me to pour you a cup of coffee before Bill hogs it all?"

Warmth spread in Hope's chest. "That would be great. I'll be right out."

Watching her teammate disappear, Hope knew that

had the situation been reversed, she would've tossed out a possibly witty, probably hurtful wisecrack. The knowledge wasn't pleasant, and she chose not to examine her behavior pattern too closely.

Instead, she made short work of packing her sleeping bag, pad and personal articles, then brushing her hair and threading the ponytail through the back of her baseball cap. She slipped on shielding sunglasses and crawled outside to get her bearings on the situation.

The early-morning air had the tangy bite of a dry martini. Hope welcomed the chilly temperature, a reviving substitute for her usual morning shower. By noon she'd be cursing the surrounding scenery. But at this hour the scrubby desert grasses sparkled with dew, the large yellow prickly-pear flowers captured sunshine in a cup of petals, the rising foothills to the west and rugged mountains beyond held a certain postcard appeal.

Wonderful smells drifted from various trail-team kitchen sites. Coffee. Biscuits. Something that her wishful nose could've sworn was frying bacon. Snatches of laughter and conversation added to the atmosphere of an awakening community. She spotted Sherry's bright blond head emerging from a tent in the distance. Dana followed close behind. They stood, stretched, turned with a city dweller's awe toward the egg-yolk sun. Sherry caught sight of Hope, nudged Dana in the ribs, and all three women smiled and exchanged friendly waves.

A haunting sense of history gripped Hope. Replace the tents with tepees, the stoves with wood fires, and she could easily imagine the extended campsite as a Native American village secure in its desert isolation. Unable to avoid the inevitable any longer, she searched for the village chief.

Jared huddled over her team's camp stove testing the contents of a frying pan with a fork. Her activated salivary glands had nothing to do with the smell of breakfast and everything to do with the deft masculine fussing of a work-roughened hand, the rhythmic flexing of a muscular forearm.

Bracing herself mentally, she headed for her teammates, who sat not far from the stove holding aluminum cups full of coffee. Without sunglasses, their personal time clocks were easy to read. Hank and Karen were morning people. Bill was not. At least they had that in common.

"Morning, Hope," Hank said, his smile easy and welcoming. His reddish stubble heightened the green in his hazel eyes. "How'd you sleep?"

She sensed Jared's stare as she settled down beside Karen. "Like a log. How about you?"

"Like a sardine."

Bill grunted over the rim of his cup. "Fresh from the net. Hell, you were floppin' around all night."

"Well, at least I don't snore. Next time I go camping I'm taking one of those." Hank jerked his thumb toward the long tubelike bivouac sack shielding Jared's sleeping bag. "My head might stick out, but at least I could straighten these suckers.'' The basket-ball-player-turned-coach slapped a powerful-looking thigh.

Hope smiled in sympathy. ''I'll bet there's a specialty line of equipment for tall men.''

She turned to Karen, intending to ask if Sports-Arama carried such a line, and caught her staring at Hank's leg as if it were a giant Milk-Bone. Hoo-boy. If all this drooling kept up, the whole team would die of dehydration.

''Is that for me?'' Hope asked, instead, nodding to the cup snugged protectively against Karen's hip.

''Mm? Oh—yes.'' She blushed. ''Here. I saved you the last of the pot.''

''Bless you, my child.'' Hope reached for the precious liquid. ''I'm adding you to my will the minute I get home.''

''Whoop-de-do,'' Bill muttered, clearly unimpressed.

A self-made man only respected one thing. Hope sat on a clump of gramma grass and lowered her sunglasses to the end of her nose.

''You know those three hundred Feast Markets you went public with, hotshot?'' They'd discussed his company's fledgling performance in the stock market during one of their friendlier moments. ''In two, maybe three months, I'll be able to buy your controlling stock outright and still be a rich woman.''

Bill's dark eyes flashed. ''Last week's NASDAQ quotes were at fifteen dollars a share.''

She did a quick mental calculation. Peanuts, compared to the dollars involved in the UroTech sale. "Really? Then I stand corrected. I could buy you out and still be a *very* rich woman. If I were Karen, I'd be whoop-de-doing to beat the band."

In the heavy silence she felt strangely hollow. Where was the triumph, the thrill of outgunning a competitor?

He's a teammate, not a competitor.

"Whoop-de-do," Karen said loudly.

Startled laughter broke the tension. As Bill and Hank settled into a discussion about the prospects for Hank's new franchise team, Hope risked a peek at Jared.

He was frowning, seemingly more disturbed than impressed by her imminent wealth. Had she intimidated him with her success? He raised his head and met her gaze.

Try as she might, she couldn't prevent the telltale heat of memory from stinging her cheeks.

His expression sharpened with interest. A knowing gleam entered his gemstone eyes. The grin he aimed her way was about as intimidated as a timber wolf spotting a staked calf. She blinked at the strong white teeth, the stubble on his jaw one shade darker than his sun-streaked brown hair, the web of fine squint lines that—in the unjust way of his gender—added to his appeal, rather than his age.

Tearing her gaze away, she gulped her coffee and looked down at her laced boots. Dear Lord, the man rattled her nerves worse than a diamondback's tail! How would she get through the next nine days without moving into his striking range?

"Come and get it," he called, an arrogant note of challenge in his voice.

Her gaze leaped back to his. Sultry blue promise confirmed that he meant more than food, and her spine slowly stiffened in outrage. Don't call his bluff again, he'd warned. Ha! He was practically *begging* her to jump his bones.

She was the last to stand and collect her plate and fork, the last in line for biscuits and powdered eggs. The closer she got to Jared, the hotter she fumed. The man knew how he affected her and was strutting his sexy stuff shamelessly. After all, if she cracked and responded to his silent invitation, he couldn't be held liable for dallying with a student.

Well, anything he could do *she* could do better. She'd never tried her hand at being desirable, and she would've preferred access to her closet, her shower and her air-conditioning before attempting the role now. But she wasn't completely unarmed.

He liked her breasts. He liked her laugh. And she thought he'd looked at her feet as if they pleased him, strange as that seemed. She knew he didn't like complaints about discomfort or his beloved land. All knowledge she could use to show him a thing or two about bluffing—starting now.

Perching her dark glasses on the top of her head, Hope stepped to the front of the line and kept her

eyes lowered, then thrust her plate next to the frying
pan.

"I've come to get it." *Big boy,* her tone added as
clearly as if she'd spoken the words out loud.

The spoon over her plate paused, then plopped a
mound of eggs in the center. A biscuit landed pre-
cariously on the edge of metal.

She didn't move.

"That's not enough?" His voice cracked on the
last word.

Hope raised her gaze languidly up six feet plus of
studly wilderness guide and met Jared's wary eyes.

"I want all you've got," she said for his ears
alone, her breathiness not entirely an act. "But I suppose that would be selfish to ask of you, what with
my—" she flicked a glance below his waist "—*appetite* being so—" she wet her lips and watched him
swallow hard "—*insatiable* like it is. You'd better
save your strength and eat your eggs."

She patted his limp hand, whirled around and
walked toward her teammates with an extra sway in
her hips and a canary-eating grin she thanked God
he couldn't see.

BY NOON THE SAME DAY the only thing Hope cursed
more than the scenery was her own stupidity.

She didn't "do" suffering anymore. If there was
something she didn't like in her life, she either
changed the something to suit herself—or steamrol-

led over it. A natural result of all this was that she didn't "do" silence anymore, either.

Yet the minute she complained Jared would see her as the shrew he could possess at the touch of a molefoam pad, instead of the unattainable woman of his dreams. So she practiced the fox walk and suffered in silence.

Far ahead through the shimmering heat waves, Bill stopped and took off his backpack, then pulled out a compass and topographical map. She didn't envy his being the designated trail leader for the day. He was responsible for getting them all to the evening campsite in good condition. Unless he endangered the group, Jared wouldn't countermand Bill's orders, and the team was expected to follow his leadership without question.

No problem. Following Bill's fast pace left her no spare breath to talk. He hadn't even looked back to check on his straggling team, and Karen had fallen way behind.

Hank reached Bill first and removed his own backpack before helping the older man spread the map on the ground. Hope could see that the two disagreed on something, but they clammed up when she got close enough to hear.

She stopped and shifted her shoulder straps. "You know, Karen could've passed out back there and you wouldn't even have known it."

Bill peered past her at the straw hat bobbing slowly toward them about fifty yards away. "She needs to learn to keep up. Besides, Jared's back there with her.'' Shrugging, he huddled over the map again.

Hank rose and frowned in Karen's direction. ''You don't think she's dehydrated, do you?''

During the last rest break, Hope had watched him cajole Karen into drinking more than she would have otherwise. ''No, I'm sure she's only drained from the heat. We could all use some shade and some lunch— *hint, hint.*''

''Nobody eats until I say so,'' Bill snapped, motioning for Hank's attention. ''So, Coach, you think we're right about here?'' he asked, stabbing his finger at a point on the map.

''No, a little to the left.''

''Well, then, hell, where's the damn creek?''

Hope moved closer and resisted looking over their shoulders. ''I don't think you're supposed—''

''Do me a favor and don't think, period. I'm trying to figure this— Hey!'' Bill rubbed one shoulder and glared upward. ''What'd you punch me for?''

''Because you're an ass,'' Hank said in a matter-of-fact tone.

Hope had never liked the amiable man more. ''No *wonder* Bill can't find himself from first base.''

Hank chuckled, Bill sputtered and she backed away grinning. She'd been rather fascinated with the navigational portion of class instruction and distinctly remembered they were supposed to look at the terrain first and *then* the map. But damned if she'd help Bill now.

Karen had almost reached the main group when Hope decided to do a little research of her own. She smiled at her lagging teammate, nodded at Jared bringing up the rear and passed them both at a crisp walk.

"Where do you think you're going?" Jared's voice boomed over her head.

"Not far," she said without turning. "I'll be right back."

He probably thought she had private business to take care of, and that was okay with her. She'd felt his probing gaze for hours and relished a break from the demanding fox walk. Slipping behind a cluster of creosote bushes, she sighed, let herself slump and made mental notes on the surrounding area.

Foothills due east, much closer than they'd been that morning. A distinctive camelback ridge to the northeast. Her roving gaze stopped at a gap in the vegetation thirty yards away, and she wandered closer to explore.

A furry shape exploded from a bush to her left. Hand over her bucking heart, she watched the biggest jackrabbit she'd ever seen race off as if her wobbly legs could actually run in pursuit. Her gaze tracked the long erect ears until she could breathe normally again, then she continued ahead. The sunken narrow passageway she found couldn't be anything other than a creek bed, but it had clearly been dry for some time. She memorized the relationship to her other landmarks before heading back toward the team.

Hope stopped on the outskirts of a situation that had gone from bad to worse. Bill was no closer to figuring out their location than when she'd left. His "discussion" with Hank had escalated in volume, and the younger man appeared genuinely angry for the first time since she'd met him.

Jared watched from the sidelines without intervention, his presence no doubt adding wounded male pride into the volatile bag of emotions. Karen stood nearby, her fingers in her mouth, her tucked-tail body language both irritating and heart-wrenching. Enough was enough. Something had to give.

"Bill, Hank, Karen," she yelled. "Get over here."

CHAPTER TEN

FOUR HEADS whipped around as Hope unbuckled her hip belt. She slipped out of her shoulder straps, let the backpack drop and scanned her immobile teammates.

"Move!"

They did, with varying degrees of speed. Bill dragged up last, his "this better be good" expression straining her patience. When Jared unfolded his arms and took a step as if to join them, Hope raised her palm and glared.

"Hold it right there, Scout. Detached observers aren't invited. Only team members are allowed at this party."

He stepped back, his thoughts unreadable behind his sporty sunglasses. But she knew darn well he wasn't thinking that she was his dream woman.

Promising herself to make up for lost ground later, she led her teammates out of Jared's hearing and concentrated on the problem at hand. "I know this is the first day on our own, but so far we're not winning any performance awards. Oh, for *heaven's sake*, Bill, quit scowling. I'm not blaming you. And *honestly*, Karen, if you don't take those fingers out of your mouth, I'm going to put yesterday's socks on each of your hands and make you wear them in this heat.''

They were staring at her as if her head had just swiveled 360 degrees. No doubt she looked like the very devil, too, with dirty hair and an all-natural pancake makeup comprised of sweat and grit.

She took a deep breath and tried again. ''I know you're the trail leader, Bill, but that doesn't mean you have to carry us all on your back. For example, Karen really knows her way around a kitchen. Hank has tons of experience gauging people's physical condition and limitations. I'm a whiz at longitude and latitude. Are you getting any ideas here, pal?''

''You want me to ask for help?'' Bill thrust out his bearded chin somewhere between belligerence and a pout.

Hope breathed deeply. *Negative thoughts have no power over me.* ''Good leaders delegate tasks all the time. That doesn't diminish their authority or their power. It increases their effectiveness. I don't know about you, but I'd sure like to show our detached observer we can get to this evening's campsite without passing out, getting hopelessly lost or killing each other.''

''Me, too,'' Hank muttered with feeling.

Karen remained silent, but at least her hands were in her pockets.

Bill whipped off his sunglasses and Feast Market Celebrity Tournament golf cap, used his T-shirt sleeve to blot his face, then glanced back at the arm-folded figure standing like Mr. Clean with an attitude beside several backpacks. Obviously Bill was afraid of making the wrong decision in front of Jared.

"Think of it this way," Hope said. "What other time will you be able to tell me what to do when I'm honor bound to obey? When my turn at trail leader comes up, you'll be sorry you blew your chance."

I'll make your life miserable, she promised with an evil grin.

He snorted, shook his head and resettled his cap and glasses.

Her grin grew friendlier.

His mouth twitched. "Okay, hotshot. Consider yourself delegated to figure out where the hell we are."

Yes! "Good decision."

Propping beefy hands on his love handles, he lifted his face to the sky. "So whaddaya think, Hank? Should we stop for a while and get out from under this heat lamp?"

Hank gave the same arm he'd punched earlier a manly slap of approval. "Absolutely. Even the lizards have gone underground until later. Want me to rig up some shade where we can park a while and eat?"

"Sounds like a good plan." Bill lowered his gaze to Karen. "How're you feeling? You up to making this crew some lunch?"

A show of concern? Well, whaddaya know?

"I'd love to try." Karen flashed an impish smile, pulled her hands from her pockets and wiggled her fingers. "It'll keep my hands occupied and out of Hope's dirty socks."

They were laughing as they broke apart to buckle into their backpacks and follow Hank. Oddly enough, Hope didn't feel so tired anymore. Maybe it was because she'd managed to refocus efforts without alienating Bill. She was beginning to suspect that once he gave you his loyalty, he'd guard your back with his life.

Ten minutes later their trail leader for the day once again spread a topographical map on the ground. Hope scanned the domestic picture behind him.

Two stunted mesquite trees offered little shade, but provided support for the tarp strung up between them. Karen worked beneath the canvas roof stirring something in a pot. Hank had delegated himself her helper, and Jared sat with his back propped against one tree trunk, his legs sprawled out and a rope of some sort in his lap. Quite a change from the scene that had spurred Hope to action earlier.

"It's all yours, hotshot," Bill said, handing her the "orienteering" compass. "Good luck."

Hope crouched down and reviewed the class instructions in her mind. *No problem.*

First, she lined up the "direction of travel" arrow on her compass with true north on the map. Then without moving the base, she turned the mounted circular housing until the etched arrow matched the *magnetic* north line on the map. "Boxing" the needle was a little tricky. She had to lift and turn the entire map—leaving the compass level and undisturbed—until the floating magnetic needle aligned with the etched arrow. That accomplished, she laid the properly oriented map down and anchored it with rocks on all four corners.

Two outthrusting V's in the contour lines identified the camelback landmark she'd memorized earlier. She found the creek bed, estimated distances and noted the red circled campsite. "Looks like we've got about six, maybe seven miles to go. If we keep heading forty-five degrees west of magnetic north, we should be okay."

"But where are we?" Bill asked from behind.

"I'm pretty sure we're ri-i-ght...*here*." She pressed a fingertip to the map.

"I'm positive we're right there," a familiar voice said.

Hope twisted sharply and looked up at Jared. He was going to give her a heart attack one of these days.

"Positive?" Delight replaced her irritation.

"Positive," he confirmed, looking taller than a mountain and too damn cute to live.

She turned to grin smugly up at Bill. "He's positive."

"I heard. I just don't understand how you did it. You didn't even look at the terrain," Bill grumbled.

"She checked out the surrounding area when you

were arguing with Hank,'' Jared explained, drawing Hope's startled gaze again. ''See, Bill, you found where you thought we were on the map and then tried to find landmarks to prove you were right. A common mistake, but one Hope obviously remembered not to make. She memorized landmarks, then oriented the map to the terrain.'' He glanced at Hope. ''You can take your finger off now, by the way.''

Hope realized she still crouched awkwardly beside the map, one hand marking their location in some bizarre parody of the game Twister.

''Come and get it,'' Hank yelled from the shade.

As Bill lumbered toward the promise of food, Hope straightened, sensed the alertness behind Jared's dark glasses and knew that he, too, was remembering their exchange at breakfast.

''Do you need me to take a look at that foot for you?'' he asked, launching a subtle weapon against her control.

''No thanks.''

Offence was sometimes the best defence. She pressed her fist to the small of her back and prolonged her arched stretch a moment longer than necessary.

Nothing. Not even a facial twitch.

''Whew, it's hot!'' she drawled, laying it on as thick as Liz Taylor in *Cat on a Hot Tin Roof*. Grasping a pinch of T-shirt between her breasts, she billowed the cotton in and out. ''How does anything survive at this time of day?''

"By finding shelter like we did. I was just about to step in and suggest to Bill that we take cover when you rallied the team. And the dirty socks on Karen's hands were just the right touch. Nice job, Hope."

She shrugged, unable to suppress a quick thrill of pleasure. "I thought a little delegation might be in order. I had to knock Bill off his throne, but a democracy works better than a monarchy, don't you think?"

"Oh, I agree. The strengths can balance the weaknesses and create a stronger unit. The question is, do *you* believe a democracy works better?"

Of all the nerve! "Why else would I have gotten Bill to delegate tasks?"

"Because you knew the game's rule—follow Bill's leadership for the day—and that was the quickest way to avoid getting disqualified and still win."

The harsh words stung any lingering pleasure right out of her. She turned to head for the tarp, but he caught her upper arm.

"If you believe in true democracy, Hope, why do you insist on making every decision at Manning Enterprises?" At her startled glance, he added, "I heard you phone your office, remember?"

It came back to her in a sick rush. She'd told Debbie not to make any major decisions in her absence.

"I see that you do remember. Don't you believe in practicing what you preach?"

"Hey, are you guys gonna eat or can I have your

pasta salad?'' Bill called while Hope's mind scrambled for an answer.

She pulled her arm from Jared's grasp and lifted her chin. ''What I practice on my own personal time is no business or concern of yours. And as far as my preaching goes, I wouldn't think of trying to compete with a pro like you. Shoot, you've got the market on sermonizing all locked up.''

He let her have the final say as she marched away and grabbed a bowl of pasta from Karen.

His words stayed with her, though. They nagged and provoked and challenged her throughout the group siesta in the shade. Sometime between watching Jared stretch out for a carefree snooze and seeing him sit up and knuckle his eyes, a trivial question popped into her head.

If her team had conducted their ''private'' meeting out of Jared's hearing, how had he known about the dirty socks?

JARED ZIPPED the tarp into its compartment, swung up his sleek backpack and shoved his arms through the shoulder straps. Weariness pressed heavier than the physical weight he carried.

Nothing like a refreshing nap to restore a man's energy, he thought wryly. Normally he could go into a meditative state under any condition, but apparently not under Hope's probing gaze. Oh, he'd feigned sleep. But he'd thought of those snapping brown eyes on his body and had fantasized that her graceful hands would follow.

Real professional.

Bill gave the signal to head out in a horizontal line, and Jared waited to bring up the rear. Hope ignored him as she passed, but he knew she was aware of him. Hell, the air practically crackled whenever they got within ten feet of each other. His attraction to Beth had been strong, but nothing as megavolt as this.

Falling into step behind the group, Jared wished that "this" was only about sex. Then after the expedition, he could've visited a divorcée in Alpine who had no desire for marriage but who welcomed his occasional company. Problem solved.

But Hope was a much more complex package. As desirable as he found the exterior wrapping, the contents intrigued him more. Conversations with her were as stimulating, as challenging as any he'd had with Ben. Jared liked having to stay on his mental toes to keep up. And his glimpses of a softer, less confident woman had triggered a surprising urge to protect her spirit from breaking.

If he'd sermonized about democracy, it was because he knew firsthand the danger of building empires. They had a history of falling and destroying everyone standing too close.

"Hey, Jared, what's that?" Hank called, pointing to a bounding mouselike animal kicking up little spurts of sand.

Jared sped up and joined the fanned line of hikers. "A kangaroo rat. That little guy is living proof of Darwin's theory of evolution. He can survive fine without water."

"He *never* has to drink?"

"Not in the conventional sense. His body makes its own metabolic water from the seeds he eats."

"Handy trick," Bill said, drawing within easy talking distance. The unnerving rasp of a snake rattle whispered in his pocket with every step. "I gotta admit the water thing out here spooks me. What if something happened to you and the remote radio? The creek on the map is bone-dry. If we can't trust the map for accurate water sources, we could die."

Facing and managing elemental danger was a key part of the MindBend Adventures experience. Jared never minimized the risks.

"I have no intention of letting anything happen to me, but for the sake of education, let's say I *was* out of commission." He gestured to the Sierra del Carmen, blue-green with forests, which rose in the group's direct line of travel. "Up there water's no problem. But in a true survival situation here in the desert or foothills, cottonwoods and willows are the trees of life. Look for them first."

"Do they always grow near water? " Karen asked.

He smiled briefly at the newest member to join his impromptu lesson. "They grow where water tends to collect, but it might not be visible on the ground surface. If that's the case, don't panic. Wait until night when the trees release some of what they've absorbed, dig several holes and watch them fill.''

"I don't see anything taller than a cactus around here," Hope piped up, walking closer to complete the team unit. "What if we all tripped on rocks and sprained our ankles and couldn't go looking for trees?"

"Then I'd point out your bones to students next year and warn them to step *over* rocks." He caught her gaze as the others laughed and saw the exact moment her surprise changed to triumph.

"No, you wouldn't. You're out of commission, remember? Your bones will be found in a little pile somewhere next to the remote radio."

So much for staying on his mental toes.

"Good one, Hope!" Bill hooted, twisting to raise his palm for a high five.

Without losing stride she slapped his hand, faced forward and tugged the bill of her cap in a satisfied "Top that!" motion.

The best Jared could do was bring the topic back under control. "Actually, in cactus country there is a better way to get water than digging for it."

"The *cactus*." Hank rapped his forehead and groaned. "Of course, how stupid. We can get water from it."

A logical assumption. "Yes and no. The Apache and Mestizos considered cactus a better source of food than of water. C'mere, I'll show you."

Unfolding his pocket knife, Jared approached a

flowering prickly-pear patch, whacked a large oval pad in half and used his blade as a pointer while the others gathered around. "See the seeds between these petals? They can be ground into flour. The pear fruit—this little reddish bud here—will be ready to eat in the fall. Pads like the one I cut here can be peeled and boiled or roasted.

"In an emergency, eating the inside pulp will gain you a few vitamins and a little water. Taking the thorns off is hell, though. Kind of like trying to skin a porcupine. And the sweat you'd lose working to get a few sips' worth of water could cancel out the benefit." Their expressions were thoughtful as he wiped the knife blade against his thigh.

"Gee, you're a big help," Hope finally said. "We can look for trees that aren't here, pray for a freak thunderstorm or sweat to death skinning a porcupine. Got any other smart tips, Scout?"

He waggled the point of his blade. "I've got a sharp tip for you right here. Any more wisecracks and I'll give you a demonstration."

Her delighted laugh pleased him too damn much. He pocketed his knife and desperately focused on the lesson.

"Believe it or not, your best bet for water in a survival situation is morning dew. Yes, dew," he added in the face of their obvious skepticism. "It's recently condensed and distilled, and probably safer than what you drink at home."

"But...how do you collect it, much less enough of it to really help?" Hank asked.

"Find something to act as a sponge—a piece of T-shirt would be fine—then get up early and work fast. Wipe everything in sight, even the sand, and squeeze the water into a container or directly into your mouth. I once used a handful of dried grass as a sponge and collected at least a quart of water out here."

The men looked fascinated, the women grossed out.

Jared smiled briefly. "Hey, it saved my life. I wasn't picky." He sensed a barrage of personal questions coming on and hedged. "You know, if we don't get our tails in gear, we're not going to make camp by dark. Why don't we get moving?"

Without any more warning, he walked off and left the group behind.

They creaked and shuffled into awkward motion as if he were the engine and they the last few cars of a long freight train. Eventually they got their rhythm and caught up. But he was ready.

Pointing out the mashed grass beneath nearby acacia shrubs, he diverted their curiosity to the piglike javelinas that had most likely bedded down there in the heat of the day. About fifty yards past the area, Bill spotted a mother with four babies and went charging off in pursuit. Seconds later he came charging back, the mama javelina hot on his heels. Her bristles erect, her grunts outraged, she abandoned the chase at the sight of more humans. Bill collapsed to his knees.

"Shee-it, that was close. Do they eat people?" he gasped.

The others were laughing by now, and Jared took pity. "No, but they eat almost anything else. Prickly pear, roots, lizards, snakes—" he turned and pointed a finger at Hope "—and no comments from the peanut gallery about Bill's genealogy."

The glance she slanted up sparkled with mischief. "No need to now. Thanks, Scout."

By the time the teasing and excitement faded, the group seemed to have forgotten personal questions and settled down to put in some serious hiking. Jared took the drag position again. Bill set a reasonable pace so that Karen was able to keep up stride for stride with Hank. Soon the two were deep in animated conversation—a little too animated for Jared's comfort. Such total concentration on each other meant little awareness of the trail. He considered speeding up to join the line of hikers.

Then Hope dropped back to join him.

"Mind if I walk with you a minute?"

Hmm. What was she up to now? "If I said yes, would you be offended?"

"No."

"Then yes, I do mind. I'm sort of in the middle of a meditation," he lied, and waited for her to do the socially correct thing. Two minutes later he glared at her.

"I said I wouldn't be offended. I didn't say I would leave." She grinned at him impudently, irresistibly.

The sight pulled at his heart, widening the crack she seemed hell-bent on squeezing through—consciously or otherwise. "You are without a doubt the most...unusual woman I've ever known."

Her grin faded. "Ditto, Scout. Collecting dew with a grass sponge, walking like a fox, *hearing* like a damn jackrabbit." She intercepted his startled glance with a knowing nod. "Unless you can read minds, that's the only logical explanation for your comment about dirty socks. I figure there's more to what Mr. Loping—*Running* Bear taught you than you're letting on. I'd like to know the full story."

"Why?"

"Call me curious."

"Okay. Why are you curious?"

She looked straight ahead, her muscles tightening, the subtle scent of fear clashing with sun-heated magnolia and the richer headier essence of the woman herself. Her curiosity obviously confused and frightened her. It was as if she wanted to run away, but some powerful force held her back.

When Jared sensed that *he* was that force, his jolt of fierce satisfaction stunned him. Suddenly his need to tell matched her need to know. He would reveal just enough to stop outrageous stunts like that "insatiable appetite" routine she'd pulled. Maybe then, at the end of the expedition, they could return to separate lives, separate commitments, without the memory of a passionate joining to haunt them.

He searched his mind for where to begin....

SKIRTING CACTUS and rocks automatically, Hope waited for Jared to continue his story. So far it'd been a real beaut.

He'd been a drifter, of all things. Hitching rides to some of the most isolated areas of the country, picking up the occasional odd job, camping in national parks when he'd had sufficient money and sleeping in roadside fields when he didn't. He'd lived off wild game and edible wilderness plants whenever possible, with survival handbooks as his guide. Incredible. Fascinating.

She wanted to know more.

"I had a chip on my shoulder the size of West Texas when I wandered into Ben's school yard," Jared finally said.

Hope released a silent sigh of relief.

"I'd thumbed a ride from Alpine but had to get out before the Big Bend National Park entrance gate. Since I couldn't afford hiking entrance fees for a week, I planned to sneak in after dark. The abandoned school looked like a good place to lay low."

Jared Austin, breaking the law? *Admitting* to breaking the law?

"The school had obviously been closed a long time. The adobe house behind it looked unoccupied from a distance, too. I thought the whole place was deserted and started walking toward the house. Then the school front doors opened and out came this old man. He just stood there staring at me, almost as if he'd been expecting me.''

Jared's silence stretched and she glanced his way. His strong throat was working and her heart contracted. Ben had been lucky. To be loved by this man would be an extraordinary gift.

A sweet yearning soared inside her, glided on a current of wonder, plummeted back down to earth.

''Have you ever seen old photographs of Geronimo?'' Jared asked thickly.

Hope struggled to regain her scattered wits. Few people who'd grown up in the Texas school system hadn't learned about him. ''I've seen pictures in history books, yes.''

''Well, focus on his image in your head. Do you have it?''

She saw the broad flat-planed face, the bold nose, the mesmerizing eyes. ''Yes, I have it.''

''Now imagine him wearing baggy worn jeans, a faded plaid shirt, a chewed-up straw cowboy hat. Picture his face with so many wrinkles there's no room for more, change his long black hair to a mixture of white and pewter gray. But leave his eyes the same, Hope. Leave them young and dark and so piercing you feel skewered and honored and humbled at the same time. Can you see him now?''

She concentrated on the vivid image he'd painted, a leader whose commanding presence was undiminished by advanced age or white man's clothes. "I see him," she murmured, impressed.

"*That's* what Ben Running Bear looked like on the school steps when I first met him. I finally got up the nerve to ask for a glass of water. He took me to his house, gave me a drink and invited me to share his lunch. I wound up sharing the final three years of his life with him."

She'd rarely heard that respectful tone from peers speaking about their parents. She'd certainly never heard it in her own voice. "Where was his family, his...tribe?"

He shot her an indulgent smile. "Tribe is a Hollywood movie myth. In real life the Apache had groups of extended families called bands. These days all groups refer to themselves as a nation. But Ben remembered and grieved for his band of Mazatzal Apache. He was the last living member."

The puzzle pieces fell into place. "Until you became his surrogate grandson."

"Yeah," he admitted after a long pause. "I guess you could say that. Ben had thirty acres free and clear, plus eighty years of knowledge and cultural history that would die with him. I was lucky enough to walk into his life when he'd decided that passing them on to a white man was better than no man at all."

"And the school?"

"Built by a do-gooder organization in the early eighties. Apparently rounding up the migrant kids, convincing decent teachers to stay, inconsistent funding—all of it was too overwhelming for the administrators. The organization finally deeded the building to Ben in thanks for donating the land.''

''So you inherited that, too.''

His head turned sharply. ''If you're thinking that I manipulated him into leaving me his property, you're dead wrong. I didn't know he owned Jacksquat until a lawyer showed up at the funeral home. Ben had told me he lived free on the land in exchange for keeping the school in working condition.''

''I didn't think you manipulated him.'' The thought had never crossed her mind, although that would've been a logical cynical assumption—the kind she normally made.

''Well, good. I didn't. I loved that old man. You can't put a price tag on what he gave me. He taught me the way of the Scout.''

Scout? Hope couldn't help her bark of laughter. ''You're making that up, right?''

'''Fraid not.'' The wry curve of his mouth acknowledged life's strange vagaries. ''He started my lessons that very first day.''

She had a feeling Jared wasn't talking about setting up a tent or orienting a topographical map. ''What kind of lessons?''

''Survival skills, tracking, awareness, the philosophy of living with the earth, instead of possessing it. I'd scratched the surface of all that when I bummed around on my own, but Ben made me see why I'd instinctively sought out the wilderness. The things I'd once owned and mourned losing…'' He looked at her quickly, as if realizing he'd revealed too much.

"The things you sold paying your father's legal fees," she filled in. How many sons would have done such a thing?

He studied the horizon. "Yeah. Anyway, those possessions had really owned me."

"'What I am looking for is not out there. It is in me,'" Hope quoted.

"Exactly! Ben taught me that meditation. He'd studied all kinds of religion, including New Age, and adopted certain teachings as his own. But he always focused most on the way of the Scout.

"And eventually I decided that there's something about living close to the earth that helps men and women get their priorities straight. By the same token, it's as if the farther removed from wilderness that mankind remains, the more inhuman—and inhumane—we become."

Heavy stuff. "So we've got to return to the earth to keep from evolving into beasts. MindBend Adventures is your silver bullet, so to speak."

He broke into a startled grin. "I don't claim to hit the heart of students all the time, but I try. I thought at first I'd missed yours."

Hope stumbled.

Only Jared's lightning reflexes saved her from eating dirt. "Are you okay?"

How could she be okay with her traitorous heart thundering against his muscular forearm? She drew herself up and away, then forced a shaky smile. "Oh, yeah, we're supposed to step *over* the rocks. Thanks for the help."

"My pleasure."

Hope could've sworn the husky words were imbued with sexual innuendo. Turning quickly, she continued walking. Hoo-boy. That'd been close. His long strides brought him to her side much too soon.

Best to confront the awkwardness directly. "What did you mean, you thought you'd missed my heart? Did you think I was a beast?"

"Not a beast. But maybe a hypocrite. That product made by your 'silent hero' is the same one that's going to make you a 'very rich woman,' am I right?"

She winced at the memory of bragging to Bill about her future wealth. "You're right. But all my ventures make products or perform services that contribute something valuable to society. That's one of my requirements for funding the venture."

"I said I *thought* I'd missed your heart."

"So...you don't think I'm a terrible person?"

"I think you're..."

She stared blindly ahead, her senses balanced on the edge of a thrilling plunge.

"No, I don't think you're a terrible person," Jared finished in a subdued voice.

Disappointment held her mute. She wanted to press for more, but pulled back mentally from the precipice. It was better this way, she assured herself. Better brought back to an impersonal level. The chasm between them was too wide.

He was as committed to his work as she was to hers; they had no time to commute cross-country; transplanting either company was out of the question. Yes, it was smart to protect herself from future pain.

She'd get over her present aching heart soon enough.

CHAPTER ELEVEN

TWO MORNINGS LATER Hope opened her eyes to the predawn darkness of the tent and frowned. A vague stir of excitement had awakened her; a subconscious alarm clock signaling a special reason to get up. Memory returned.

Today was the day *she* was the team's designated trail leader!

If Debbie had dared tell Hope eight days ago she would look forward to such a thing, she would've forged a trail for the VP right out her office door. But she saw things a little differently now. Ever since Jared had spoken about living close to the earth, in fact.

From that point on, she'd stopped treating the land as a commodity—something to consume, to cross over as quickly as possible in order to reach a campsite and possess it—and had begun *seeing* what she'd only looked through before.

Plant and animal life scattered widely in sparseness, in simplicity, and bathed in the extreme clarity of pollution-free light. The sprinting roadrunners pausing intermittently to lift their brushy topknots; the scuttling lizards hotfooting it across the sand like barefoot tourists on a scorching beach; the soaring hawks wheeling high overhead.

And the flowers! Distant splashes of scarlet and yellow became works of art up close. The creamy white yucca petals could be eaten raw, the leaves dried and twisted into cordage. The roots made a good soap when mashed in water, so Jared had told them. As he'd told them so many interesting things.

His tidbits of information had made the miles pass quickly. He was a walking Discovery channel, and she thanked fate for making him angry enough the first day they'd met to assign himself her trail leader.

They'd left the desert behind the day before, and she'd been shocked to feel regret. Yet the grassy slopes footing the Sierra del Carmen were new territory waiting to be explored. Today she had a chance to prove her own leadership ability, to practice the democracy she'd preached. She wanted to do well almost more than she wanted the UroTech sale to go through. And the implications didn't bear thinking about.

Wriggling out of her sleeping bag, she dressed as quietly as possible and reached for her sweatshirt. Karen remained a motionless pupa in her warm cocoon. The temperature had lowered with the team's climb in elevation. Hope wouldn't miss the desert heat at all.

She crawled out of the tent and stood, then waited a moment to orient herself as she had every morning on the trail. Only this morning was darker. Colder. More special.

Not a whisper of wind stirred. The stars had faded, hinting of dawn, but shapes were barely discernible in the dense gray light. Hank and Bill's tent huddled twenty yards to her left. Scattered piñon pines stood sentinel throughout the grassy clearing of their campsite. Her breath plumed visibly in a slow steady rhythm, then stopped altogether.

Then plumed shorter and faster than before.

She'd know that particular shape across the field anywhere. Tall, broad-shouldered, lean-hipped—all man. The stuff women dreamed about but often found lacking in brains and/or morals in the waking world. Jared possessed both attributes in abundance. All three, if you counted his shape. Which, personally, she did.

He didn't move, just stood there watching, pulling her forward on the strength of his charisma alone. She found her feet moving through knee-high grass and then stopped an arm's length away. Too close. Not close enough.

"Couldn't you sleep?" she asked in a soft voice, which still sounded much too loud.

"I don't need a lot of sleep. I'm surprised *you're* awake. It usually takes the smell of coffee to draw you out of that tent." His teasing voice was deep. Hushed. Lovers-in-the-dark intimate.

A shiver rippled through her.

Instantly he whipped off his pullover sweater,

draped it capelike over her shoulders and looped the sleeves beneath her chin. The wool embraced her in his heat and masculine smell, as if he'd wrapped his arms around her from behind. Her eyelids drifted lower.

"Better?" His thin dark T-shirt was little protection from the cold.

Inexplicable tears clogged her throat. "How has a man like you managed to stay single all this time?" *Way to keep it impersonal, genius.*

"What kind of man am I?"

Thoughtful. Gorgeous. "Heterosexual."

He chuckled. "I was engaged once."

Don't ask. "What happened?"

He shrugged, the movement visible if not his expression. "Beth was sweet and shy, very unworldly. That's what attracted me to her at first. I fell in love and decided to help her gain a little social polish. Forced that first ice-breaking cocktail into her hand at a party, as a matter of fact." His self-mocking tone bordered on scathing. "Pretty soon she was the last one to leave every party, and by then I'd have to pour her into my car."

"Beth drank too much?"

"Beth never stopped drinking, once I showed her how to relax and get over her shyness."

He blamed himself. But that was ridiculous. "Alcoholism is a disease, not a bad habit. You couldn't have known the way drinking would affect her system."

"I could've accepted her, *protected* her instead of trying to change her. But by the time I realized the extent of her problem, she already loved booze more than she did me. Look—" he rumpled his hair in a dismissive gesture "—it was a long time ago. I've come to terms with what I did—and didn't—do. Let's just drop the subject, okay?"

Nodding, she watched the first rays of dawn touch the hard planes of his cheeks, the uncompromising squareness of his jaw. The chiseled effect was softened endearingly by the glasses askew on his nose and his tufted hair. She clutched the sleeves of his sweater to keep from straightening the frames and finger-combing his hair, liberties only a mother—or lover—could take.

Suddenly he stiffened, his attention focused on something behind him, then he flashed a smile. Raising a warning finger to his lips, he turned and pulled her down to crouch beside him in the tall wheat-colored grass. She followed his gaze to the edge of a thick stand of pines about fifty yards away.

The shroud of night had lifted from the clearing, yet she didn't see a thing that would have caused his reaction. She kept still, anyway, trusting his extraordinary senses, and was rewarded an instant later.

The mule-deer doe emerged from the dark woods as if from the flat page of a storybook. She picked her way delicately through the thick undergrowth, paused with her beautiful gaze alert and long ears pricked, then lowered her head to graze on the tender green blades. The silent signal flagged a fawn from the safety of the woods. Tentative at first, growing bolder with each step, the tiny spotted creature soon gamboled on pogo-stick legs around its mother.

Dewdrops trembled and glistened on the grass. Birds warbled and chirped good-morning to pals in neighboring trees. It was an idyllic scene. Sentimental and placid. The antithesis of the frenetic business environment Hope loved.

She was entranced, utterly and completely. The quiet pleasure emanating from Jared served to increase her own.

For the first time since leaving her family's ranch, she understood something simple and sad. By cutting herself off from anything "close to the earth," she hadn't defied her parents—she'd punished herself.

Nostalgic longing pierced the last of her defenses. The bluebonnets would be blooming in the grazing pastures now. Maybe after the expedition she would swing by the ranch for a quick visit before returning to New York.

The rasp of a tent zipper cut through her musings. The doe's head came up high and she froze.

"*Damn,* it's cold," Bill muttered from in front of his tent.

Both deer sprang toward the woods with their tails held high and slipped back into the storybook page. The only sign they'd ever been there was grass knocked bare of dew.

"Well, *damn,* did you see those deer? Hank, get out here and look at the deer."

Hope met Jared's eyes and saw a reflection of her own exasperated amusement. Unable to suppress a grin, she stood and faced the golden sunrise, her anticipation and good humor restored.

The magical storybook moment had shattered, but the whole day remained. And she, for one, chose to make it wonderful.

ON A PRIVATE AIRSTRIP outside Del Rio, Stan Lawler hoisted his backpack from the Lincoln's trunk and slammed the lid. He took a minute to admire the sleek white car in the morning sunlight before dropping his pack to the ground. No more luxury cars or hotels for him in the next couple of days. The chopper was due any minute. Time to take care of business, pick up his scratch and head back to north Chicago.

A sneer curled his lip at the thought of his dingy one-bedroom apartment. The first thing he'd do was find a classier place. Or maybe he'd move to another city altogether. Yeah, one where he didn't freeze his ass off six months out of the year.

He was smiling as he crouched on the tarmac and unzipped his backpack. He'd loaded up carefully last night, but he prided himself on good planning. So he double-checked the contents now like any businessman would check his briefcase before an important meeting. Not that he'd need half this shit. The job was hardly a challenge. Taking out a woman with an M21 was never as much fun as up close and personal. He'd included his .22 caliber Ruger Mark II and buck-hunting knife—just in case. The knife had sentimental value and went with him everywhere.

He'd required a few facts before accepting the contract. The sexy redhead in the file's photo was a real ball breaker, according to his employers. It was important to do her before some FDA-approval thing went through. More information than that he hadn't needed—or wanted—to know.

Once in the backcountry he would eavesdrop on the morning radio check-ins, get the woman's exact team location and blow out of Mexico while the others were still freaking over the hit. Orders were orders.

Then again...

This was a landmark contract. Maybe he had time to make the occasion memorable, to have a little fun. If one of those faggot wilderness instructors got in his way, hell, so much the better.

A muffled whir alerted Stan before the AS 350B Ecureuil flew into view. Designed for high speed and low vibration and noise, the chopper was perfect for transporting cargo in and out of Mexico that certain parties would prefer remain undiscovered. He watched the ski-like landing gear touch down and felt the first welcome stir of excitement in his gut. The sun shone bright in a cloudless sky, but it could've been overcast for all he cared.

Any morning that brought him closer to that ultimate moment of power was the start of a good day.

THE TEAM'S MORNING ROUTE had taken them up the grassy slopes skirting the mountains. The trees were growing thicker now, and Hope noted ponderosa pine and Douglas fir in addition to the piñons of lower elevations. The spicy fragrance and cool breeze were invigorating and sharpened her hunger. She hadn't eaten much breakfast. The others were probably ready for lunch, too.

She started to call ahead to Karen and suddenly realized there'd been no muttering from the back of the hiking group for the past fifteen minutes. *Well, whaddaya know?*

Had Jared noticed, too? She forced herself not to glance at the drag position and seek his approval.

Bill had been much more vocal an hour ago when Karen had started to tire in the lead position. He'd protested long and loudly that she was slowing up everyone else and therefore should switch her assigned spot with him.

Of course Hope had wanted the team to set a pace based on the energy of its weakest element. She frowned now at the "weakest" element hiking gamely five yards ahead. Karen had started her period the night before and wasn't feeling too swift. Yet she hadn't breathed a word of complaint.

"We'll stop for lunch soon," Hope promised Karen. "How are you doing?"

"Better than Bill. Putting him in charge of map reading for the day really shut him up. Thanks, Hope."

"Anytime."

Hope had suspected that assigning Bill a task he hadn't mastered yet would increase his sympathy for the slower hiker, and she'd been right. It seemed, in fact, that when she pushed aside her own fear of appearing weak, she had a knack for reading human nature, as well as numbers.

Pride filled her with renewed energy. She forged ahead of her weary friend and five minutes later found the perfect spot for a break. The grassy meadow was surrounded by forest and the peaceful cooing of doves. By the time the others reached the clearing, she'd already removed her backpack.

"So how about it, troops, are you ready for some lunch?" Hope asked.

"Are you kidding? Even that fruit-nut pemmican stuff in my emergency bag is starting to sound good," Bill said. "Who's got chef duty?"

All eyes, including Hope's, turned to Karen.

Before Karen could respond, Hope remembered her responsibility. "We can't expect Karen to do all the cooking for us. I'll throw something together."

Bill groaned and looked pained. No one else met her gaze. Just because she'd burned the oatmeal that morning and made the coffee a teensy bit too strong...

"How much water do we have?" she asked haughtily.

Backpacks came off and were unzipped. A quick inventory showed that canteens and containers were low. Four stares turned her way with varying degrees of accusation.

Just because she'd used a teensy bit too much water in the second batch of oatmeal and pot of coffee...

Hope sniffed, asked for the map and pointed out the creek running parallel to their route. "Why don't the rest of you go refill our supply while I set up the kitchen?"

"I'll stay and help you," Karen offered.

"Hallelujah," Bill muttered, then glanced hastily at Hope. "I mean, shoot, there's no reason all of us have to go. Karen looks kinda beat, anyway, don'tcha think?"

Hank made a low noise of protest. "She looks gr—" He ducked his head. "She looks fine to me."

"Excuse me, but why are you both talking like I'm not here?" Karen asked.

Go, girlfriend! "Bill, your concern is...touching. And actually, Karen, I could use your help." Hope arched a brow at Jared. "That plan okay with you?"

"Makes good sense to me."

She'd made good sense to him. Hope smiled.

Jared smiled back. "I would've suggested the same thing."

He would've suggested the same thing. Hope's smile became bigger, she couldn't help it.

The wattage in his smile increased.

"Okay already," Bill grumbled. "It's a great plan. You're a great trail leader. So are we gonna go get water or not?" He and Hank held collapsible plastic jugs in both hands and stood watching Jared expectantly.

Jared's smile collapsed flatter than the jugs. His complexion grew dusky. He crouched on one knee and rummaged busily in his backpack. Rising with two more containers in hand, he nodded at Hope without meeting her eyes. "We'll be back in about thirty minutes."

Be careful, she came so close to saying. "Okay," she said, instead.

Silly woman, she thought as the men walked away. He was a wilderness guide, for heaven's sake. *Be careful.* How stupid. How inane. How *revealing.* That was something only a mother—or lover—could tell him.

Subdued and oddly depressed, Hope helped Karen unload the stove and foodstuffs. A bare slab of limestone served as a countertop. The blonde studied the supplies with a competent eye and pronounced they would make quiche for lunch. Hope shook her head.

"You're amazing. You should write a camping cookbook when you get home." Picking up the stove's spirit cup and fuel, she carried them a safe distance and began filling the cup. "I mean it," she called over her shoulder. "I'll bet a gourmet camping cookbook would really sell well. How many millions of people did Jared tell us camped at national parks each year?" She paused. "Was it three hundred, do you think?" Silence. "Karen?"

The hair at Hope's nape prickled. She turned around slowly and dropped the spirit cup.

Karen stood with her back to Hope as if turned into a pillar of salt. Forty yards ahead of her a large black bear lifted its snout and sniffed the air.

The facts Jared had recited on Sierra del Carmen bears flashed in Hope's mind. *Shy of humans. Frightened off by loud noises. Burn—don't bury—meal scraps.*

"Heeyah! Get out of here!" she shouted, rising and waving her arms wildly.

Why wasn't he running? The food was sealed and odorless. *The odor of a woman's period attracts— and sometimes angers— wild bears. Let your trail guide know if you're menstruating.*

Oh, dear God.

The beady dark gaze hadn't wavered from Karen. Black fur spiked the animal's ruff. A menacing rumble rolled from his cavernous chest. This was no zoo animal performing safely behind a moat.

"Hope?" Karen said, mindless terror in her tone.

"I'm right here. Back away slowly."

Rooted in horror, Karen didn't move.

Advancing a step, the animal raised his head, bared vicious-looking yellowed teeth and roared.

Adrenaline surged through Hope. Her body braced for flight. Karen swayed on her feet.

The movement triggered the bear into a deadly forward lope.

Hope launched into a sprint. She passed her friend, scooped up a backpack without breaking stride and heaved it about ten feet into the bear's face.

Veering off, she yelled, "Move, Karen!"

Behind her, Hope heard the enraged bear ripping the pack to shreds. The diversion wouldn't occupy him for long.

She ran toward the woods as she'd never run before. Her heart exploded in sync with her pounding boots. A sudden terrible thought made her turn.

Karen was running awkwardly across the clearing in the opposite direction. A slow easy target, and closer than Hope to the bear. Just then the animal looked up from the destroyed pack and spotted Karen.

"C'mere, you ugly bastard!" Hope shouted through cupped hands.

Uh-oh. That got his attention.

Fear pumped her legs. She heard the sounds of maddened pursuit through the roaring in her ears. Crashing undergrowth. Snarling pants. So near she expected to feel the hot breath on her neck any second.

She hit the woods and kept running, looking for branches she could reach. *There!* Launching herself high, she grasped the lowest limb of a slender pine and scrabbled, scraped and sobbed her way up the tree. A mighty roar preceded a tremendous jolt of the tree trunk. She screamed and nearly fell, then wrapped her arms around the rough bark. Why hadn't she picked a bigger pine? She prayed for a miracle, promised to become a better person, peeked down and moaned in terror.

The bear was trying to climb! A lower branch cracked. The massive body tumbled down. *Thank you, little tree,* Hope thought, and hugged the trunk tighter. None too soon. Thwarted from climbing, the animal tried to shake her loose from her perch. Pine needles and dead wood showered over her shoulders. She closed her eyes in grim hysteria.

This was crazy. This was preposterous. People died of cancer, auto accidents, assault with a deadly weapon. Nice civilized things. To be eaten by a bear was...barbaric. She would've laughed, except her teeth were clicking like castanets while her lungs worked like bellows.

Thunk!

The bear grunted. The tree stopped shaking. Hope held her breath and waited.

Thunk!

A barking roar sounded below. She looked down as the bear lowered to all four paws.

Thunk!

This time she saw the rock hit. Shaking his snout as if stung by a bee, he lumbered away from the tree trunk. Hope watched his swaying backside disappear into the thickening forest the opposite direction of camp. It was a trick. The minute she let go of the tree he'd come charging back. She pressed her cheek against the bark and hugged even harder than before.

"He's gone now, Hope. Can you make it to the ground by yourself?"

The voice she'd waited for unconsciously absolved her of the need to be strong. She looked down and had one thought, one goal, one purpose in life.

To reach Jared.

In her haste to get to him she lost her balance five feet from the ground. She shrieked and grabbed air, fell against his solid warmth, was turned and pulled into his arms.

Thank you, God. Hope clung more gratefully to Jared than she ever had to the tree trunk. He was safety, he was saneness, he was everything she wanted and needed. He was man enough to absorb her weakness and not use it to make himself feel stronger. The heart beneath her cheek beat faster than his calm voice had let on. She breathed in his wonderful smell and started to tremble in delayed reaction.

His hands rubbed her back in small circles. "Are you all right, honey?"

Honey. Contentment soothed her frayed nerves. She could've stayed in his arms quite happily until moss grew on them both.

"I'm all right...now. But Karen—"

"Shh. She's back at the camp. Bill and Hank are

with her by now. Throwing the pack was quick think-ing. That was a brave thing you did, Hope. Foolish, but brave. Karen would never've made it to a tree in time.''

His admiring tone warmed her almost as much as his arms. ''You saw what happened?''

''Yeah, I saw.''

''But…you went to get water. What made you come back?''

''The doves.''

The doves. ''What about them?''

''When they flew past, I knew something had stirred them up. I headed for camp and broke from the trees just as the bear charged Karen.'' His arms tightened fiercely. ''I couldn't get to you in time. I could only watch… God, I thought…''

He'd thought he hadn't protected her, as he hadn't protected Beth. She snuggled closer and heard his heartbeat speed up, then felt his lower body stir. The aftermath of danger probably, but her own body re-sponded.

''You *did* reach me in time,'' she reminded him. ''When I was in the tree, I knew you would come. It's what kept me holding on.'' Hope pulled back and looked into his beautiful eyes.

They were dark with guilt and something stronger, something mesmerizing, something that was surely more than the concern of a teacher for his student. She reached up and lightly stroked his bristled jaw, exulting in the corresponding surge of pressure against her stomach.

"Thank you for protecting me, Jared."

The jaw beneath her palm clenched once. He muttered, "Hell."

Then his head swooped down.

CHAPTER TWELVE

HE WAS ONLY HUMAN, and he'd almost lost her. When she looked at him as if he was her hero, Jared gave up his internal battle and accepted the inevitable.

Her mouth was water in the desert, bread in the midst of famine. He devoured her in a ravenous orgy of lips and teeth and tongue. No finesse, much less tenderness. The pounding pressure in his loins wasn't interested in either. There was no future, only the here and now. And now he needed to cross that ancient line that would proclaim her his to protect above all others.

Her spine was long and lithe, her waist narrow, her rounded bottom a perfect fit for his cupped palms. He squeezed the firm flesh and lifted her up and in, showing her exactly what she did to him, exactly what could relieve the terrible wonderful tension always strumming between them. The dig of her fingernails through his shirt inflamed him. The incoherent sounds in her throat drove him wild.

She'd kissed him once before, the aggressor out to prove she was his equal. Now he backed her against the nearest tree, his mouth locked on hers, and pressed home his own blunt point.

I want you. You can't escape me. This was meant to happen and time is up.

Ah, jeez, he was losing control.

Releasing her mouth, he buried his face in her neck and drew in sharp ragged breaths. Her quick pants reminded him of a rabbit in a snare, and suddenly he was aware of how fragile and small her body was in comparison to his. Not her spirit, though. Ben would've recognized her warrior's heart and shown her the highest respect.

Jared could take her standing up against the tree—he was that aroused, that close to the edge. But he didn't want a quick coupling. He wanted... His mind erased the dangerous thought.

Her skin was soft, smooth and fragrant beneath his nose. He rumbled his approval and nuzzled the sensitive spot beneath her ear. When she shivered and cocked her head, the better to give him access, he smiled and nipped the plump flesh of her earlobe. Her gasp increased the pressure against his zipper to near pain.

Nudging her legs apart, he stepped in closer, reveling in the yield of her breasts and belly, the cradle of her hipbones. She sighed, her obvious pleasure feeding his own, satisfying something within him beyond mere lust. He brushed his mouth tenderly across her jawline and plucked succulent kisses from her lips, each one longer and deeper than the last, until he was drinking her tiny moans and making another salient point.

I want you. I care about you. When this happens it will be good for you, for me—for us.

"Jared? Hope? Where are you?"

The shout penetrated Jared's ardor. He identified Hank's voice.

Jared tore his mouth from Hope's and stared down. Her passion-drugged eyes were nearly black, her thoroughly kissed lips coral pink. A cloud of auburn curls cushioned her head against the bark and would no doubt look glorious against the forest floor. For one reckless instant he considered dragging her deeper into the woods.

"Hope? Oh, God, please answer." Karen's voice broke on the last word.

Hope's dazed expression vanished. She shoved hard against Jared's chest. "They're coming!" she whispered, her eyes frantic.

"Lucky them," he muttered, pulling away from her body.

Hope cupped her mouth. "We're here, Karen. I'm all right."

Speak for yourself, Jared thought. He quivered like an uprooted yucca, its life force ripped from the nurturing soil. He'd made a huge mistake, one he would pay for when she returned to New York, but there was no turning back now. He would make love to her before the end of the trip because if he didn't, he would die. It was that simple and that complicated. And he would just have to accept the consequences.

Seconds later he and Hope were swept up in the hugs, handshakes and babbling relief of the other team members. When Jared learned about Karen's period, he soothed her blushing embarrassment. Hank handled the intimate topic with his usual sensitivity, and even Bill apologized for complaining earlier about Karen's slow pace. He gruffly offered her two aspirin, and Hope sandwiched his bearded cheeks between her palms and planted a loud kiss right on the smacker.

His blush put Karen's to shame.

Once back at the clearing, Hope refused to let anyone continue to fuss over her actions. They were packing up after lunch when Bill shot her an admiring glance.

"I'll tell you one thing, Hope. At first I wasn't too happy to be on your team. But you sure keep life on the trail from getting dull."

She laughed along with the others. "That's it for me, I've provided my quota of excitement. It's somebody else's turn to stir things up." Meeting Jared's gaze, her expression grew satisfyingly flustered.

She obviously knew that what he had in mind would stir her up real good.

LATE THAT EVENING at the campsite, Hope acknowledged to herself that Jared was more dangerous than cranky rattlesnakes and pissed-off bears combined.

The smoldering looks he'd sent her throughout the afternoon had reminded her of his kiss—if you could call what he'd done to her something as bland as a kiss.

She touched her cheeks now. Yep, as hot as a schoolgirl's. She wasn't an innocent virgin, but damnation, he made her feel like one! Fortunately Bill was occupied draping his washed laundry over the lower branches of a pine tree. Hank and Karen were busy cooking dinner. And Jared, the source of her ridiculous blushes and unease, was taking his turn bathing at the creek.

The image that brought to mind made her blush spread downward. He'd pressed his fully clothed body against hers and made her forget her own name. Naked, the man could probably perform the first lobotomy on record without surgery.

In her admittedly limited sexual experience, she'd never almost climaxed from merely kissing. But Jared's kisses made other men's seem uninspired and amateurish. He made her want all the kinds of gratification he'd boasted of knowing when he'd bandaged her foot. And he'd as much as promised her with his mouth and body that she would receive what they both wanted at the earliest opportunity.

Hoo-boy, she needed that cold bath.

They'd set up the tents about a five-minute walk from water. Wet, wonderful, never-to-be-taken-for-granted-again H_2O. Hank, Bill and Karen had already filled their jugs and bathed the ecologically correct distance from the creek.

Hope glanced at Bill's laundry and considered, then discarded, the idea of snatching his underwear when he wasn't looking. Banana-breath was actually a pretty nice guy beneath the chest-pounding bluster.

Raising her arms to the sky in a joint-popping stretch, she inhaled the sharp aroma of pine and...something wonderful. Her stomach rumbled. She slumped into a boneless mass and turned toward the camp kitchen.

Hank sat by the stove like a great big adoring hound. The object of his devotion hovered over a pot, adding bits of this and that to the contents, looking miraculously revived and happy after her traumatic encounter with the bear.

Maybe it was her own recent awakening that opened her eyes to Karen and Hank's sexual attraction now. The relationship had obviously progressed faster than Hope had realized. Damn, why did fate have such a rotten sense of timing? Those two were headed for heartache.

With deceptive casualness Hope wandered to the stove and sniffed the air. "Yum. What are you making?"

Hank raised his head. "Hungarian-goulash soup—with dumplings."

Hope searched without success for opened cans. "Where's the Campbell's?"

Karen paused from rummaging through a sack,

cast Hope an affronted glance, then continued digging.

"She's making it from freeze-dried vegetables, Bisquick, bullion cubes and I won't know what else until I hand her the ingredient. There's no recipe," Hank added, looking proud enough to pass out cigars. "Amazing, huh?"

Hope saw Karen's quickly hidden smile and blessed him for his praise. "I'm impressed, but not surprised. The quiche at lunch was delicious, Karen. Thanks for volunteering to make dinner, too."

Her smile broke free. She made a flustered shooing motion. "Oh, y'all are so easy to please it's a pleasure to cook for you."

Hope had a pretty good idea who *wasn't* easy to please.

Pouring a ladle of soup into a cup, Karen blew the hot liquid, sipped hesitantly and gestured to a bag of spices nearby. "Pass me the salt, would you, Hank?"

As the tall man obliged, Hope quelled an irritating pang of guilt. Her mama would never've sat back and watched a man do "women's work." After leaving the ranch, Hope had taken great satisfaction in doing a "man's job" well and leaving traditional fetch-and-carry roles behind.

But Hank didn't expect to be waited on—and that made all the difference.

"Need any help?" she blurted.

"*Two* offers to help cook a simple meal? I could get used to this spoiling." Karen added salt to the pot, stirred, dipped the ladle again. "Thanks, but I think everything's under control."

Not everything, Hope thought, noting Hank's hungry gaze and seeing details she'd missed earlier.

The past four days of demanding physical activity had given Karen hollows beneath cheeks glowing pink and dewy from steam. Her plain black T-shirt and jeans called attention to generous curves rather than glitter or appliqués. Honey blond hair, freshly washed and wavy, reflected slanting sunlight in a lovely golden nimbus around her head.

She took a sip from her cup, looked up and caught Hope staring. "What?"

"It's bad enough that you cook like an angel, but do you have to *look* like one, too?"

"An angel?" Wedgwood blue eyes lit with pleasure, followed quickly by skepticism. "I wish. Now the Pillsbury dough girl...*that* I could believe."

Karen set down her cup and reached for the ladle. Hank's hand shot out and grabbed her wrist. "Why do you cut yourself down so much? Does *he* fill your head with that crap?"

Karen looked as shocked as Hope felt from her front-row seat.

When Karen didn't answer, Hank shook her fisted hand and leaned down nose to nose, his hazel eyes glittering. "Well, does he?"

"He...teases me a little."

"Teases? Do you feel like laughing when he calls you names?"

Her mouth thinned. "I *am* too fat."

Hank's succinct curse word echoed the one in Hope's head. "He's an idiot, Karen. He doesn't deserve you and it's making me crazy. If I had anyone half as smart and sweet and pretty as you, I'd..." His Adam's apple bobbed. He stared into her eyes a long yearning moment.

Karen's fingers unfurled slowly as if to touch his rigid jaw.

With an unintelligible sound of frustration, he released her wrist, surged to his feet and strode off into the trees.

The stove burner hissed loudly in the silence.

The whole incident had happened too quickly for Hope to have made a graceful exit, but she felt like a voyeur, anyway. Then she met Karen's stricken eyes.

Her embarrassment forgotten, Hope rushed forward, sank to her knees and gathered the trembling woman into a hug. For aching seconds she was simply there, offering silent unconditional support. Life was just too sucky for words sometimes.

At last Karen drew a shuddering breath and pulled away. "Oh, Hope, what should I do?"

Hope didn't pretend to misunderstand. She scanned the campsite and noted with relief that Bill had left. Willing all three men to keep themselves scarce a few minutes longer, she lowered the stove-burner flame and then sat back on her boot heels.

"I'm going to ask you a personal question, and I

hope you trust me enough to be honest. You understand that I'll hold anything you say in the strictest confidence?''

Folding her legs to one side, Karen averted her gaze and nodded.

"Has Jim ever hit you in anger?"

The golden lashes fluttered. "No."

Hoo-boy. "You're sure about that?"

Karen met Hope's probing gaze with resigned stoicism. "Yes, I'm sure he's never hit me."

And suddenly Hope knew that hitting might have been kinder. Hot acidic anger roiled up from deep inside and harshened her voice. "But he yells at you, doesn't he, Karen? He calls you a clumsy moron and the Pillsbury dough girl and whatever else punches your button and makes you feel crummy at the time. He criticizes everything you do and complains about every penny you spend and demands complete obedience from the family because that's the one area of his life he *can* control."

Hope's anger faded and she swiped at two fat tears spilling free from anguished blue eyes. "Oh, Karen, I don't want to hurt or embarrass you, but you see, I know what it's like. I know how it feels to never be as pretty, as accomplished, as *anything* that Jim might admire in other women, because I was never what my father admired in other daughters."

Karen blinked twice, her wet lashes dark and spiked. "Wh-what?"

"You heard me. My mother never crossed him—

she had enough grief from him as it was—and I lived for eighteen years trying to meet impossible standards. It took years of therapy for me to believe that I could've been perfect and I *still* wouldn't have met his standards.''

''I don't understand.''

Victims of verbal abuse usually didn't—until they broke free from the constant battering of their self-esteem.

Sighing, Hope reached out and tugged down the fingers rising to Karen's mouth. ''Dad needed me and Mama to be imperfect so that he could feel superior. The same reason that Jim finds fault with you and the boys, I'll bet. You're not the only one he makes miserable. Take it from me, Tommy and Lee are suffering, too. If you want to save them years of therapy as adults, insist on joint marriage counseling when you get home. Only a trained professional can help you and Jim change existing patterns of behavior.''

''Counseling?'' Karen blanched, then shook her head. ''He'll be furious. He won't do it.''

''If he won't, then that's his choice. But you've got a choice, too. You don't have to keep the status quo. You can get out of a destructive relationship. I'm not saying that's what you should do,'' Hope added hastily, alarmed at her friend's increasing pallor. She grasped Karen's hands and squeezed. ''I'm saying don't let fear of the unknown decide for you.''

''But where would I...what would I... Oh, God.''

"There's that fear again, thinking for you. Look, any number of employers would snap you up in a minute. I'll help you explore your career opportunities if it comes to that. The point is to make a decision and change the situation. Remember, you are the power in your world. You do have choices. Pick one and quit being a victim. That's what I did."

"You're stronger than I am, Hope."

"Excuse me, but I had a worse case of weenie-itis than you ever thought about. If it weren't for my grandmother, I'd probably be a dutiful rancher's wife right now and hating every minute of it."

Hope rubbed her thumbs over ragged cuticles, her eyes growing unfocused with memory. "Grandma died my junior year in high school and willed me her secret blue-chip-stock portfolio. Seems I wasn't the only mathematical whiz in the family, and she'd always regretted apologizing for her 'unwomanly' talent, instead of cultivating it. She'd left a letter telling me to use the money for college expenses—preferably a business college."

Her focus clearing, Hope held Karen's turbulent gaze. "My dad—Mom, too, probably—resented the hell out of me for not giving them that money. Dad called me..." The horrible names came flooding back and she shuddered. "Well, you can probably imagine after living with Jim. I almost cratered several times, but somehow I made it through graduation. I got out, with the help of my grandmother. If you want out, I'll be there for you. You're stronger than you think, Karen. And you're not alone.''

A tiny spark flared amid the swirling blue emotions. Hope watched the light of determination flicker, grow steady, gain strength and intensity with each passing second.

A sense of immense well-being expanded in her chest. ''Go, girlfriend,'' she said quietly.

Karen's mouth curved up in a mirror image of Hope's.

The popping sputter of the stove burner drew their startled attention. Before either woman could react, a strong masculine hand reached into view and fiddled with the fuel valve.

Jared straightened his torso, naked to the waist, and looked directly at Hope. ''Are you ladies okay?''

How could she be okay with her heart beating like hummingbird wings? How could she be okay with his hair seal-slick wet, his jaw just-shaved shiny, his torso mountain-man brawny and bared to her stunned gaze?

While Karen murmured something and fussed busily over her soup, Hope looked her fill and was not okay.

His swelled biceps and sculpted shoulders had the well-rubbed sheen of golden oak. Her fingers itched to polish his contours, to pet his silky brown chest hair, to stroke the thin arrow of pelt bisecting his hard ridged stomach. A drip from his hair rolled to his chest and trickled slowly through the silky forest, broke free to race down lean ribs and into low-slung jeans that confined an obvious and impressive erection.

Her gaze jerked up.

His eyes were a ferocious midnight blue, magnificent without his glasses.

Hoo-boy-hoo-boy-hoo-boy.

"Like you said," he murmured in a low dangerous voice, "we've all got choices. I made an important one today."

The next time the choice is between being your lover or your enemy, you can bet the family ranch which one I'll choose.

His warning replayed in her mind and she couldn't speak. This man wouldn't settle for her body and second billing to Manning Enterprises. This man wouldn't settle for anything less than her very soul. Hope was terrified that if he made love to her, she'd give up everything she'd worked for, everything she was, without a whimper.

Emotion yanked one hand, logic the other, in a brutal tug-of-war. She would have to release one grip soon or she'd tear apart under the pressure.

Karen made a sound of distress. "You heard our conversation, Jared?"

His gaze released Hope's and gentled. "What I heard stops with me."

"But how... I mean, you weren't anywhere close that we could see."

"That you could see," he agreed.

Rising quickly, Hope moved away from the stove, slapped the grass from her pants and threw up her defensive shield. "When do we get to learn the radar-ear and disappearing tricks? It would be so much more useful in my line of work than walking like a fox, don't you think?"

"Maybe. But it took me years of practice and meditation in the backcountry to learn. You'll be listening to taxi horns and disappearing into pedestrian crowds in eight days."

The heart that had beat so quickly moments ago lurched to a sickening stop. She kick-started the sluggish muscle by sheer force of will and feigned nonchalance. "Oh, well. Maybe you'll come to New York one day and continue my lessons there."

"Not a chance," he said flatly, stopping her heart for the second time.

When she could breathe again, she managed a wan smile. "It's your choice. But you don't know what you're missing."

"I wish like hell I didn't."

They exchanged a raw pained look that acknowledged glorious horizons and bleak dead ends.

She tore her gaze away first. "Don't wait dinner on me, Karen, and don't send out a search party, either. I decided to take my bath last so I wouldn't feel rushed."

"I'll save you a bowl of goulash. Take your time," Karen said, her eyes warm with sympathy and understanding.

Hope swallowed hard and nodded.

The shoe felt really lousy on the other foot.

THE NEXT MORNING no subconscious excitement tickled Hope awake. Only Karen's increasingly vigorous prods managed to rouse her from her deep sleep.

Jared had honored her strong hint the night before and hadn't sought her out at the creek. But she'd stared at the tent ceiling into the wee hours feeling restless and confused and resentful. Debbie was in for one nasty surprise when Hope returned to New York. The expedition that was supposed to have relieved stress was pushing her over the edge into a nervous breakdown.

By the time she dressed and dragged herself to the stove for coffee, the others were waiting for her in order to recite the daily meditation. Hope knew it by heart now, and took it to heart, as well. As the words echoed in the pristine mountain air, she gained some measure of peace.

At precisely 0700 hours the other trail teams began radioing in their locations and campsite destinations. One by one, Jared marked them down on a master map he'd spread out on the ground. Matt was the last trail guide to check in, and the one to whom Jared gave his own team's coordinates for safety's sake.

"So Jared, have you been seeing as much bear scat as we have? I keep expecting— Hey, gimme that!"

"Yo, Karen, Hope, are you guys there? It's me,

Sherry,'' a feminine voice said. ''And Dana's right here, too.''

Hope met Karen's startled gaze across the stove, and they both broke into huge grins. Rushing over to Jared, Hope grabbed the CB radio from his hand and waved Karen close.

''Hiya, guys—''

''Push down the transmitting button,'' Jared interrupted, sending his two male teammates a long-suffering look.

Hope did as he said, too excited to do more than stick out her tongue first. ''Hiya, guys, it's Hope.'' She held the radio to Karen's mouth.

''Hi, Sherry, hi, Dana. It's Karen. How're y'all doing?''

''Dana's boots got chewed up by a porcupine—''

''After Sherry left them outside the tent,'' Dana piped up.

''*After* Dana got a little too close to the bear poop Matt showed us. How was I supposed to know salty leather attracted animals? Anyway, other than that we haven't run into any problems. How about you two?''

Hope met Karen's wry gaze and knew an angry bear wasn't the only problem she was thinking about.

''Nothing we can't handle,'' Hope said, as much to reassure herself as her friend.

Recovering, Karen jumped in with an account of her narrow escape from the bear. Hope squirmed while she was painted as a heroine, then answered a half dozen questions. After several failed attempts to change the subject, she noted Jared pointing to his wristwatch.

"Hey, listen up," Hope ordered. "Looks like Scout wants us to wind things down, so say goodbye, ladies."

"Goodbye, ladies," they chorused.

"And Karen?" Dana added in a mischievous tone. "I know how troublesome those little toes of yours are, especially when they get hot. Soak them in a cold stream if they swell up, okay?"

"That'll shrink 'em down to size fast," Sherry seconded.

I've created a couple of monsters, Hope thought proudly.

Muttering, Jared strode forward and confiscated the hand-held receiver. "Dana, Sherry, put Matt on the mike, please. Over."

Static hissed, followed by "Sorry about that, boss." Feminine snickers escalated in the background. "I don't know what's gotten into these two. Over."

Gazing thoughtfully from Karen's blush to Hope's carefully blank expression, Jared sighed. "I have a feeling you're better off not asking them, Matt. Look, I'll talk to you same time tomorrow…*alone.* Do you copy? Over."

"That's a big ten-four, boss."

"Good. Over and out."

Suppressing a smile, Hope watched Jared fold the

map, pack up the radio and gesture for everyone to return to the morning routine. Her mood had lifted, thanks to Sherry and Dana's banter, and Hope thought she might make it through another day without falling apart at the seams.

Breaking camp was not nearly the chore it had been those first few days on the trail. The team worked efficiently and smoothly dismantling tents, washing pots, purifying drinking water, loading backpacks. Prior to buckling up they scattered duff and dead grass over scuff marks, replaced a few rocks originally moved from the kitchen site, and in general camouflaged the evidence of their presence. The surrounding forest seemed to approve.

This was the time to chug water, stretch cold muscles and mentally prepare for the long hours of hiking ahead. Hope went through the minimal motions, propped her rear against a towering pine and waited for the signal to gear up. The terrain behind her rose steeply. They would all be tired tonight.

Bill stood about twenty feet away with map and compass in hand, conferring with Jared on the day's route. To their left Karen and Hank talked quietly.

A mosquito on Hope's calf drew blood. She twisted and bent down to slap the little sucker.

Ping!

The bark above her head splintered and she jerked back.

Ping!

The bark spit fragments again and she gasped in pain.

Jared rammed into her midriff in a flying tackle, whooshing the air from her lungs. Her back slammed hard against the ground. His body slammed hard on top of hers. She lay there with her mouth working like a goldfish out of the bowl and knew she would suffocate any minute.

If she didn't bleed to death first.

CHAPTER THIRTEEN

JARED PULLED HOPE behind the big pine, curled protectively over her body and searched the down-slope treeline. This was no accident. Two shots with a silencer made it deliberate. Shooting at Hope made it personal and the bastard's last mistake.

Turning, Jared glanced up the slope at the craggy boulder thirty yards away. Safety. A place to plan his next move and check Hope's wound. The blood from it was dark and spreading slowly. The bullet hadn't nicked an artery, but it had to hurt like hell.

"Someone shot me." Hope's voice sounded muffled—and little-girl bewildered.

"I know. Hang in there, honey," he soothed absently, looking for a glint of sun on metal, a shadow that moved.

"Do you sweet-talk everyone you tackle?"

He almost smiled. "Only the tight ends."

Ignoring the weak punch against his chest, he sought out Hank's stunned gaze. Jared pointed to the massive rock up the slope and Hank nodded. He would herd the others from behind the trees to the boulder.

Now for the fun part. "All right, Hope. On the

count of three, I want you to put your arms around my neck and hang on tight.''

''I don't need to be carried.''

''One—''

''Get off and let me—''

''Two—''

''Would you listen to—''

''Three!''

Jared scooped Hope up in his arms and sprinted from pine to pine, a fox on the run, fluid and close to the earth. The thick forest protected them but paid the price. Bullets chewed into tree trunks, cracked into low limbs, bit deep into mulchlike duff. She squeaked in his ear at every near miss and damn near choked him to death. The lady had one helluva grip for someone who was wounded.

Harrowing minutes later he rounded the boulder, sank onto his knees and lowered Hope to the ground. He peeled back her fingers from his neck and listened. Abrupt eerie silence. The guy wasn't out for mass slaughter—only Hope. Jared tensed.

Save your anger until it can be used against the enemy. Then release the animal within.

Ben's advice calmed the primitive call to battle roaring through Jared's veins. He smoothed back tangled curls a shade brighter than the blood soaking her sweatshirt sleeve. ''How're you doing?''

''Just dandy. I've always wanted to be a maniac's clay pigeon.'' Every ounce of color had drained from her cameo complexion.

Trust Hope to be flippant under gunfire. She would never admit to being afraid.

Propping her back against the rock, he unfolded his pocketknife and carefully cut off her fleece sleeve at the shoulder seam. The bloody gash furrowing across her upper arm was nasty, but superficial.

Thank God, he thought, looking up as Hank, Karen and Bill barreled around the rock and fell panting and shaken behind cover. Jared noted the emergency fanny pack and larger backpack Hank had grabbed. The man really came through under pressure. He would make a great NBA coach.

Karen gasped, her shocked gaze fixed on Hope's wound.

Not now, Jared begged Karen silently. He didn't have time for her to faint. She met his eyes, drew a deep breath and nodded. *Good girl,* his look told her, and she flushed.

Bill crowded closer. "Damn, Hope, you're bleeding like a stuck pig."

She smiled wanly. "I see that dodging bullets hasn't affected your delicate tact."

"Hell, he wasn't shooting at *us*. I think the nut is after *you*. Is there something you haven't been telling us?"

Hank glared at the older man.

"What?" Bill said. "A big shot like her probably has enemies."

Hope's pale face grew even paler. "I'm sure I do. I just didn't think they wanted to kill me."

Hank cast Jared a worried glance. "The guy's already had his kicks. He's probably run off scared by now."

"Would you hand me the canteen and first-aid kit?" Jared asked Karen, ready to ring both of the men's necks. False assurances were as bad as dire predictions.

She rummaged in both packs and handed him the items. "What can I do to help?"

Her face was almost as ashen as the patient's, but her eyes were steady. He untwisted the cap of the canteen and wet an unstained portion of sweatshirt sleeve. "Take this and clean the blood from around the gash, but don't touch the wound."

She accepted the cloth with a trembling hand.

"You don't have to do this," Hope told her fiercely.

"Yes, I do." Karen sounded equally fierce.

She proceeded to do what needed to be done while Jared pulled iodine, gauze and tape from the kit.

The rifle fired again in rapid succession, louder with each shot. The sniper's silencer had worn out and he obviously didn't care.

"He's shooting your backpack all to hell!" Bill said in outrage, peering above the pocked limestone.

"Get *down*," Jared ordered, then caught Karen's eye.

"Go," she said. "I'll take care of Hope."

He gauged her expression, decided she could handle it and laid the medical supplies by her knees. "Thanks, Karen. You're somethin' else."

Spinning away, he crawled to the other end of the boulder and peered around the corner.

Bullets smashed into his backpack with sickening results. Water spewed, pots clinked, down puffed, plastic cracked. A bullet finally exploded the liquid-fuel tank, sending shock waves outward and a mushroom of fire roiling high into the air.

"Holy shit," Bill breathed, peeking once again above the boulder.

"There's nothing holy about the guy out there," Hank said grimly.

Amen. With a sickened stomach, Jared watched the CB radio, large first-aid kit and food supply go up in flames.

Bill whirled around and slid his spine down the rock. His rump hit the ground and he sighed. "Maybe somebody will report the noise."

Nobody answered, including Jared. In more than forty expeditions to the Sierra del Carmen, he'd never seen a soul in this particular area. The other teams were too far away to hear. The sniper had done his research.

But then, so had he.

Jared turned around and went into command mode. "Hank, Bill, I want an inventory of the backpack supplies in three minutes. Give me the map and compass first."

A quick indrawn hiss caught Jared's attention.

Karen had just poured iodine on the open wound. Hope met his eyes and attempted a valiant smile. "Don't mind me, Scout. Karen will have me patched up here any minute."

He hoped so. They didn't have much time. The sniper would circle around and attack from behind—or pull something deadlier out of his bag of tricks. Jared wanted to be gone by then.

Spreading the map, he marked down Matt's trail-team destination from memory and plotted the quickest course to get there. About eighteen miles of hard hiking. Damn.

"Okay, what do we have in the packs?" Jared asked the men.

Bill spoke up. "One half-full canteen, one empty collapsible jug, five packs of oatmeal, six granola bars, six Heath bars, multiple dried flies—" he dangled a bag of dried raisins and wrinkled his nose "—five packets of hot cocoa and one pack of spearmint gum."

Not enough calories for hard hiking.

"Then there are the 'ten essentials' in my fanny pack," Hank added. "The main pack has the tent, assorted clothing, a sleeping bag, a mug and bowl…oh, and about thirty water-purifying tablets."

Finally some good news. "Do you have something warm in there Hope can use?" Jared asked.

Hank dug through his pack and tossed over a thermal-underwear top.

Jared caught it in one hand, then fisted the material. "Here's the situation, and I won't pretend it's good. Hope, Karen, listen up. The trail leaders won't radio in for another twenty-two hours. When they can't reach us, they'll wait another five hours and give us a chance to remedy minor problems we might've had with equipment. At that point they'll kick into emergency procedures and call in the cavalry."

He studied their solemn faces one by one. "We can't wait that long. Bill, Karen, Hank, I need you to go get help. I've marked the route to Matt's campsite, but you'll have to travel through the night to reach them before they break camp. If you can't, you can't. Use good sense. You'll be no help to us if you get injured. Just get to their campsite and head due east. You'll catch up eventually."

"But why don't you two come with us?" Karen blurted. "Isn't there safety in numbers?"

"This guy is after Hope." Jared's cold rage seeped into his tone. "I can protect her better if I don't have to worry about anyone else. If we split into two groups, he'll follow her. And to get to her, he'll have to get through me." He paused and met Hope's eyes. "That ain't gonna happen."

She was looking at him the way she had after he'd run off the bear. As if she could see into his soul and trusted what she saw with her life. And in that instant she became his woman. The sex, talk and complications could wait until later.

Rifle fire and thudding bullets widened her eyes.

"He's creaming the other packs," Bill reported. "What a sicko."

Jared narrowed his eyes. *He's messing with our heads*.

"Show us our route," Hank told Jared firmly, "then mark where you and Hope are going. We'll do our part and get to Matt's campsite by morning."

Three chins squared. Three gazes full of heart and determination turned to Jared.

He couldn't have received a better affirmation of his life's work than if the president himself had endorsed MindBend Adventures. Pride thickened his throat.

"Where *are* we going, Scout?" Hope asked quietly.

Somewhere off his regular expedition route. Somewhere few white men had seen. Somewhere he could keep Hope safe or stand and fight if necessary.

He jerked his thumb at the mountains behind him. "We're going up."

HOPE FOLLOWED one step behind Jared's broad back like a good little woman. Screw women's lib. There was a bullet out there with her name on it, and she was only too happy to have a big strong man's help. Since the big strong man was Jared, she even thought the trigger-happy maniac might have bitten off more than he could chew. She hoped he choked and suffered horrible agony.

Nobody said good little women couldn't be vindictive, too.

She'd given her situation plenty of thought in the past hour while climbing steadily upward. Thinking took her mind off her throbbing arm, her laboring lungs, her straining muscles.

Could UroTech's incontinence-control implant be at the root of her problem? Nothing else made sense. Offhand she knew of three other similar but inferior devices that were in various stages of development. The first one to receive FDA approval would lock in the largest market share. The dollars involved could establish small countries. And without her spearheading the approval process, her company's product would fall by the wayside.

It had to be UroTech. In essence, she was worth as much dead to her competitors as she was alive to her investors. Comforting thought.

As comforting as wondering if her teammates were okay. Jared had instructed them to wait behind the boulder thirty minutes before heading out. He'd figured that was as long as the sniper would listen to their decoy noise before coming in closer to investigate. Hope prayed that once the killer realized she wasn't with them, he would follow her without making her friends pay.

Slipping her hand in one pocket, she fingered the awful diamondback rattle Bill had insisted she take for good luck. She'd never forgive herself if anything happened to her teammates.

Jared stopped suddenly, grew still and tilted his head. Hope's heartbeat accelerated, as it had every time he'd listened for the sniper behind them. When Jared relaxed and pulled out his canteen, she released a long breath. She knew firsthand the accuracy of his hearing and trusted that they were safe—for the moment.

He untwisted the cap and extended his canteen. "Here, I want you to drink at least a cup. More hikers get dehydrated in the mountains than the desert."

Remembering the unrelenting heat down below, Hope arched a brow. "With all due respect, Scout, that's gotta be a crock of bear scat." Good. She'd almost made him smile.

"Not that I don't love it when you talk dirty, but it happens to be the truth. People don't feel as hot in the mountains, so they forget to drink enough."

She lifted the canteen. Pain streaked down her arm, forcing her to transfer the container to her other hand.

"Do you want another aspirin?"

She'd have to remember that he noticed everything. He looked as if her pain hurt him more than it did her. "No thanks, I'll save 'em for later." He only had four more tablets.

Chugging dutifully from the canteen, she handed back his water, then watched the ripple of his strong throat as he followed his own advice. "You... haven't even asked why someone would want to kill me."

His gaze moved over her face, lit briefly on her bandaged arm, met her eyes with renewed grimness. "Doesn't matter why, just that someone's trying."

She didn't know whether to be flattered or insulted.

"The trail gets steeper from here on out," he continued. "I know that arm is hurting like hell. I'll do what I can to help you, but we've got to keep going. The best way to conserve your energy is to use the 'rest step.'" He shoved the canteen into his pocket and demonstrated on the wooded slope ahead.

Hope watched him lock one knee and bring the opposite foot forward, then reverse the process in a stiff forward motion.

"See how my locked leg transfers all the weight to my skeletal system? The other leg gets a few seconds to rest. This is *serious*," he said sternly, squelching her beginning smirk. "You'll last hours longer if you climb this way. Now you try it."

She did, then rolled her eyes. "I can't move fast walking like Frankenstein's monster."

"Yeah? Well, pretend that the villagers are right on your butt and the sniper is carrying the lead torch."

The image gave her a major attack of weenie-itis. She suppressed a shudder. "I'd rather just focus on *your* butt, if you don't mind. I've always thought you had a tush worth following."

He scowled and opened his mouth, then seemed

to take a closer look at her face. She tried for a cocky grin and failed miserably.

"Aw, hell," he muttered, stepping down the incline.

A steely arm circled her waist and pulled; blunt fingers thrust into her hair and tugged her head back. She stared up into narrowed blue eyes and felt her stomach drop away.

"I'd die before I let him hurt you," Jared said gruffly, then captured her mouth in a deep kiss.

He went to her head faster than three martinis. How could Beth ever have preferred booze over him? Hope's eyes drifted shut as his tongue did delicious things that made her want him around her, inside her, mixed with her until she couldn't tell where his skin ended and hers began. He shifted and spread his legs apart to bracket hers, his thighs rock-hard where they met her hips. Pressing her closer, he massaged her skull and made hungry masculine sounds deep in his throat.

And she kissed him back.

With all the hunger of too many late nights at her office, too many Sundays reading the paper alone. She kissed away a hundred faceless dates and claimed the one man whose features were burned into her memory, whose approval filled her with joy. She kissed Jared, only Jared, forever and always Jared.

He lifted his mouth with a groan.

"Jared," she murmured, straining toward his lips for more.

He clasped her hips and set her back firmly, his expression almost pained. "I have the damnedest timing. We *will* finish this. You know that, don't you?"

She was breathing as fast as he was; she'd nearly swallowed the man's face whole. Yet he acted half-afraid that she wouldn't want to "finish this." Hope folded her hands demurely, a good little woman.

"Yes, Jared."

"Good." He nodded for emphasis. "Because I mean it." His eyes glittered thrillingly. "Did I hurt your arm?"

Her nerves and blood seemed to have pooled in another location. "No, Jared."

He looked unconvinced but let it stand. "All right, then, use the rest step and call out if you need help."

"Yes, Jared."

With a last possessive glance, he turned and headed up the mountain.

She stuck to his prime grade-A tush like shrink-wrap to a rump roast.

He followed no trail, used no compass or map—he'd given both items to Hank. But Jared seemed to know exactly where he was going, and Hope was determined not to slow them down.

The heavily wooded slope was slippery with pine needles and studded with partially buried rocks. As the climb grew steeper, the footing rockier, her appreciation for the rest step grew.

She'd been hearing the rush of water for the last half mile or so when Jared veered sharply to the left and headed straight for the sound.

Ten minutes later she saw that it wasn't a stream so much as a series of waterfalls channeled inside a deep ravine. Virgin forest filtered the sunlight into distinct beams filled with mist. The smell of pine and compost and water hung heavily in the air. She walked to the edge of the ravine and absorbed the awesome beauty of the scene. Jared moved up beside her and she smiled, her world complete.

She was Pocahontas, she was a daughter of the earth, she was a reformed and repentant litterbug.

"We're going to cross the ravine here," Jared yelled above the thunderous roar.

Her smile dissolved. She *wasn't* a fool.

He walked twenty feet farther along the edge, then motioned her to join him.

She shook her head.

He motioned again, his murderous look saying that if the sniper didn't kill her, he would.

So much for vows of dying for her. Approaching him with caution, she saw what he had in mind and wondered if a bullet might not be preferable. The fallen tree spanning the thirty-foot chasm looked slick and too narrow to support Jared.

He hopped up onto the snarled roots and was halfway across the ravine before she could react. The frothy water eighty feet below pounded no more loudly than her heart. On the opposite bank he turned, flashed her a jaunty thumbs-up and hurried nimbly back to her side.

"I can't do that," she shouted in his ear.

In answer he steered her to the makeshift bridge and vaulted onto the roots. Reaching for both her hands, he helped her up, then walked backward, his warm grip pulling her forward.

Time and water had eroded the tree's bark. The smooth surface was as slick as it looked. *Hoo-boy.*

"Don't look down," Jared yelled. "Place your boots carefully and feel the wood."

His glasses had misted. She couldn't see his eyes. Panic locked her knees.

He wouldn't allow it and tugged her steadily, so that she either moved with him or stumbled. She stared at his blurred glasses and imagined the eyes she knew were as unfaltering and confident as hers were scared. Her boots inched forward. She clung to his hands grimly.

"I won't let you fall. You're doing great. We're almost halfway there."

Hope looked down. And her feet slipped off the log.

Somehow Jared caught her wrists and held on. A scream that must've been hers pierced the water's roar. Frantically pedalling air, she swayed beneath his grip like a trapeze artist, her stomach level with the fallen tree.

"Don't move!" he shouted.

Against every instinct, she obeyed.

He pulled her up as if she were a barbell, an amazing act of strength and coordination. Her boots met wood and fumbled for purchase. She found it and straightened, only realizing as his muscles relaxed how bulging and strained they'd been before. True to his word, he hadn't let her fall. He'd kept her safe—again.

Shaky but determined, she followed him the rest of the way. She would've followed him into fire if he'd asked her, as long as he held her hands. When they reached the bank, she wanted nothing more than to collapse against his chest. Now that the adrenaline rush had worn off, her wound throbbed like an abscessed tooth.

He wiped the beads of water from his lenses, glanced at her arm and bit off a curse.

She stared at the fresh blood soaking her bandage. "I'm okay. It looks worse than it feels," she yelled. Which was true, as long as his eyes held that gleam of admiration.

He nodded and left her to scout the forest floor for branches. He'd discarded several before dragging back a stout specimen. Jamming the branch under the trunk of the fallen tree, he prepared to lever it up.

"How can I help?" she shouted, ignoring her aching arm.

"Move out of the way."

She stood firm. "How can I help?"

The respect and approval in his gaze deepened, and her pain dissipated like the mist once more blurring his glasses.

He placed her hands on the branch. "Push down. When the trunk lifts, I'll shove it forward." He crouched and moved into position, his palms beneath the sodden wood. "Okay, now!"

Pushing down with her hands didn't cut it. She had to ride the branch like a seesaw before the trunk lifted even fractionally.

Jared heaved. The trunk crashed down a measly six inches or so forward.

"Again," he ordered.

The work was slow and grueling, especially for him. She sneaked admiring peeks throughout the ordeal. She'd never been particularly turned on by a man's muscles before. But my, oh my, she was learning to change.

At last the top of their tree bridge hovered on the edge of the ravine. She sank onto her knees beside Jared and pushed with him for all she was worth—which in her present condition wasn't much.

The treetop shuddered over the edge, the roots and base ripping from the opposite bank and hitting the water with an impressive splash. She exchanged a tired grin with Jared.

Her arm ached incessantly now, her bruised stomach hurt with every breath, her overused muscles burned from lactic acid. But she definitely felt safer with the ravine between them and the maniac.

Good thing they could go easier on the pace now.

Jared rose and pulled her up by her good arm. "Come on, let's go. This took too long."

She narrowed her eyes at his departing tush, not nearly as inspired to follow it now as she'd been an hour earlier.

Sighing, she forced her body into motion.

STAN GLARED with impotent rage at the frothy water eighty feet below. The job had gone sour. And he had no one to blame but himself.

He would've taken out the woman with one shot, but she'd reached down to scratch her leg. Fate, he'd thought at the time. A sign that he was meant to bend the rules and make the kill that much sweeter. And the game had been fun—at first.

Sort of like squeezing off shots in an arcade shooting gallery. Then watching an action movie where a backpack blows up, instead of a car. He'd pictured the group quivering like rabbits behind the rock and gotten a kick out of making them sweat. But the joke had been on him.

When he'd finally circled behind the boulder and peered around a tree, the redhead was gone, along with the big guy who'd carried her earlier. The faggot with the glasses who had to be the leader "Jared" from the radio. The first man to dare mess with Stan since he'd discovered the ultimate power.

If he hadn't been worried about future references, the three rabbits behind the rock would have been buzzard bait now. Instead of venting his anger, he'd slipped away unseen and picked up the woman's tracks.

He kicked the ground viciously. Fresh dirt sprayed forward and dropped out of sight. A few snapped-off roots remained buried near his boots. Directly opposite on the lip of the bank was the imprint of a tree. He'd scouted thirty minutes in each direction looking for another tree bridge without success.

Jared had destroyed the only crossing in miles, and there were only two hours of daylight left. Stan kicked another dirt fan into space. God*dammit*, he couldn't believe this!

Dropping his backpack, he sat on his heels and unzipped the largest compartment. The woman was hit. At the very least nicked. She'd probably collapsed just beyond sight on the other side of the ravine. If he could find a way across soon, there'd still be plenty of time to fulfil his contract and get away. The chopper wasn't due till ten tomorrow morning. And according to his map, the rabbits were a long way from the nearest team, the one that had checked in by radio this morning.

He pulled out a versatile woodsman's hatchet, tested the blade with his thumb and smiled at the welling bead of blood. It paid to be prepared. About a mile up the ravine there was a tall pine tree rooted along the edge. He'd chopped enough cords of wood in his life to know how to fell a tree the right direction. The inconvenience was minor, but the redhead would pay big time.

He flipped the handle like a pistol butt, caught it on the second spin and narrowed his eyes. *After,* that is, the asshole with the glasses learned exactly how good Stan was with an ax.

TIME BLURRED as the going got tougher and Hope grew wearier. Jared paused periodically to listen in that peculiar animallike way she'd come to trust. He stopped once at a tumbling stream to fill the canteen and share a stale granola bar with her.

So tired she could barely chew, Hope asked if he actually thought the maniac was hot on their tail. He said probably not, but he didn't want to take a chance with her life.

The man really knew how to kill a good whine.

She followed him up, always up, her lungs dragging in the thin air, her legs screaming for a rest despite her faithful use of the rest step.

At some point since they'd left the stream she'd decided that Jared wasn't human. No man could do what he'd done already without showing any sign of fatigue. She didn't know if she could "finish" anything with him, after all. Sex with an alien had never been one of her fantasies.

When he stopped again, she didn't care why. Lowering her knees to the ground, she slumped in sheer bliss. A vague part of her saw him notching sticks, unwinding a thin length of rope from his pocket, do-ing something with a supple tree that rustled the leaves...

He prodded her good arm until she opened her eyes groggily.

"Come on, let's go. This took too long."

A bullet would definitely be preferable. Ideally one between *his* eyes.

Somehow she dredged up the discipline to keep her mouth shut as he helped her stand. Drooping like three-week-old celery, she waited to follow where he would lead.

He pulled her into his arms.

One hand pressed her head into the hollow of his shoulder. "Poor Hope. It's not much farther. Stay strong a little while longer." He kissed the top of her head, his touch, his words, his tone so tender that she blinked against the sting of tears. "Will you do that for me, honey?"

That and more. That and anything. She nodded, loving the feel of his scratchy wool sweater beneath her cheek, loving the weight of his hand against her head, loving... Her eyes widened.

Loving *him*.

Her heart had known for some time. Admitting it with her brain opened a floodgate of stored emotion. Warmth poured into all her cold empty spaces and filled them up, overflowed, spread throughout her body with dizzying speed. Stupid or not, as doomed as the relationship was, she loved Jared Austin with her heart and soul. And she allowed herself this one moment of pure undiluted happiness.

He tightened his arms, then released her quickly. "I'm sorry, Hope, but we have to climb one last stretch."

Giddy with the need to tell him, unsure enough of his response to hesitate, she tilted up her face and smiled. "Come on then, let's go. This took way too long."

CHAPTER FOURTEEN

JARED PEELED OFF his sweater and tied it around his waist. He didn't remember the trail being this narrow, this vertical, this broken by crevices plunging down anywhere from five to thirty feet. In another two hours darkness would make hiking suicidal. He had to get Hope up to Eagle Watch before then.

Twisting, he extended a hand down and grasped her fingers. The nails were short, their red polish chipped. Her hand felt small and deceptively fragile. That same hand had thrown a backpack into a bear's face and comforted a confused friend. There was strength in that hand. The kind a man could count on through good times and bad. He helped her clamber to his level, then climbed higher to start the process again.

She hadn't complained about her wound, hadn't asked to rest or eat or drink. She hadn't faltered in the face of extreme danger or his relentless physical demands. He now knew she'd overcome an upbringing that would've crushed a weaker spirit, then gone on to champion others in need of encouragement.

His woman was a woman of remarkable courage and compassion. As tough and beautiful as the

Apache corn basket on his kitchen table. Like the basket, Hope might not be his for long. But while she was he intended to treasure her as she deserved.

Hauling her up by her good arm, he grimaced at her obvious pain. *This is no way to treasure a lady, Austin.*

"I'm all right, Jared," Hope murmured, her gaze understanding and gentle.

A smudge of dirt stamped one pale cheek. Half-moon shadows bruised the delicate skin beneath her eyes. She'd turned her baseball cap with the bill in back, suppressing—but not confining—the auburn curls he loved.

He remembered the bored sophisticate who'd slouched in the back row at orientation, and marveled at how much he'd misjudged her. This was the real Hope Manning. The one he would love regardless of what the future held. The woman he would love until he died. He couldn't stop staring.

Hope raised her hand and tucked in a curl self-consciously. "I must look pretty bad."

"You look beautiful."

Her eyes went soft and shy and sexy. "So do you, Scout."

Jared glanced down at his clinging undershirt, soaked from the strenuous climb. He hadn't shaved that morning and he'd needed a haircut for weeks. But he liked the way she was looking at him. He liked it a helluva lot. His desire to reach Eagle Watch increased to an urgent need.

Climbing another tier, he reached down to help her up. "Bet you sweet-talk all the guys you hike with."

"Only the tight ends," she said, her undaunted grin familiar and dear.

Those were the last words they spoke as the trail grew little better than a deer track. At one point the sound of rock hitting rock about a half mile back froze his blood. He motioned Hope to stay still and closed his eyes, opening himself up to the spirit-that-moves-through-all-things. The distinctive snort of a lone buck on the move slumped his shoulders with relief.

Jared honestly didn't think the sniper would take the time to find another ravine crossing, but he couldn't dismiss the possibility. Smiling at Hope, he started forward again, but from her dazed expression she was operating on empty.

Arizona cypress, Douglas fir and juniper clung to the steep slopes on either side of the track. At about seven thousand feet the air held a nip that would bite deeply tonight. Before he could think about shelter and food, there was one last precaution he wanted to take.

The next crevice they approached was perfect. About five feet wide, sheer walls straight down. A floor of crumbled rock. Eleven, maybe twelve feet deep.

He leaped across and stretched out his hands for Hope. She bit her lip, but didn't hesitate to grasp his hands, didn't cry out when he yanked her the final six inches. He dropped an apologetic kiss on her injured arm and she smiled tiredly, increasing his guilt.

He led her to a tree and propped her back against the trunk. "Rest here a few minutes."

She didn't ask questions, but simply closed her eyes and sighed. Two minutes later she'd nodded off to sleep.

He worked quickly, efficiently, thankful once again for the hours spent under Ben's tutelage. The secret to a successful trap was good camouflage, and Jared spent at least fifteen minutes covering the dead branches he'd gathered with pine needles, duff and small rocks. Animals using this track knew it like people knew their own homes. They would either jump or avoid the suspicious change in footing altogether.

But the animal Jared was concerned about wouldn't be suspicious.

When he could barely distinguish the false floor from the rest of the path, he walked to Hope and prodded her good arm.

She slapped his hand away and mumbled, then lifted her head as if it were unbearably heavy. Her eyes focused slowly. "Did we take too long?"

Tenderness welled in his chest. "No. And I *promise* we're almost there."

Her expression said, *Yeah, right.* But she rose and shuffled behind him without comment.

He'd lied. Not purposely, but it *had* been four years since Ben had led him up this trail. When he finally broke into a level meadow, they'd hiked nearly a mile from the trap.

He paid little attention to the beauty of the place. Twilight descended quickly in the mountains, and there was much to do before then.

"We're here," he told Hope, frowning as she swayed on her feet.

She lowered to her knees on the thick spring grass, toppled sideways and curled into a fetal position. "Good night," she murmured, her cap askew, her lids drifting shut. Within seconds she was out to the world.

Remorse pricked his conscience. He'd pushed her too hard, but she'd recover, he assured himself. She'd be as comfortable sleeping here as anywhere until he built a shelter. Untying the thermal underwear from around her waist, he draped it gently over her. With one last tender glance at her sleeping form, he set to work.

A lean-to would be fastest. He'd used the last of his cordage on the spring snare, but he could make do without. The forest guarding this mountain oasis was thick, the floor carpeted with fallen branches from periodic storms.

He found two with forked limbs, cut them to match in length and propped each against trees ten feet apart. Another trimmed branch fit inside the forked notches, forming a pole parallel to the ground. Long sticks propped at a slant along the pole supported the brush he layered like shingles from bottom to top.

Without sleeping bags their body heat would flow straight into the cold earth. A brush mattress would provide insulation and more cushion than the most expensive bag. The Douglas fir, with its dense needles, furnished exactly the material he needed.

Breaking off only the soft tips, he jammed a row of coarse broken ends into the ground with the boughs curving upward. The next row leaned against the first, and so on, always with the soft tips on top. By the end of his labors he'd constructed a mattress nine feet long and four feet wide fitting snugly beneath the lean-to. Not the Hilton, but adequately comfortable.

He headed for Hope and stared down. She hadn't moved a fraction that he could tell. If he'd harbored an ulterior motive for building a cozy shelter, it vanished in the face of her exhaustion. She'd been so brave, so stoic. She'd earned her rest. He would content himself with holding her close throughout the night. Amazingly, the thought *did* fill him with contentment.

He crouched down, scooped her into his arms and carried her to the shelter. She stirred a bit when he placed her on the mattress, but sank deep into healing sleep again.

Straightening, he scrubbed his face in his hands, then surveyed the mountaintop meadow. Accessed only by the narrow track they'd climbed, this had been the safest place he could think of to bring Hope. Once he rigged up an alarm across the entrance to their hideaway, he would have done the best he could to protect her.

With the realization came weariness and hunger. A quick bath would help the first symptom. Foraging through the woods should assuage the second. The sun had melted into the treetops, but his night vision was excellent. He'd let Hope sleep until he had a meal of some kind to offer.

Not even a maniac would risk his neck climbing the dangerous track under the dubious light of the moon.

STAN STARED at the slanted "bridge" in disbelief. The goddamn treetop had fallen two feet short of the opposite bank and lodged on an outcropping of rock fifteen feet below. He hated chopping trees, he hated heights, he hated mistakes, and he was starting to hate the redhead and her wilderness guide with a passion he hadn't felt since his daddy died.

He could always call it quits and try again when the woman went back to New York. But she'd report this to the cops; she'd be spooked and on the lookout. Besides, if he screwed up now, his employers might not give him another chance.

Slipping the hatchet into his backpack, he pictured what he'd do when he caught up with the two. Excitement rushed through his veins. He hoisted the heavy backpack as easily as the bags of peat moss he'd gathered to sell as a kid. The power would be strong this time. He could feel it in his bones.

Buckling his hip belt, he straddled the fallen tree and slid his butt forward inches at a time. There was no one to see, and he wanted across this mother *now.* Branches and pine needles entangled his legs and jabbed through his clothes. His crotch met a vertical tree limb that forced him to stand and maneuver around it carefully.

By the time he'd reached the other side, sweat soaked his shirt, he felt like a human pincushion, and he still had fifteen feet of rock and earth to scale. Again, his backpack produced what he needed. Dynamic eleven-millimeter rope, rock hammer and metal pitons he'd thrown in at the last minute.

He'd kept himself in shape. Physically, the climb was no big deal. But shit, he hated heights. Pulling himself up over the edge and onto safe ground, he lay with arms spread, his heart pounding like a damn faggot's in a redneck bar. As his pulse slowed, his anger returned.

He'd show these frigging clowns what happened to people who screwed with Stan Lawler. Vengeance beat in his blood as he rose and walked the mile back to the original tree bridge. He'd left the rope and pitons behind and intact, ready for a fast escape from the site.

Picking up the cooling trail was child's play—or at least picking up the woman's trail was easy. There wasn't a trace of the man. Had he fallen into the water? Abandoned her and run off? Whatever had happened, it was probably for the best. Stan had earned a little reward. And the guide might've cost him valuable time.

He checked the sun's position. About an hour of light left. She couldn't have gotten far.

Her tracks showed dragging feet. She'd be weak, scared and ready to bargain. But no tears or mewling would stop him from teaching the bitch a lesson. And he wouldn't have to hold back today. Not like he'd had to with the blonde at the hotel.

His groin stirred. He picked up his pace.

Her trail led straight up with no sign of her resting. She had to be just up ahead. Her big brown eyes would fill with terror when she saw him. If not, his pistol would do the trick. The Ruger Mark II had made grown men beg. The redhead would do more than that before he was done with her.

His erection swelled. He hurried up the steep slope. Something cinched his ankle and yanked.

The world turned upside down. He whooshed high into the air. Blood rushed to his head as the ground six feet below swayed back and forth. Stunned, he realized that he dangled by one foot from a rope tied to a treetop.

His body hit the young pine and glanced off. He was ready the second time and grabbed the trunk. Twisting, he managed to unzip his backpack and pull out his buck knife. Lifting his weighted torso strained his ab muscles, and he swiped the blade savagely above his boot. The rope snapped. He plunged, back-pack first.

The M21, cartridges, hatchet, hammer and assorted other tools jabbed into his spine and shoulder blades. He blinked up at the sky, assessing his injuries. Nothing was broken, but everything hurt. He sat up slowly, got to his feet like an old man and took a tentative step. God*dammit!* His ankle was sprained.

He'd been setting snares since he was ten years old. To step right into one was more than he could stomach. Forcing himself to calm down, he examined the trigger mechanism. Two hooked sticks, all fresh cuts rubbed with dirt to blend in. The "rope" was some type of tanned hide, braided by hand and almost invisible against the earth tones. The young tree had been chosen well. Surrounded by saplings, it would be hidden when bent.

Whoever had set this snare was no faggot wilderness guide who only slept in tents and cooked with fuel stoves. No, this guy was good. And he was probably laughing right now at the thought of Stan strung up like a ham in a smokehouse.

Humiliation heated Stan's face, followed by hot killing rage. He might not know the right fork to use in a fancy restaurant, but *nobody* knew more about the woods than him. He'd find the man who'd done this and have the last laugh, goddammit. It was no longer a matter of money alone. His pride was at stake, too.

Come ten the next morning, he'd get on that chopper with his head held high—or he wouldn't get on it at all.

Ignoring the twinge in his ankle, he headed up the trail with grim determination. The light was fading fast, but the moon would rise soon. They wouldn't expect him to travel at night. He'd get the jump on them for sure.

Ten minutes later his boot slipped on a loose rock, and he went down hard on one knee. The throb in his ankle grew worse. Common sense told him to wait until the moon rose high enough to light his path, but the need for vengeance drove him on.

He climbed steadily, jumping crevices and grunting in pain. When he found them, he'd make them pay. When he found them, he'd—

The ground collapsed. He plunged feet first and hit rock. His sprained ankle crumpled on impact, his shoulder and head slammed into the rock wall. He toppled onto his side and groaned as sticks and pine needles and dirt sprinkled down like rain.

A trap, his brain jeered in self-contempt, before unconsciousness shut down his thoughts.

HOPE DRAGGED UP into wakefulness and scratched her nose. Something tickled the tip again. She buried her face in her fragrant pillow and rubbed from side to side. Her eyes popped open. She struggled upright, disoriented and vaguely frightened.

Awareness returned by degrees. It was dark. She sat on some sort of...pine-needle mattress. Under some sort of...pine-needle shelter. She'd been escaping from the sniper, so tired she'd lost all sense of urgency, when Jared had finally said, "We're here." She'd curled up on a bed of sweet-smelling grass. After that her mind was a blank.

A meadow stretched ahead of her now. The one she'd slept on earlier?

"Jared?" Her voice whipped back in her face, carried on a chilly mountain breeze.

Shivering, she flipped off her cap and pulled Hank's thermal underwear on over her head. Every movement hurt. She could hardly distinguish the ache from her wound among the thousand other sore muscles screaming "Ouch!" She needed the aspirin in Jared's pocket. She needed some food in her stomach. Who was she kidding?

She needed Jared. Needed to see him and know he was safe.

Searching the dark meadow frantically, she told herself she was being foolish. Jared was fine. He was out doing something useful or he-man brave. He'd be back when he was finished, and her world would be right again. But in the meantime she wished she knew where he was.

So why am I wringing my hands like some helpless female?

Scrambling out from under the shelter, she studied the small meadow. Moonlight transformed the swaying grasses into a rippling silver sea. Beautiful—if Jared was safe.

Hope started on her left and walked the perimeter of the clearing, calling his name softly into the trees. Nothing. Only the hoot of an owl, the three-note chord of wind through boughs, grass and her tangled hair. The woods were dense and dark. She'd be stupid to go charging into the unknown. Jared could hear like a bat. Why wasn't he answering? Oh, God, if anything had happened to him...

Her mind rejected the thought. Queasiness rose and subsided.

Was this what it was like to be in love? To feel incomplete and lost and physically sick without the one you loved?

She'd been so happy earlier. Happy was good. This was bad. This was hideous. She didn't like this feeling at all. She'd spent her entire adult life establishing her identity and self-worth, independent of other people's desires or opinions. Love could go take a hike. Love could go smite some other schmuck upside the head and leave her in peace.

"I'm over here, Hope," a deep voice called.

Her heart surged weightlessly. It was her love!

For the first time in her life Hope understood why unplanned pregnancies still occurred, secretaries still had doomed affairs with their bosses, neon wedding chapels in Las Vegas still thrived. Love couldn't be controlled. It controlled *you*. The best a woman could hope for was that the feeling was reciprocated. But even if it wasn't, that didn't prevent this spontaneous and overwhelming reaction.

Hope followed Jared's voice into the woods because she couldn't do anything else.

Her body knew where its other half was and guided her unerringly through the dark forest. Occasional streaks of moonlight kept her from walking headlong into trees. The spongy carpet of compost muffled her steps, but she knew that he heard her. She knew that he waited. Anticipation quickened her pulse.

The smell of water drifted from somewhere close. The expedition had done that for her, sharpened senses grown dull from disuse. She saw a mist floating around tree trunks ahead. Another waterfall? No. There was no distinctive roar of pounding water.

She hurried forward, broke out of the trees and stopped, her heartbeat suspended.

Her boots edged a free-form body of water about the size of a small swimming pool. Moonlight glittered on the surface between patches of rising steam. Delicate ferns sloping into sandy soil lined all the banks but one. The far end of the pool appeared carved out of solid rock, with natural stepping-stone benches a landscape designer would charge a fortune to construct.

All the details faded as she focused on the man sitting chest deep in water, his hair slicked back, his features enshrouded in steam. He wasn't wearing his glasses, which made him seem all the more naked.

"You're awake." Jared's voice rumbled across the surface, curling her toes inside her boots.

If she'd been any more awake, she'd have died of a heart attack. She nodded once and swallowed hard.

"What do you think of my private spa? A hot spring keeps it nice and warm."

Think? Her brain was oatmeal. Her tongue was full of drool.

He frowned and stood up. Water streamed down his powerful torso and into the pool at navel level. The hair on his chest, stomach and forearms plastered dark and sleek against hard muscles and sinew.

"You must be starving. Give me a minute to get dressed and I'll fix us something to eat."

She didn't move.

"What's wrong?"

Hope's gaze roved helplessly over his tensing body, then met his alert eyes. "I woke up and you were gone. It...scared me." Her voice came from deep in her chest, a voice she'd never heard before.

"I'm sorry," he said carefully. "I didn't think you would wake up before I got back. We're safe here, Hope. You don't have to worry about the sniper."

He didn't understand. She had to make him understand. "I was afraid something had happened to you. I needed to see you. I needed...you, Scout."

Jared grew very still.

Pride be damned. "I *need* you."

A fierce exultant gleam lit his eyes from within. "Come here, Hope."

She'd never heard that voice before, either, but she thrilled to its unmistakable message. He needed her, too. Right here. Right now. She took one step into the water and jumped back, her boot dripping.

Her clothes. Of course, how silly. She bent down and untied her laces, slipped off her boots, unpeeled her socks. Would he watch her the whole time? She peeked through a screen of red hair at his unwavering gaze.

It appeared that he would.

She straightened, her cheeks heating as her fingers fumbled with her snap and zipper. Her past liaisons had been businesslike affairs. No smoldering looks. No extensive foreplay. No lingering once the meeting was over.

She'd never undressed for a man before. It was unnerving and, yes, exciting. The loose khaki pants pooled at her feet. She kicked them off, conscious of the thermal-underwear shirt falling to midthigh. Not exactly sexy, but Jared didn't look bored. He looked...dangerous. Intensely masculine.

She shivered, but not from the cold. Grasping her shirt hem, she lifted—and yelped. Pain streaked down her wounded arm. Her hands fell.

Jared waded noisily through the water and up the bank. Wet fingers tugged hers from the hem and gently pulled both her sweatshirt and thermal underwear up over her head. Steamy heat radiated inches away from her exposed skin as he unthreaded her good arm from the sleeves, then oh-so-carefully did the same with her injured arm. One quick pull and her head popped free.

She blinked at his bare chest, his taut stomach, his... "Hoo-boy," she breathed, startled, flattered and highly aroused by the state of his voluptuous erection.

"Yeah," he said hoarsely, his gaze scorching the scraps of turquoise lace she'd picked up on sale at Victoria's Secret.

Best money she'd ever spent, Hope thought, slipping out of her panties, unclasping her bra and tossing them both on top of her boots. One step brought her breasts into full pillowing contact with his hard wet chest. Her eyes drifted shut on a blissful sigh.

He drew in a sharp breath and stepped back. Their skin parted with an erotic suction that ripped a moan from her throat.

"Damn." He flung back his head and squeezed his eyes shut. "I need a minute..." Every muscle stood out in rigid relief. He was obviously fighting for control of his body.

Her dismay turned to understanding and shy feminine pride. "It's all right, Jared. Take your time." Hope turned and walked into the pool. "We've got all night," she added over her shoulder, then chuckled when his eyes flew open.

She dived under the water and wallowed on the sandy bottom, ignoring the sting of her wound in the greater pleasure of taking a bath. A full bath, a *warm* bath. What sinful glorious luxury! She rubbed sand— nature's exfoliating scrub—over her legs, stomach and arms, careful not to disturb the sodden bandage.

Bursting up for a gasping breath, she smiled and waved at Jared, who now sat on the submerged rock bench where she'd first seen him. Then she drew a deep breath and sank underwater again.

She scrubbed her face and scalp, she rubbed her teeth with her finger, she surfaced, floated lazily on her back and contemplated the sky. The ink-black backdrop showcased a luminescent white globe. A lovers' moon. If only Jared would make the first move...

Her soreness had eased considerably. She felt refreshed and squeaky clean. But the tension low in her belly had tightened with every minute he'd watched her. And he'd watched her every minute from his bench seat. She could feel his eyes on her now.

"Are you trying to kill me?" Jared asked in a near growl.

She bobbed upright and treaded water. "Excuse me?"

"I'm dying here and you're looking at the moon."

A thrill leaped across her nerve endings. "You said you needed a minute..."

His eyes glittered. "The minute's up. Now I need you."

The repeat of her own words sent heat flooding to the parts of her body that needed him most.

"Come here, Hope." It was a command, nonnegotiable.

The mating dance was over. All her coyness fled,

replaced by a soul-deep sense of rightness. Standing shoulder-deep in water, she walked slowly forward, watching his eyes narrow, his heavily muscled chest rise and fall, the cords of his neck grow taut as she approached. The water circled her waist when she came to a halt before him.

"I'm here, Jared," she said softly, and opened her arms.

He rose to his feet, Poseidon tall and strong, and met her chest, stomach and thigh. The *feel* of him... A shudder of pure ecstasy rippled through her at the hard planes and ridges pressing into her yielding flesh. He didn't pull away this time. His arms wrapped around her waist tightly and he rocked her back and forth, as if the moment was as unique and precious to him as it was to her.

"I've dreamed about this," she confessed, her voice muffled against hair-roughened skin. "I'd wake up aching for you. One time I nearly crawled into your bivouac sack with you."

"If I'd known..." He groaned, widened his stance and pulled her in a step, his erection pressing hot and insistent against her stomach. "Do you feel what I've been living with since I met you? Hell, if you knew the kind of dreams I've had, you'd run scared right now." His arms tightened possessively. "Oh, honey, I don't think we're gonna sleep much tonight, either."

She lifted her head for a kiss and got one—open-mouthed, tongue-thrusting, wildly exciting. His hands were everywhere, but so were hers. He was a tactile smorgasbord, lean and muscular and as arousing to touch as he was to look at. She gripped the bunched muscles of his buttocks with one hand, reached between them with the other and cupped his velvet softness. He broke the kiss and stepped back, his breath choppy, his eyes hard and predatory, a man pushed to the limits of his control.

''I wanted to go slow,'' he said, pulling her down with him, seating her on a stone bench in belly-deep water. ''I wanted to make this last.'' Positioning her elbows on the bench behind her, he bridged her body with powerful arms and stared down, his wet hair falling forward. ''Don't touch me or I'll explode. Let me do the touching.'' His gaze bored into hers. ''And the tasting.''

Her protest died as he dipped his head low and captured a puckered nipple in his mouth. The pleasure was exquisite. She told him so with a moan. He flattened his hand against her stomach, slid the heel of his palm into the water, into her curls, then rubbed around and around and around. Her head tossed. The discomfort of the rock became nothing. The ache of her wound became nothing. Heat spiraled out from his massage, creating a throbbing pressure that was part pleasure, part pain.

He moved his mouth to her other breast. His fingers slid into her body, which was as wet now inside as out.

She tried to arch against his chest, but he pressed

her back down. She tried desperately to touch him, but he clamped her wrists easily with one hand. She felt wanton and wicked, spread upon a stone banquet table for him to feast on at will.

He hadn't boasted idly about knowing how to gratify a woman. His mouth, teeth and tongue knew exactly where to roam, how hard or soft to wield their magic in order to take her to the edge. She didn't want to fall alone.

"Let me touch you," she begged shamelessly. "I have to touch you."

He growled incoherently, a denial.

"Jared, *please*. I want you inside me." She twisted her hands sharply. "I *love* you, dammit!"

His head came up. He released her wrists.

She pulled him forward, stared into his stunned face and said more softly, "I love you."

Joy leaped in his eyes, followed by a possessive tenderness that took her breath away. He spread her thighs apart and snugged up close. "That's good, honey. Because I love you, too." With one powerful thrust he embedded himself deep inside her.

They both moaned.

Hope clutched his shoulders, her laugh half sob, her body too aroused to withstand his sensual assault for long. When she clasped her legs around his hips and met his next stroke fiercely, he picked up the pace and gave her what she'd never thought to receive. His beautiful body, his magnificent heart, a sense of worthiness no business deal could—or ever would—provide.

Her explosive climax shattered the old Hope into a million separate pieces. Jared's swift thrust and hoarse cry pulled the fragments all together again, more whole and complete than before.

"I love you, Jared."

"I love you, Hope. We'll work out the rest of it somehow."

She tightened her arms around his waist and smiled through her tears.

CHAPTER FIFTEEN

HOPE AWAKENED by degrees, frowned and scratched her nose. Something tickled the tip again. The brush mattress. She flopped onto her back. The tickle persisted.

Her lids opened and her eyes crossed at the sprig of pine brushing lightly across the tip of her nose. Jared.

Shivering in the cold, she nudged the sprig away and rolled toward him in the first rays of dawn. His hands reached out and lifted with effortless strength, and suddenly she lay sprawled on top of six feet plus of muscled virile male. Unfortunately he wasn't naked, and neither was she.

She crossed her arms over his wool sweater and propped her chin on top. "Mornin', Scout."

He folded his hands behind his head and grinned, his teeth white against his dark stubbled beard. "Mornin', Hope."

His bass voice sent delicious vibrations through her abdomen. Her sore muscles absorbed his warmth gratefully. She studied him with unabashed pleasure. He really was gorgeous, with those golden sun streaks in his shaggy brown hair, those Elvis-thick lashes and sultry blue eyes that his glasses usually muted, that uncompromisingly masculine nose and jaw.

"Keep looking at me like that and I'll take you back to my private spa," he warned in a raspy voice.

"Promises, promises." Her voice was equally husky.

He shifted her lower on his body until she knew his promise wasn't idle. Amazing, after the night they'd spent. Maybe he *was* an alien. She squirmed now just thinking about what they'd done. How many times they'd done it.

"Quit wriggling. I can't take you there now." Regret and frustration harshened Jared's tone. "I need to build a signal fire. If Hank and the others made it to Matt's camp early, they could be sending a bush plane out to look for us."

She stilled, then sighed and rolled off, pulling his arm around her stomach so that they lay spooned together facing outward. "Okay, but just hold me and enjoy this view a minute. I don't think I've ever seen anything so beautiful."

And truly she hadn't. Verbena and buttercups sprinkled the lush green grass with purple and yellow confetti. Blue gray sawtooth peaks of the Sierra del Carmen picketed them on all sides. From a tree on the northern perimeter, a large bird flapped its wings and launched into flight with a piercing cry.

"That's a golden eagle," Jared said. "Several pair nest up here at Eagle Watch."

Ben had brought Jared to this meadow four years ago, he'd told her. His vision quest had produced the seed for MindBend Adventures. Knowing the area's significance for Jared increased its beauty for Hope.

She snuggled back against his solid warmth. "I'm so happy that it scares me, Jared. What if this doesn't last?"

"What I am looking for is not 'out there.' It is in me," his deep voice rumbled in her ear. "The past has no power over me."

Her voice joined his and they spoke in unison. "Negative thoughts have no power over me. I am the power in my world. Today is a wonderful day and a new beginning. I choose to make it so."

The meditation rang true and strong with shining promise. Promise of a future that included an incredibly special man's love. When Jared tightened his arm in silent empathy, her heart was too full to contain her emotion.

"Oh, Jared, I—"

Thrashing tree limbs cut off her sentence. Jared's entire body tensed.

"Move!" He pushed her forward off the mattress, followed close behind and grabbed her hand. "Run!"

She obeyed his urgent tone and plunged with him into the woods. Jared had insisted that they sleep with their boots on, and now she realized it wasn't only to ward off the cold. He'd wanted them ready to escape.

He dragged her deep into the forest, past the point of her ever finding her way back to the meadow alone. At last he stopped, glanced around as if to get his bearings, then settled her against a towering Douglas fir.

Breathing hard, she stared up into his grim eyes. "What happened?"

"I rigged an alarm across the trail last night. Something set it off. I'm going back to see what— or who—tripped the spring mechanism. Stay here."

She clutched his biceps. "Stay here with me."

He was distracted, his mind already focused on returning. "If it's nothing, I'll come right back. If it's the sniper—" his expression hardened to that of a chilling stranger's "—I'll be a little longer."

Her nails dug through wool to rock muscle. "This isn't some spiritual exercise Ben is putting you through, Jared. This man will try to kill you."

"This man already tried to kill you. I'm not feeling very spiritual right now."

He *wanted* to run into that maniac. She could see the light of battle in his eyes.

"Don't worry, Hope. The bastard won't even see me until his throat is in my hands."

Men. "I just found you, dammit! I don't want to lose you now." Her voice broke on the last word.

His features softened, became the face she knew and loved more than her life. He cupped her cheek and brushed his thumb over her lower lip. "You're never going to get rid of me, Hope. Trust me. And don't move from this spot.''

His hard swift kiss drove her head back against the tree.

Then he was gone.

She blinked in surprise. She'd been looking right at him and he'd simply...melted into the trees. The way of the scout, he'd called his training. Hope placed her faith in the Apache she'd never met and sent up a fervent prayer that he watch over his protégé from the spirit world.

The next minutes were the longest in Hope's life. She paced up and down the same ten-foot path, listening for gunfire, imagining the worst, hating the position women had endured since man first fought for possession of his neighbor's cave.

If she knew the way back, she'd head for the meadow. How dared he leave her here to stew and worry! She wanted a piece of the sniper herself. In fact, she'd take a piece out of Jared's hide when she saw him...if she saw him...

''Miss me, honey?''

Hope whirled around and catapulted into Jared's open arms. She breathed in his wonderful smell and felt her heart pump blood through her deadened body once more.

He nuzzled the top of her head. ''You really did miss me, didn't you?'' The smile in his voice oozed masculine smugness.

''Don't *ever* leave me like that again if you want

me on your team, understand? I do my part, dangerous or not." She punched his shoulder, but stayed in his arms. "Understand?"

He held her quietly as a major term for their relationship sank in. "I understand," he murmured, properly solemn.

Hope released a long breath. "So...did you strangle the bastard?"

He chuckled, squeezed her tightly, then pulled away. "It was a doe," he said, grabbing her hand and walking in the opposite direction she would have picked. "I followed her tracks from the trip cord and found her drinking at the springs. The sniper's crossed the Mexican border by now, if I had to make a guess. But, Hope, you'll have to continue to be on my team when we get to the States."

She glanced up in surprise.

"You'll have to give up some of your independence and cooperate with the authorities. I just found you, dammit." He repeated her own words softly. "I couldn't stand to lose you now."

Sappy tears threatened again, but she managed a shaky smile. Had any woman ever been so lucky? She thanked God and Ben both for her good fortune.

Back at the shelter they sat on the mattress side by side and ate raisins and the last granola bar. Ambrosia. Last night's hot cocoa, dewberries and oatmeal had only taken the edge off her hunger.

"I miss Karen's cooking," Hope said, then frowned. The rest of her team had gotten the short end of the stick. They'd been hiking over Lord knew what kind of terrain all night while she'd been safe in Jared's arms. What if...

A hundred terrible possibilities crowded her guilty conscience.

"Hey, now, none of that. Don't underestimate those three. I'll bet they're eating one of Karen's omelettes at Matt's campfire as we speak." Jared slipped on his glasses, reached into one of his bountiful pockets and smiled teasingly. "What have we here?"

He pulled his hand out with deliberate slowness, diverting her worried thoughts, then waved two Heath bars in front of her nose. She snatched hers, tore off the wrapping and moaned in ecstasy at the first bite.

When the final swallow had been savored, she realized Jared had finished his candy bar long ago and was watching her as if starving—for her.

"I'd better go make that signal fire," he said, averting his gaze and rising swiftly. He'd walked four steps before her mouth caught up with her libido.

"Wait," she commanded, her pulse quickening.

He stopped and turned as she moved up close, his expression curious and a bit impatient.

"You've got chocolate on your mouth," she explained, bracketing his bristly cheeks with her palms. Pulling his head down, she flicked her tongue twice over the seam of his lips. "Mmm, nice."

She released his head and started to step back.

His eyes flashed. A muscular forearm whipped around her waist and pulled her flush with his body. "Oh, no, you don't, woman. Come get what you came for."

Their mouths met with equal greediness. She sank into the kiss she'd craved, the one she'd blatantly teased him to receive. She'd never get enough of "what she came for"—not with this man, not if she lived to be a thousand. He angled his head for a tighter fit, his tongue plundering deep and shallow and everything between. The roar in her ears pounded louder than the waterfall they'd crossed, an untamed rush of passion she'd only experienced with this man.

Jared's body went totally rigid. He lifted and turned his head.

Hope blinked up and struggled to focus.

"Leave some of that for me, lover boy," a male voice sneered, penetrating Hope's sensual fog.

The palms on her back slid down fractionally.

"Keep those hands where I can see them!"

She followed Jared's riveted gaze.

A tall muscular man stood twenty feet away pointing an ugly black pistol their way. Dried blood streaked his broad face and congealed in a deep gash on his forehead. Dirt and debris dulled his short blond hair, littered his backpack, clung to his ripped black turtleneck and tight black pants. He looked as if he'd been dragged along the ground behind a running horse. And from the direction of his murderous glare, he'd guessed exactly who'd been in the saddle.

"Step back nice and easy, bitch, and maybe I won't pull this trigger."

Her heart bucked. The roar in her ears returned, but the difference was obscene. Her hammering heart and coursing blood were part of a surreal nightmare now, separate from her thoughts. Jared's intense focus remained on the sniper.

Begging him silently to please, please, not be a hero, she broke from Jared's embrace and moved away.

"Atta girl. They told me you were smart, honey."

Shivering at the endearment she'd learned to cherish, Hope wondered who "they" were.

"Come on over real slow now, ya hear?"

Southern accents were supposed to sound friendly. The sniper's voice was as frigid as his ice blue eyes.

"Don't do anything stupid," he warned Jared. "She gets a bullet the minute you move."

Instinct told Hope to keep her expression meek, her demeanor terrified. It wasn't a hard act to pull off, she admitted, stopping a foot away.

"Come closer." He reached behind with one hand and fumbled in his backpack, the gun barrel never wavering from her heart.

"You're going to tape lover boy's wrists and ankles for me, Red, and then we're going to get acquainted." Pulling out silver duct tape, he handed her the roll, then inspected her with detached interest.

"You're better-looking than in your picture." His insolent chilling gaze lowered.

A scratched and filthy hand fondled her left breast.

Jared lunged—then stopped abruptly.

"Ah-ah-ah," the pig warned softly, pressing cold metal against Hope's temple. He pinched her nipple hard.

She couldn't prevent her gasp.

Jared's rage was palpable. He looked as lethal and inhuman now as any hired killer.

The sniper smiled and groped her right breast. "You don't like it when I touch her, do you, lover boy? That's good. You put me through hell, and now you're going to watch me take your woman. Is she as hot as she looks? Is she a screamer? I promise she'll scream before I'm through with her, asshole."

Jared wouldn't let her be hurt. He'd make a suicidal move first. He'd be killed because of her—no, because of this blond maniac. This overgrown bully who'd assumed she was weak and helpless, who'd dismissed her as a threat.

"Did you think your pit trap would really stop me? Once the sun rose, it was only a matter of time before I climbed out. I'm the best there is, wilderness boy."

The voice close to Hope's ear was as sinister as a diamondback's rattle. Her heart lurched at the thought.

Jared made a feral sound. "Let her go, tough guy, and put your money where your mouth is. We'll see who's the best man without a woman to hide behind.''

Hope slowly withdrew Bill's good luck gift from her pocket.

The sniper quivered, his gaze locked with his challenger's in a deadly battle for dominance. "I'm tempted. Mi-i-ghty tempted. But I want you in shape to watch all the fun." He raised the gun from her temple and used the barrel to lift curls gently from her neck. His mouth lowered to the tender spot beneath her ear.

She tossed the diamondback tail behind his boots. The rattle shook on impact with the ground.

"Son of a—" Whirling, the sniper aimed his gun at the rattle and stiffened. "Bitch!" He spun back around to face Hope.

The toe of her heavy hiking boot caught him full force in the crotch. He dropped as if cut off at the kneecaps and teetered.

A powerful fist in his jaw snapped his blond head back. His body followed. He landed heavily and didn't move.

Jared stood with his fists clenched and his chest heaving, his face pale beneath his tan. Hope moved closer and nudged her boot against the sniper's rib. He was unconscious, all right.

Turning, she caught Jared staring at her foot. His gaze rose to meet hers and filled with wary awe.

She shrugged and broke into a shaky satisfied grin.

"They don't call me the Nutcracker for nothing, Scout."

One year later

HOPE LEANED BACK in her leather executive chair and propped navy Bruno Magli pumps on one edge of her desk. Across the sleek cherry-wood surface, Debbie crossed red Gucci heels on the opposite corner. They saluted each other with martinis and sipped in celebration.

Nine in the morning was a bit early for imbibing, but then, the UroTech sale had been later coming through than expected. Having signed the final papers ten minutes ago, Hope cut herself some slack.

"Congratulations, boss. You laid the biggest golden egg of your career today. What does it feel like to be a rich goose?"

Hope considered her mood. She was happy for Dr. Hiller and the investors who'd trusted her instincts. But... "I was rich in every way that counts before I signed those papers."

Rolling her eyes, the sophisticated VP of Manning Enterprises made a gagging gesture with her French-manicured fingernail.

Hope took a sip to hide her smile. "When did you get to be so cynical?"

"Let's see... What year did we meet?"

"Now, now. Is that any way to talk to someone who got you a piece of that egg?"

"You're right. Getting me to invest before the scandal broke was very Mother Goose of you, and I'm grateful," Debbie purred, resting her blond head against the delft blue chair back that matched her satisfied eyes. "But you know, if I hadn't insisted that you go to Texas—"

"Blackmailed me, you mean."

Debbie waved slim fingers airily. "Semantics. You went there because of me. And changed that gorgeous Viking into a soprano—"

"He was a *hit* man, for heaven's sake! You wouldn't have thought he was gorgeous facing his loaded barrel."

Delicate blond brows waggled. "That depends entirely on the caliber." She smiled at Hope's groan. "Anyway, you exposed the scuzziest plot to manipulate the market in years. In a way, you owe Uro-Tech's rise in value to me."

Investors' faith had been so shaken by a major medical-industry conglomerate's criminal activity that trust in the victim—UroTech—had gone up by default.

"You're not getting a raise," Hope said evenly.

Debbie lifted a toothpick and bit pointedly into an olive. "You're funding scholarships to hick-town high-school kids. I just thought you'd like to give money to someone who'd know how to spend it with finesse." She pouted, then had the grace to look guilty. "I know, I know, everybody focuses on urban kids and forgets the ones stuck in places like Hopeful, Texas. I'm a horrible, greedy person. You're a saint of a boss. I don't deserve you." She took a sip and peeked over her martini glass.

"You're still not getting a raise." Hope checked her watch. "Oh, damn!" She set down her glass. Her legs came off the desk. Hurrying to the television set nestled in a cherry-wood bookcase on the opposite wall, she flipped on the TV, switched channels and backed up grinning.

The female host of "Good Morning America" sat interviewing the NBA's rookie Coach of the Year and his honey blond bride.

"So tell me, Hank, what gave you and Karen the idea to collaborate on your new cookbook, *Eating on the Run: High Energy Snacks to Make and Take?*"

The couple gazed at each other as if sharing intimate memories, then took turns telling the story of their expedition experience.

Debbie choked on a sip of martini and stabbed a finger at the TV. "They're talking about you!" she finally managed.

"Shh!" Hope propped herself on the desk and strained to hear.

Hank had segued into their cookbook recipes described from an athlete's perspective. Karen supplemented with comments from a mother's viewpoint on the importance of nutritious fast food in today's society. The newlyweds deferred to each other with respect and obvious love, and the host warmed to their charm.

Karen looked stunning and slim in a Givenchy scarlet suit that matched her long red fingernails. She glowed from within, a striking change from the timid woman Hope had first met. Jimbo the Jerk had refused to consider counseling, and within three months of his divorce had married his secretary.

Love. There was no controlling it.

According to Karen, Hank was wonderful with the boys, and they adored him. How could they not? Hope had asked her friend, and hadn't gotten an argument.

The interview was wrapping up when Hope's telephone rang. And rang. Transfixed by the TV, Hope rounded her desk and lifted the receiver.

"Manning Enterprises, Ms. Austin speaking."

"Hello Ms. Austin. This is Mr. Austin speaking."

"Jared!" Hope caught Debbie's knowing glance and realized her body's instant response was transparent.

"Are you watching these two?" he asked. "Book sales will go through the roof after today."

"I know. Can you believe how poised they are? You'd think it was the hundredth interview on the book tour, instead of their first. Hey, I thought you were going to tape the show. Who's taking over your class?"

"Matt of course. I've gotta give him a raise soon. He never complains, always comes through for me— the guy lives and breathes MindBend Adventures. I wish I knew someone who could shake him out of his rut. Ah, well.'' He paused. ''I miss you, honey.''

She thrilled to his husky voice. ''I miss you, too.''

Debbie drained the last of her martini, rose and walked to the TV. ''I'll leave you two lovebirds to talk alone. All this cooing is making me nauseous.'' Switching off the closing shot of Hank and Karen holding hands, Debbie fluttered her fingers over her shoulders and left. Hope hadn't missed the touch of wistfulness in her voice.

''Was that Debbie?''

''Who else? You know, I was just thinking how she needs a break from her routine, too. A little forced vacation, maybe. Somewhere with lots of sand and sun—and lonely studly wilderness guides.''

''Don't meddle, Hope. She could barely make it through our wedding without complaining about sand blowing into her contacts.''

Their desert-sunset ceremony eight months ago had been perfect, and Debbie had told Hope so later.

''She wouldn't last a day on an expedition,'' Jared predicted.

''That's what you said about me when I first started the course, and look what a happy camper I turned into.''

His pause signaled an alarm inside Hope.

''I forgot to congratulate you on the sale,'' he said carefully.

That again. Hope relaxed. ''I wouldn't change a thing in my life, Jared. I'll almost be sad next month when the new house is finished. But then again, it will mean fewer trips to New York, less time away from you.''

The Spanish colonial-style house faced a spectacular view of the distant Sierra del Carmen range. Her home office would feature state-of-the-art business and communications equipment. And an empty nursery waiting to be filled when the time was right.

''When are you coming home?'' His voice had dropped an octave.

She braced herself against its pull. ''Tomorrow morning. We discussed this. I have a meeting with that new software company Bill told me about. Feast Markets are testing the company's new inventory system, and he's convinced it will revolutionize the business.''

''Let Debbie handle the initial interview.''

''Jared, I can't.''

''You can. She can get the preliminary information. If she thinks it's worthwhile, she can schedule a second meeting. You trust her judgment, don't you?''

''Yes, but...''

''But nobody does it better than you?''

Damn. He'd caught her again.

''Delegate, Hope. You believe in democracy, remember?''

''You're not playing fair.''

''What's not fair? I miss my wife. I want to hold her in my arms and make love with her tonight. And that's something she does better than any woman I know.''

Hope twisted the phone cord, closed her eyes and laughed softly. ''You might want to rephrase that, Scout.''

''You're the *only* woman I love, the only woman I want. And I want you now, honey. Real bad.''

When he used that dark seductive tone she was weak, weak, weak.

''This sale...I need to hold you...I need to know... Ah, hell, never mind. I'm being selfish. I'll see you tomorrow like you planned.''

Selfish? He'd taught her to live close to the earth in concrete canyons or scorching desert. He'd enriched her life in a thousand ways and made each day wonderful. And her big handsome husband was feeling a bit insecure, now—because of her.

''No, I've changed my mind. I'm telling Debbie to handle the interview and then I'm catching the next flight out.''

''You don't have to—''

''I *want* to, Jared. Anyone can ask questions at that meeting. But there are some things only we can do.'' She smiled at his low whoop and thought of his waiting arms and the empty nursery.

The time was definitely right.

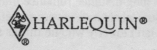

HE SAID

♥

SHE SAID

Explore the mystery of male/female communication in this extraordinary new book from two of your favorite Harlequin authors.

Jasmine Cresswell and Margaret St. George bring you the exciting story of two romantic adversaries—each from their own point of view!

DEV'S STORY. CATHY'S STORY.
As he sees it. As she sees it.
Both sides of the story!

The heat is definitely on, and these two can't stay out of the kitchen!

Don't miss HE SAID, SHE SAID.
Available in July wherever Harlequin books are sold.

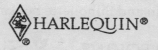

HARLEQUIN®

Look us up on-line at: http://www.romance.net

HESAID

On the plus side, you've raised a
wonderful, strong-willed daughter.
On the minus side, she's using that
determination to find

A Match For
MOM

Three very different stories of mothers,
daughters and heroes...from three of your
all-time favorite authors:

GUILTY
by Anne Mather

A MAN FOR MOM
by Linda Randall Wisdom

THE FIX-IT MAN
by Vicki Lewis Thompson

Available this May wherever
Harlequin and Silhouette books are sold.

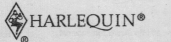 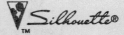

And the Winner Is...
You!

...when you pick up these great titles
from our new promotion at your
favorite retail outlet this June!

Diana Palmer
The Case of the Mesmerizing Boss

Betty Neels
The Convenient Wife

Annette Broadrick
Irresistible

Emma Darcy
A Wedding to Remember

Rachel Lee
Lost Warriors

Marie Ferrarella
Father Goose

HARLEQUIN® *Temptation*

and

HARLEQUIN®

INTRIGUE®

Double Dare ya!

Identical twin authors Patricia Ryan and
Pamela Burford bring you a dynamic duo of
books that just happen to feature identical twins.

Meet Emma, the shy one, and her diva double,
Zara. Be prepared for twice the pleasure and
twice the excitement as they give two
unsuspecting men trouble times two!

In April, the scorching **Harlequin Temptation** novel
#631 Twice the Spice by Patricia Ryan

In May, the suspenseful **Harlequin Intrigue** novel
#420 Twice Burned by Pamela Burford

Pick up both—if you dare....

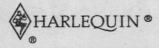

HARLEQUIN ®

Look us up on-line at: http://www.romance.net   TWIN

HARLEQUIN SUPERROMANCE®

A trilogy by three of your favorite authors.

Peg Sutherland
Ellen James
Marisa Carroll

A golden wedding *usually* means a family celebration.

But the Hardaway sisters drifted apart years ago. And each has her own reason for wanting no part of a family reunion. As plans for the party proceed, tensions mount, and it begins to look as if their parents' marriage might fall apart before the big event. Can the daughters put aside old hurts and betrayals...for the sake of the family?

Follow the fortunes of AMY, LISA and MEGAN in these three dramatic love stories.

April 1997—AMY by Peg Sutherland
May 1997—LISA by Ellen James
June 1997—MEGAN by Marisa Carroll

Available wherever Harlequin books are sold.

SIS

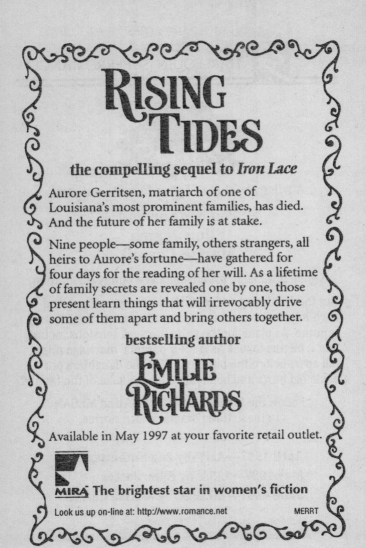